A PSYCHOPATH MURDERS YOUR WIFE.
THE POLICE CAN'T HELP.
DO YOU JUST WISH FOR HIS DEATH
—OR DO YOU MAKE IT HAPPEN?

You read it in the papers. See it on TV. It's still remote until you walk into your living room and find your wife murdered—horribly mutilated—by someone who was obviously a psychopath.

Choking, you stumble to the phone. Punch out three digits. Sirens scream, and the police rush in and chalk up another victim to the killer they can't find—a killer who strikes and disappears, leaving no clues to his real identity.

What do you do? If you're like one man, you commit suicide. If you're like another, you dedicate the rest of your life to a revenge—which certainly isn't legal—but which may be the only meaningful action left for you to take.

SHADOW
OF THE
KNIFE

BY KENNETH R. McKAY

PLAYBOY PRESS
PAPERBACKS

SHADOW OF THE KNIFE

Copyright© 1978 by Kenneth R. McKay.

Cover illustration by Eraldo Carugati: Copyright© 1978 by Playboy.

Published simultaneously in the United States and Canada by Playboy Press, Chicago, Illinois. Printed in the United States of America. Library of Congress Catalog Card Number: 78-58395. First edition.

Books are available at quantity discounts for promotional and industrial use. For further information, write our sales-promotion agency: Ventura Associates, 40 East 49th Street, New York, New York 10017.

ISBN: 0-872-16485-3

Thou shalt not kill.

Exodus 20:13

Who so sheddeth man's blood, by man shall his blood be shed.

Genesis 9:6

Thou shalt not kill.

Deuteronomy 5:17

The revenger of blood himself shall slay the murderer: when he meeteth him, he shall slay him.

Numbers 35:19

The righteous shall rejoice when he seeth the vengeance: he shall wash his feet in the blood of the wicked.

Psalms 58:10

ONE

Alice Quinton came home from work this Tuesday at twenty minutes after five. She was horny. It was a word she did not particularly like. When she was young it had been a borderline word, not really a dirty word, but not really clean either. Nice girls did not use that word. Young? She laughed. She was younger now, at 42, than she had ever been in her life. Right up there with all the modern unmarrieds. And she used all the modern flat-out dirty words when appropriate, although inside herself she might wince. But these days "horny" was downright respectable: they even used that word on the TV talk shows.

She undressed, hung away her things, slipped on a housecoat. The apartment was spotless. She was a proud housekeeper. And a fine executive secretary. She worked for Ira Newton of Newton Realty, Rockville Centre, New York. It was a small firm but it did an excellent business. The storefront office on Maple Avenue employed five people: Ira, Alice and three sales people. Alice's desk was the desk nearest the door, so in a manner of speaking, she was not only the executive secretary, she was also the receptionist. "Hell," Ira said, "I'd have to be out of my mind to hide a gorgeous *punim* like yours behind a desk somewhere in the rear." He was a sweet, gentle man, Ira Newton, and she was devoted to him.

She shook up a Scotch sour, made a salad, put on a steak to broil. It was a large apartment—two bedrooms—too large, really, for one person. But until two years ago Wendy was home and two bedrooms were necessary. Then Wendy, at age 18, married her college professor and left Long Island when he transferred to the University of Arizona at Tucson. Before the apartment, there had been the house in Locust Valley.

Like mother, like daughter. Alice Quinton also had married early: age 20. She was red-haired, blue-eyed and beautiful, and at 18 she went to work for a firm of architects on Wall Street. There she caught the eye of one of the partners, Gordon Quinton. He was twice her age and twice divorced. They got married, moved into the house in Locust Valley, and lived happily ever after—for 14 years. Then again it was divorce time for Gordon Quinton. He was a gentleman: he withdrew without argument and before recrimination. And he was exceedingly generous. Alice received a settlement of $75,000 tax-free. She also received, in full deed, the house in Locust Valley; for the benefit of the child Wendy, then 12, Gordon committed himself to the sum of $300 a week until Wendy was 21. For financial advice Alice's lawyer recommended one of the best accountants in Nassau County, Ralph Haskell. His advice was simple but solid: $25,000 went into a savings bank; $25,000 went into common stock—AT&T; and $25,000 went into preferred stock in General Motors. Then Alice retained a housekeeper to care for Wendy and went off for a full refresher course in stenography and typing. She resisted the compromise of complaisant matron. She was not going to sit quietly in Locust Valley and watch the grass grow; not at age 34 with all her blossoms blooming.

After six months with Ira Newton, real estate, she knew, and he knew, that they fit, and she talked to him about getting rid of the house in Locust Valley and moving to Rockville Centre. Ira himself handled the deal, and of course he refused any commission. He sold the house at the highest possible price—$125,000—and once again Ralph Haskell was brought in. This time $25,000 was added to the savings accounts and $100,000 went into government bonds. Only Ira Newton knew that she was a rich lady, but he never once mentioned it; as far as he was concerned, and she loved him for it, she was the executive secretary with the desk up front.

It was at that period, before disposing of the house in Locust Valley, that she obtained this apartment in Rockville Centre. And it was a godsend. There was an excellent school for Wendy only two minutes' walk from the house. And the drive from house to job—ten minutes. Many a time, *many* a time, she awoke at eight-thirty from a tinctured slumber and was at her desk at Newton Realty, drowsy and perhaps for her even frowzy, at nine o'clock on the button. Of course, nothing is ever perfect. It was a fine apartment house of chrome and steel and glittering windows in a high-rent neighborhood and the rooms were lovely, but the landlord pinched pennies and cut corners: no doorman, and occasionally in the winter there was insufficient heat. The advantages, however, far outweighed the disadvantages.

She ate, washed the dishes, drew a tub, sprinkled in bath oil. Tonight she was going to *move!* We will try to make some new acquaintances. I've been a virgin for at least three months, she thought. She removed the housecoat, smiled at herself in the mirror. Thank you, dear Lord, I mean I know how old I am, and that's not 42 looking back at me from the mirror, and I'm not one to kid myself. When I tell them 35, nobody even thinks to lift an eyebrow. Maybe I eat right or something—meat and potatoes and vegetables. And I jog, play tennis, dabble in the health foods, and pop vitamins like the kids pop pep pills. Whatever, at 42 I look young, I feel young, and I'm so sexy today I can attack a pillow in bed. And my figure there in the mirror, I can't complain, can I? A big pair of boobs, but firm, and a slender waist, round buttocks, strong thighs, long legs, and all smooth and supple. She slid into the tub for a good long hot soak.

In Garden City, at seven o'clock, Donald Wharton Cranford locked the front door of his shop and turned off the front lights. He continued turning off the store lights as he walked to the rear, through the stockroom and into the large square office, which contained solid expensive furniture and every necessary appurtenance—including a pink-tiled lavatory with a stall shower. He removed his clothes. He hung his suit and tie in a closet, then dumped shirt, socks and underclothes into a hamper. In the bathroom he shaved with an electric razor. He had a tough, dark beard. He was 28, but looked older. And he was good-looking. He had a firm jaw, a strong chin, regular features. He was six feet tall and had broad shoulders.

When he finished shaving, he stepped into the stall shower and let the water run at good speed. He came out refreshed. He toweled. He rubbed on underarm deodorant, applied cologne to his body. He dressed in a white shirt, striped tie, and a custom-tailored suit, one of many in the closet. Whatever had been in the other suit he transferred to the suit he was now wearing, and then he added the items he would need if he got lucky. It was always a long chance because his requirements were special, precise and exclusive. Which was why there were such great gaps of time between successes.

He went to the phone and called home.

Diana answered. "Hello?"

"Hi, babe."

"Hi, Don."

"How're my kids?" Twins, Adam and Walter, four years old.

"Great. How's my husband?"

"Rather be home where he belongs."

"Honey, what you have to do, you have to do."

He explained these nights as out with the boys. The boys were supposedly customers, and out-with-the-boys was necessary to stimulate business; as she damn well knew. Since he had taken over the business, it had boomed as never before.

"I'll try to be home early, but you know how it is." He laughed. "Don't bank on it."

"I know. Please remember to eat, Donald. Eat good."

"Right. Love you. Take care." He hung up.

He put out the lights and went out the rear door into the alley. A desolate alley. He locked the door. His car was parked in the alley. A late-model Mercury, gleaming, shining. All except the license plates, which were dirty, somehow always caked with mud. He unlocked the car, climbed in, turned over the motor, put on the headlights. The car purred out of the alley. First stop would be a restaurant. He knew just where. He was in the mood for sauerbraten with red cabbage and potato dumplings. Then afterward he would try that new joint he had heard about on Sunrise Highway.

Alice Quinton selected a simple dress, not cut too low. She had what Ira called a *zaftig* figure, and she didn't want to exaggerate it: she didn't want to be too conspicuous. She was going out on her own, alone, and hoped she hadn't lost her touch. It was a long time since she was last out hunting. She knew where she was going. A few of her friends casually had mentioned a tavern recently opened in Merrick, Pemberton's Pub, on Sunrise Highway. The drinks were expensive, which kept the kids out. Pemberton's, she'd been told, catered to sophisticated singles. She smiled. Sophisticated singles means married. Good enough. On this Tuesday night Alice Quinton was not seeking a husband.

At ten to ten she rode down in the automatic elevator. In the car she rolled the windows down. It was warm for October. A lovely night, clear, stars in the sky. She drove at a steady pace, no swerves. She was a good driver. She hoped she would meet a nice man, somebody to her taste. If not—nothing. Alice Quinton was a very particular lady.

In 20 minutes she was there. She locked the car in the parking lot and then entered a really beautiful room. The lights were soft, the walls were red velvet. In front there was a long bar. In the rear there was a separate, wider room with tables for couples and a small dance floor. The music was romantic, none of that disco rock. The bar was crowded. She was nervous. She needed the kind of drink that would get to her quickly and she knew just what that was. She ordered a vodka martini, straight up. She consumed it quickly and almost at once felt good. She was on her second vodka martini, this one on the rocks, when she saw him.

It was an L-shaped bar. She was on the long part. He was at an angle to her, at the short end of the bar. Nice! Tall, dark, young, intense-looking—a straight nose and a high forehead. She glanced at him and he glanced at her and click: barroom eye contact. She did not smile and neither did he, but somewhere between them there was a smile, tentative, distant: the no-smile barroom smile. A man offered to buy her a drink; she politely refused.

Another man offered; she refused. Men talked to her, men asked her to dance; she refused politely. She nursed her martini on the rocks and sent out silent messages to the tall man at the short end of the L-shaped bar. And she was receiving messages. He approved that she refused the men offering to buy drinks. He approved that she refused the invitations to dance. But he certainly took his time. At least a half hour. Momentarily she was looking the other way, but then when she turned, he was no longer there at his place at the bar: he was right here near her.

"You're a beautiful woman," he said. Not embarrassingly. Quietly. At her ear.

"Well, thank you kindly, kind sir."

"No, please, honest, I really mean it."

"Well, thank you." But more with it. Earnest.

"You don't dance?"

"Of course I dance."

"I mean, I noticed people asked you."

"I don't dance just because people ask." She smiled broadly. She was proud of her teeth.

"Would you dance with me?"

"I'd love to."

He was a good dancer, strong. She judged him about 30. The dance floor was small and it was crowded and therefore they danced closely. She felt his tumescence at the fork of her thighs. She did not discourage it. In fact she encouraged it, by a few little pelvic thrusts of her own.

They returned to the bar.

"Look," he said. "Can we, should we, a table,

you know? I'd like us, I mean, to get acquainted. I mean, all right, if you please—?''

"I please. I'd like it very much."

She opened her purse to pay her bar bill. He did not permit it. He paid and led her back to the rear to a table where a waitress in a skimpy skirt inquired, "What'll it be, folks?"

"What would you like?" he asked his red-haired lady.

Time to shift. "Vodka and tonic," she said to the waitress.

He ordered a bourbon and Coke, tall glass, lots of ice.

And then they talked, the get-acquainted barroom talk, most of which, as she knew from the old days, was bullshit. But she liked this guy. And knew of course what she was liking him for! And knew what he was liking *her* for. Kid, she thought, we're going to get laid, you and me, but first we must perform the necessary rituals, huh? We must look serious and talk serious and lie through our teeth at each other.

"You didn't mention your name," she said.

"Corbin. Don Corbin. You?"

"Alice Quinton."

"A lovely name." He was a smooth worker. And so sexy and handsome. Thick black hair, big, dark, liquid eyes. And that soft, calm, whispery voice. You're elected, Mr. Corbin. I mean I wouldn't really trust you as far as I could throw you, but for an affair, a little sexual satisfaction, you suit me where I feel you most. And he was not

some little *schnook*. Definitely not. She knew
men's clothes. The lapels on the suit, the way the
collar lay, the way the sleeves were set in the shoulders. That's a custom-made job and had to cost a
pretty penny.

"Are you married, Mr. Corbin? And let me has-
ten to say—I don't care. Let your wife worry."

The waitress delivered their drinks and went
away.

"Married but separated," he said. "You?"

"Married but divorced. And in case you're thinking about age, I'm happy to tell you my age. I don't
lie because I simply don't care. Thirty-four."

"You sure don't look it."

Oh, the bullshit artist. "Thank you," she said.
"You? Wish to confess age?"

"Thirty-five."

And then of course they were into their signs and
she was Pisces and he was Aquarius and that combination, as all the world knows, is most compatible. She told him she was an executive secretary.
He told her he was an airline pilot. He asked if she
was here with girl friends.

"No. I came alone." She laughed. "Looking for
trouble."

She had passed the first test. There were other
answers he needed, but he would mix those pertinent questions into the whole mishmash of the conversation as they went along. He waved to the
waitress and ordered a repeat of their drinks.

"Do you have any children, Donny?" He *hated*
when anyone called him Donny. He was Don.

"Luckily, no," he said. "You?"

"None. Whereabouts do you live?"

"Woodmere. Near Kennedy. I share an apartment with my brother." When you share a pad, you can't ask the lady to go there to shack up with you. And he would *never* ask the lady to go to a motel. "How about you?" he said. "Where you from?"

"Rockville Centre."

"House? Apartment?"

"Apartment." She drank. She was beginning to sound slightly bombed.

"How many roommates?" he asked.

"No roommates. Me alone."

Another test properly passed. His heart thudded. Jesus, did the luck finally come around? Was this going to be the night? They drank. They danced. She told him she was born in New York City, never went to college. He told her he was born in Los Angeles and was a graduate of UCLA (not a word of which was true). He was dying to know if there was a doorman at her apartment house, or an elevator man, but he could not get the conversation around to that, and he didn't dare press or he might frighten her. So far, she was perfect. At long last, perfect. Don't do anything to scare her. Easy. Take it easy. At one-thirty she looked at her watch and said, "Oh my, the time. I didn't think it was this late."

He called the waitress. He paid the check. They went out into the warm October night. She clung to his arm.

"I like you, Donny. I like you very much."

"You're a doll, babe. Tell you true, I'm crazy about you."

"Look, you live with your brother. I don't live with anybody. We'll go back to my place. For a nightcap. Or coffee. Or, if you want, I'll cook you ham and eggs. Whatever you want."

"You're sweet. You're so damn sweet." He kissed her neck.

In the parking lot, there was a momentary drunken problem. She had a car. He had a car. "Do we leave one here and go together?" she asked.

"No," he said. "You drive yours and I'll drive mine behind you. But don't go too fast. I wouldn't want to lose you."

They arrived, a procession of two, at the apartment house in Rockville Centre. There was no doorman. He could see that the elevators were automatic. Had there been a doorman or elevator man he would have gone, as he had gone before to other apartments, up into her apartment. He would have had a drink and then begged off because of the late hour. He would have taken her phone number and promised to call, and she would never have heard from him again.

They entered an elevator; she touched one of the buttons. He did not know which button. He could not see; for the moment his eyes were glazed. He could hear the sound of his blood pumping in his ears. This is it. Finally after such a long time; I know it, I feel it. Oh, sweet Jesus. Oh, sweet Jesus God. Oh, this is it! His penis pained him, swollen, turgid against his trouser leg.

In the carpeted living room of the apartment, a richly furnished apartment, she offered booze, coffee or coffee and eats. He said booze. He said a bourbon and Coca-Cola, if you please, but when she brought it, he did not touch it. He was experienced. He did not touch any hard surfaces. He touched the soft surfaces of Alice Quinton. He held her, he kissed her, he took off her clothes and let them fall. Jesus, this broad has a real wild body. Jesus, look at those crazy bazooms.

"Hey, baby, Donny boy, you're still all dressed up. Like you're at a wake or something. Come on. Join the party. Let's get some clothes off, hey?"

His right hand slid inside his jacket and came out with slender, rolled-up strips of leather.

"What the hell?" she said. "What's that?"

"Thongs." He unrolled them.

"Thongs? What's thongs? What's with thongs?"

The soft whispery voice. "I'd like to tie you up. You know—bondage. Discipline. I get off on that kind of thing. Fantasy. Everything is in the mind, you know, fantasy. I'm into a little S & M. But I won't really hurt you, sweetie. Wouldn't hurt you for the world."

She laughed, naked, swaying drunkenly. Of course she knew about "that kind of thing." Restraint, some of them called it. Discipline, others called it. S & M. Sadomasochism. Everybody has their thing. Their gig, their bit. "Donny, baby, with me you don't need no thongs. No bondage, no discipline. I only happen to be the greatest piece of ass God ever created, and there are experts that'll write me testimonials. So put away your leather, put away your thongs. If you tie me up you won't be able to get my real action, and *you'll* be missing out. So take off your clothes, kid, and come and get me, and by tomorrow morning you'll be into a nervous breakdown."

One of his hands went behind him, to a rear pocket of his trousers, and then the switchblade knife was out front, the extruded blade gleaming. He moved to her quickly and the point of the knife touched her neck and she felt a trickle of warm blood. She was gasping now, inhaling breath, frightened to death, but his deep, soft, easy voice was reassuring. "It's a game, baby. It's a game I need to play. A sex game, sweetie. Fantasy. The fantasy of sadism, the fantasy of rape, the fantasy of a bound and helpless victim. We all get off in different ways. Please, let me do it my way. All I want to do is tie your wrists behind you, and tie your ankles. Tell me okay. If you tell me okay, I don't have to hold this knife to you."

"Okay, okay. Jesus, you never know what you meet. You look like such a nice guy."

He scowled, aggrieved. "I am a nice guy. I'm going to put the knife down, and then I'll tie you up like I said. Play my game with me, Alice. You'll enjoy. You'll see."

"Heck, I don't have any alternative, do I?"

He smiled. "Nope."

"Okay. Play. Maybe you're right. I'm just drunk enough. Maybe I'll like it, whatever it is. Hell, there's always a first time for everything, right?"

"You're a doll, babe."

He laid away the knife. He tied her wrists behind her. He tied her ankles. "Now go down on your knees," he said. He helped her. He held her arms so that she wouldn't tumble as she went down.

On her knees she looked up at him wondering what his next move would be.

"So? Now?"

"Now you'll suck me off." His hands trembled as he opened his fly. He produced his penis, put it to her mouth. "Do it easy, babe. Nice and slow and easy."

She was proficient at fellatio, and the dark young man grunted. She used her lips, tongue, palate, throat, even her teeth lightly. And had to admit she was enjoying a weird, crazy rapture. The posture of obeisance. The fettered wrists and ankles. The playact of the rape-compulsion. Maybe they did have something going for them, these whacked-out S & M people. Occasionally he pulled it out, and she knew why. To prolong the pleasure. To keep back from climax. And when he put it back in, she did him gently at first, until he was grunting up there again, shivering, panting, holding her head and thrusting. And finally when he came it was a massive load, most of which she swallowed. A little dribbled out of a corner of her mouth. She looked up at him. She was smiling.

"Good?" she asked. She repeated: "Good?"

He didn't answer. Then she saw in amazement that his thing was still standing. She couldn't believe it. This guy had just shot a lump like a bull;

yet that was a rigid erection sticking out of his pants. She had been told about men like that. Extraordinarily virile, abnormally virile. There was a word. Like for women there was the word nymphomania. For men—yes, she remembered. Satyriasis. And another word. Priapism. Whatever the heck the words, guys like that could fuck all night. Which was all right with her.

"Look, Donny, get me up, will you? We've had it with your bondage, with the restraint, right? Now untie me and we'll go to bed and we'll have some sex you'll be able to write home about. Man, you're all dressed, you've got all your clothes on, for chrissake. Now get undressed, and get me untied, and let's get into bed and have some *real* action, right?"

"Right."

He undressed. He carefully laid his clothes away, far away. The man had a good body, strong, muscular. Just a little hint of a paunch. He must like to eat. Maybe she'd cook him a real meal one day.

"You're a nice-looking guy, Donny. Real nice. Now go get your crazy knife and slice me out of my leather shackles." She laughed. "But kindly be careful." And laughed again. "I bruise easy."

He took up the knife and went to her. He cut her throat from ear to ear. He kicked her bound feet from under her until she was lying supine. He bent and slashed her breasts, stabbing, hacking, and as he rose from her his ejaculate upon her body was involuntary.

He wiped the blade of the knife on her scattered

clothing, closed the knife, tossed it on his clothes. He went to the bathroom and cleansed himself with a towel and water. In the living room he dressed and pocketed the knife. He used a handkerchief on the doorknob when he went out. He knew how to be careful about fingerprints. He knew he never left fingerprints. But even if somewhere by chance he had left a print, it would not be of any use to them. He had never been arrested, he had never been in the armed services: there was no file of his prints for comparison. But he was certain, quite certain, he had never anywhere left a fingerprint for any such comparison.

Downstairs he climbed into the shiny Mercury and drove home to his neat little house in West Hempstead. He hoped the rolling garage door did not disturb any member of his small family. In the house, he first went to the children's bedroom. A tiny night light was burning. He fixed Walter's cover. Adam was fine. He tiptoed out and into the big bedroom, and there he clicked on another tiny night light. Diana stirred in her sleep, but did not awaken. He undressed. He doused the little light and groped his way to the bed. He never wore pajamas. Diana never wore pajamas or a nightgown because he had taught her not to wear pajamas or nightgown. She was a good girl. She listened. She had listened to her father, and she listened to her husband; as she had listened to the nuns who had been her teachers in parochial school. She was good. Not some kind of bum like them broads that hung out in bars. Not like that cunt in the house in

Hicksville who used to strut around in the five rooms with her naked tits bouncing like basketballs.

He slipped into the bed and under the cover and took his wife in his arms and he held her like that, face to face, close to him. He had never once touched his fingers to her vagina. He had never once kissed her breasts. Now he kissed her mouth and pressed his penis to the hot place between her legs; he could tell by the wetness, the feel of the lubrication, when she was ready to receive him. Then he turned her on her back and mounted her and they had intercourse as always in that one position: he was on top. But he was a good husband. He did it slow and easy. He always let her come first. He regarded her as a good and proper wife; she always accepted the husband's will. It could be once in a night, or five times in a night, or no times at all for a week. She never made the move. Not like them bums at the bars. If he did not make the first move, she did not make a move at all. Tonight he did it once and then he let her sleep. She was good. She was pure. She was obedient and respectful.

TWO

On this bright Wednesday morning in October Ira Newton arrived at ten o'clock at the Maple Street storefront which was Ira Newton Realty, Inc. Of the four desks in the front room of the store only one was occupied, Seymour Roebling's. Ira knew that today Dick Rochelle was out supervising repairs in one of Newton Realty's apartment houses, and Freddie Blackwood was showing a house for sale in Baldwin.

"Good morning, Sy," he said to Seymour. He glanced at the desk nearest the entrance. "When our lovely lady returns from our lovely ladies' room, kindly tell her the boss has some dictation for her." He proceeded toward the rear, to his enclosed private office.

"Mr. Newton!" Seymour was their youngest employee.

Ira turned. "What?"

"She's not in the ladies' room."

"Well, wherever she is."

"She didn't come in."

"She didn't come—what?"

"Figured you knew. Figured you gave her the day off or something."

"Who opened? You opened? What time?"

"Five to nine."

19

"Did she call?"

"No. That's what I meant when I said I figured—"

"No show? No call? That ain't Quinton." Ira marched into his office and slammed the door. He sat at his desk and lit a cigarette. Not Quinton. Always in there on the ball, strictly dependable. Was something wrong? When they're young and beautiful, anything can happen. Hell, these days, if they're old and ugly anything can happen. He pulled the phone to him and called her. No answer. He let the phone ring ten times, hung up. He called again, ten rings. He hung up and sat there.

This was not Alice Quinton; if she didn't feel well, if she were ill, she would have called in. But perhaps she was too ill to call; maybe she's had some kind of seizure. Should he put in a 911? Now hold it, Ira. No answer in her apartment—maybe she's in someone else's apartment. Maybe she went out with a guy last night and they got good and smashed and they're still sleeping it off at *his* place.

He rubbed out his cigarette. He slammed out of the office.

"I—I don't know. Hunch. Something. I—I'm worried about Quinton. Going over to her place; check it out. You stay just where you are, Seymour. Stay put. I'll be in touch."

In the car he thought: better than calling the police. If she's with a guy and they're both laid out drunk in her apartment it could be an awful embarrassment. If she's not in the apartment—a forced entrance by the police could also be an awful embarrassment when she learned of it (which of course she would). He stayed in control; he refused to panic. He certainly could get there as quickly as the cops. And he knew the building superintendent, a stolid young man named Mike Bradley.

He drove fast and was there in seven minutes. Mike's wife told him that Mike was downstairs in the laundry room. He found Mike and explained the situation.

"We'll give it a try, Mr. Newton, but don't expect you're gonna come up with no royal flush. What I mean, all I got is a key to the bottom lock, period. She's also got a top lock and an inside latch. If she's in there, locked on top and latched—the only way, we'd have to call the cops. If she ain't in there, like out somewhere, and she used both keys, we still can't get in there without the cops knocking out the locks for us. And from what you tell me, Mr. Newton, just because she don't come in to work and don't happen to answer her phone, I just don't think that would give the cops the right to break into her pad. Christ, with any half-ass lawyer she could sue the sonsabitches."

"Let's get up there, Mike."

"You rang downstairs?"

"Of course. Now please, let's get up there."

"Okay. Like I said, Mr. Newton, we'll give it a try."

The apartment was 8-B. Mike inserted his key in the lower lock, turned it, tried the knob, and the door opened. They glanced at each other and went in, both of them stopping in the small foyer.

"Alice," Newton called.

Then louder: "Alice!"

Silence. Mike Bradley shrugged, grinned.

Newton, followed by Bradley, traversed the foyer and turned left and they entered the living room and saw her.

"Oh, my God," Newton cried. "Oh, my dear God!"

He heard the thump beside him. Mike Bradley had collapsed.

Ira Newton stepped over the man and ran to the phone.

On this bright Wednesday Franklin Demarest, a veteran political reporter on the newspaper *Newsday,* was strolling along West Street in Mineola when he was startled by the sudden screeching sirens of the squad cars hurtling out of the garage of police headquarters. He watched them fly by, then shrugged them off. He had his own troubles.

He was on his way toward the Executive Building for his appointment with S. Lloyd Jutland, the Nassau County Executive. He had come in early from Washington, had had another argument with Bill Oradell, his managing editor, and although it was still morning several belts of Scotch were already seething in his belly. He had an appointment with the County Executive because he needed a verification—Bill Oradell refused to print Demarest's story without Jutland's verification. Which was dumb. Frank Demarest had received his information from the proverbial unimpeachable source and he knew it to be straight goods. And if Demarest had the goods now it should be printed now; that kind of goods could flow elsewhere and he would be scooped on his own story because the intransigent managing editor insisted on the verification.

Demarest did not oppose verification. He was all for it whenever possible, and it was damn possible now, because Jutland was an old friend—but that was not the point. Point was, if no verification, no story. And the reason Bill Oradell was giving him this hard time was the Moscow assignment.

It was still a long way off, but the boys were already scrambling for it and Frank Demarest was one of the boys—except he was not Bill Oradell's boy for the Moscow job. However, good old Bill did not have the final say. On top of him in descending order was the publisher, the general manager and the executive editor—which was why the managing editor was sticking in the pins whenever a cushion presented itself. He preferred the seasoned Frank Demarest on the Washington–Long Island shuttle. Frank was good, Frank knew all the right people and the conservative Bill Oradell was against making nuts-and-bolts changes when the machinery was running well.

The S. Lloyd story was not the biggest ever to have occurred on the North American continent. In that context, it was minuscule. It was New York State up for grabs. Next year was an election year and it was rumored the present governor would not run again, so a hell of a lot of hats were already in the ring. The next hat to be tossed, according to Demarest's information, was S. Lloyd Jutland's.

In the County Executive's reception room Frank Demarest said hello to the beautiful Puerto Rican receptionist. Jutland was a smart politician. He maneuvered his ethnics like a field general maneuvered his troops. Jutland had them all, and many in high places: Blacks, Hispanics, Jews, Catholics, Germans, Poles, Italians, even WASPS—nobody had cause for complaint. He was a smart apple, S. Lloyd. Smart enough for governor and young enough for ambition beyond that office.

"How goes it with The Man?" Demarest inquired.

"Waiting for you. He's all yours for the next thirty minutes."

"*Grácias.*"

He pushed through swinging doors, greeted the outer secretary (black), greeted the inner secretary (Italian) and entered the sanctum sanctorum.

"Hi," Jutland said. They shook hands and Jutland returned to the swivel chair bchind his desk.

Demarest sank into a comfortable chair opposite.

"I'm here on business, Lloyd."

Naturally, Jutland parried. "How goes it with your brother, the good doctor?"

"Goes great. Matter of fact I'm having dinner at his home this evening."

"Please convey my regards. And my love to his beautiful Lori."

"Shall do. Now, I would like to ask: When are you going to announce, Mr. County Executive?"

"Pardon?"

"Governor of the Empire State."

Jutland peered across at the reporter from *Newsday*. The reporter spread his arms and did a sort of a bow while sitting in a chair. He admired Lloyd Jutland. The guy was 40 years old, with the face of a fox, the eyes of a dove and the rapacious capacity of a hungry lion. A born politician.

"Announce?" Jutland said.

"Hat in the ring for the candidacy. There's gossip floating all the way to Washington that your organization is all geared to go."

"Gossip also floats in reverse." Jutland did a toothy smile. "I've heard that Franklin Demarest is anxious to go over to Moscow as correspondent for *Newsday*. True or false?"

"Very true."

"I might be able to help with that."

"You'd have my deep appreciation, sir."

Jutland pointed a finger, winked imperceptibly, nodded. The politician had made a deal. "You see, Frank, we simply cannot be premature. An announcement involving public office must be carefully managed, properly orchestrated."

"Lloyd, will you please listen—"

"We can't jump the gun. Confidentially, we know exactly when—"

"I'm afraid you're not going to have the luxury. I know you're going to announce—unimpeachable source—and thus far it's all mine. Exclusive. But, as you know, there's no exclusive control on *any* story. I've got it all now, but if somebody else catches up with it, that wouldn't be good for you, my friend. I mean with me it would be better. Would you want that story to break in the *Washington Post* under the by-line of a reporter who thinks of S. Lloyd Jutland as some little asshole in a county seat called Mineola? Or would you prefer the story broke in a Long Island newspaper under *my* by-line, and I happen to think you're as close to a statesman as any politician can get. It's out there, Lloyd, and it's going to happen before your 'orchestration' and I say it's better that it happens through me. But Oradell won't let me write a single word without, first, your verification. And that's why I'm here, Mr. County Executive.''

Jutland took a pipe from a rack, filled the bowl with tobacco, lit it, puffed, remained silent for minutes. Then he said, "You win."

"But do I lose Moscow?"

"No." Jutland's smile was stern. "Now *you* listen to *me*. You do the story, but it's going to have to contain certain facts that this whole damn state should know about."

"Lloyd, please remember that my managing editor can prune my story."

"Don't worry about Bill Oradell. I'll talk to him, personally."

"What facts, Mr. County Executive?"

"The governor of a state is not a legislator; he's an executive. S. Lloyd Jutland is not a legislator; he's an executive. And a *major* executive; not some little asshole in a place called Mineola. The County Executive of Nassau County presides over an area of three hundred square miles and a population of a million five hundred thousand human beings. Nassau is the most populous suburban county in the United States. It has a higher population than all but six cities in the entire country. In fact, in population this suburb actually outranks fifteen of the *states* of these United States. Which means that the County Executive—''

The phone rang. Jutland glowered, disregarded it, but it kept ringing. He seized the receiver. ''I gave instructions! I specifically told you I was not to be dis—''

His eyes opened wide. His jaw dropped. The color drained out of his face. He listened for a long time, and then he hung up. He sat there.

''What?'' Demarest said.

''Jesus Christ.''

''Lloyd, what—?''

''Jesus Christ,'' Jutland said.

''What the hell's the matter? What's happened? Lloyd!''

''Slash,'' Jutland croaked. ''That fucking Nassau Slasher. At it again. Another woman. Trussed up. Throat ripped open. Slashed. One breast practically amputated.''

''Oh, no,'' Demarest said. ''Oh, Jesus Christ, no,'' he said.

THREE

In the Quinton apartment the man in charge was Lieutenant Mark Andover of Homicide. The moment he saw the mutilated woman, her wrists and ankles bound in the leather strips, he recognized the modus operandi. This case belonged to Jake McVail. He put through the call to McVail's office. Then he called the Commissioner. The Commissioner said he would inform the County Executive. In the meantime, in the Quinton apartment, Andover's people did their work: the fingerprint experts and the police photographers. The room was crowded with detectives. The uniformed policemen kept the press outside. Andover had quickly dismissed the shaken Mike Bradley. Now in the bedroom he was questioning Ira Newton. Newton told him all he knew about Alice Quinton (including the present whereabouts of Quinton's daughter) and Andover expertly reduced the data to succinct notes in his notebook. A detective came in to tell him the medical examiner was here. Andover went out to the medical examiner and told him he was not to touch the body until Jake McVail showed up. The medical examiner grumbled, then he sat down in a chair and smoked cigarettes. Twenty minutes later McVail arrived and with him was his aide and able second, Detective-lieutenant Pamela Medford. The medical examiner looked up at McVail but said nothing. He sat there and waited.

He was an awesome figure, Captain Jackson Brendan McVail, mostly because of his bulk. He was an immense man, with a hell of a lot of loose fat on him. The medical examiner judged him to weigh about 260. The medical examiner was a movie buff who liked to watch the old films on late TV. Captain Jackson Brendan McVail was a combination of Charles Laughton and Lee J. Cobb, but the captain was bigger than either of them. The medical examiner knew McVail's age, 59, and knew he was with the Department for 37 years. The guy was jowly, paunchy, shaggy, wrinkled. Nobody really knew the man: he was not what you would call garrulous. On the other hand, maybe he was; the medical examiner simply did not know him well enough for an opinion. (Who did?) The medical examiner, like everyone else, had a hell of a lot of respect for Jake McVail; it was universally acknowledged that the captain was an absolutely brilliant police officer. But the medical examiner, in his meditative moments, admitted to being a little bit afraid of the guy; he believed McVail to be rigid, a martinet, strictly law and order. We're all entitled to our opinions, right? Free country.

Andover led McVail to the body.

"Looks like your boy's loose again," Andover said.

The big man squatted. He looked at the gaping hole that was the throat, the slashed breasts, the ankles tied by the thongs. He stood up. A sigh rattled out of him. He faced Andover. He spoke quietly, but it was a rasp. That was his voice: as though there were sandpaper in the larynx. "I really thought this son of a bitch was finished. Dead somewhere. I really thought, by God, we were rid of the bastard. Ten months. It's been ten months since the last one. They croak. People croak. I really thought, honest to God, this bastard, somehow, somewhere, had finally croaked on us." He turned from Andover to the medical examiner. "What's with you? You on vacation?"

The M.E. stood up. "Lieutenant Andover asked me to wait until you arrived."

"Well, I've arrived, haven't I?" Then to Andover. "Your boys have looked over the thongs?"

"Yes."

To the medical examiner: "When you untie the leather strips, you'll please give them to me."

"Yessir, Captain."

"Thank you."

The medical examiner went to work on the body. McVail talked with Andover, got all of the story that Andover knew, and took Andover's notes. Then McVail pointed to the tall glass on the coffee table.

"Smells like bourbon and Coke," Andover said.

"Prints?"

"Only one set, and the boys say, from the prints all over—the kitchen and all—they're hers."

"When the M.E.'s through with her, let the boys make sure."

"Right."

"And get that glass and contents down to the lab—just in case."

"Right."

"No sign of break-in, of course. Nothing has been stolen."

"Correct."

"The son of a bitch," McVail growled.

Ira Newton said, "May I call my office, please?"

"Sure. If the lieutenant's men have finished dusting the phone."

"Yeah, it's okay," Andover said.

"Hell, it was me who called the police," Newton said. "I was the last one to touch the phone."

"Cops are crazy, huh?" McVail grinned. Newton made his call. Then McVail asked him, "Did she drink bourbon and Coke?"

"I don't really know. Sometimes she drank Scotch, sometimes vodka, but I don't really know."

"Did she say anything about having a date last night?"

"No sir, not to me."

The medical examiner came near. "I'd say, give or take an hour either way, she's dead about twelve hours. There's semen in the mouth and on the face, and semen on the body." He turned over the thongs to McVail. "Can we take her now, Captain?"

"All yours." McVail looked at the notes, looked at Newton. "Daughter in Tucson. Ex-husband in Manhattan. Do you know how long she was going with that Allendale, the boy friend?" —

"About a year. Broke up about three months ago."

"I'll want to talk to him," McVail said to Andover.

"Right."

"Now, Mr. Newton, I'd like you to sit down with a pen and paper and write down the names, and the addresses if you know the addresses, of everybody that you know that she knew, including the people at work."

"Yessir."

"After that, you can go back to your office."

"Thank you, Captain."

"Mark, you'll attend to notification of next of kin."

"Right."

"She had an address book?"

"Yes."

"We'll want to talk to everybody in that book."

"Right."

"Pam." McVail touched her elbow and took Lieutenant Pamela Medford to a corner of the room. "I want you to go see Marge. Tell her Leather Boy's with us again. Tell her to clear her decks so we can have a full review tomorrow afternoon."

Medford nodded and left.

"Any snapshots of Quinton?" McVail asked Andover. "That we can make duplicates to show around?"

"Yes, I've quite a batch."

"Good."

McVail watched as one of the detectives carefully carried away the glass of bourbon and Coke.

McVail knew that nothing would show up on that glass except Quinton's fingerprints. It was a part of the modus. And even if Quinton never in her life had drunk bourbon, it did not mean that they had a clue to Leather Boy—that he was a drinker of bourbon and Coke. That was also a part of the modus. Sometimes there would be a glass of Scotch and soda, sometimes rye and ginger, sometimes brandy, sometimes a cup of coffee—but no lips would have touched that glass or cup and any fingerprints would be solely those of the occupant of the apartment. And they were not going to discover any incriminating fingerprints *anywhere* in the apartment. McVail sighed. His jowls shook. He lit one of his gnarled black cigars. "Okay," he said sourly. "Let's give the press boys their stories, and then we go back to the office and solve our case."

There were three important persons in Pamela Medford's life: Tom Stockton, who was her husband and whom she loved; Captain Jackson Brendan McVail, whom she worshiped; and Dr. Margaret Wyckoff, whom she adored. She had of course called first, and now she sat in the waiting room, which was on the ground floor of Wyckoff's house in Cedarhurst. Wyckoff was in there with a patient.

Pam Medford had always wanted to be a cop, all the way back to early youth. She was a bachelor of arts from Adelphi and there she had also taken her master's in criminal justice. At age 21 she had applied for a job with the Nassau County Police

Department, at a time when they were anxious for a few token women on the force. That was 16 years ago and the lady who was applying to be a cop was a college graduate with a master's. They grabbed her, and in short order she made sergeant. She passed the test for lieutenant but remained there high on the list while males were promoted over her and received appointments. It was Captain Jake McVail, with a heavy clout in the Nassau Police Department, who had studied the list and then selected her as his first assistant in the then newly established Sex Crime Squad. Ten years ago Detective-lieutenant Pamela Medford had married Thomas Stockton, born the same year as she, and they lived in a house in Roslyn Heights, with no children. He was a lawyer with offices in Mineola.

Now Pam Medford smiled inwardly. She had not seen Marge Wyckoff in quite some time and the purpose of this visit was awfully gruesome business, but she had a little surprise to impart to Marge and she knew how pleased—

The inner door opened. The patient, a pale man, walked quickly past her, opened the outer door, went through, and then Dr. Margaret Wyckoff was there in the waiting room.

"Pam. It's been a long time." She was in her 50s, tall, plump, a connoisseur of food and wines. Unmarried, a renowned psychiatrist, she was a consultant to the Nassau Police Department. "Please come in." And in the inner office she said, "Emergency. But on the phone you didn't state—"

"Leather Boy came back to the fold last night."

"No! God, it's ten months! I thought we'd had the last of him. Destroyed somewhere. Dead—"

"That's what Jake said."

"Sit down, Pam."

Medford sat. Wyckoff went around and sat at her desk.

"All right, tell me," she said.

Pam Medford imparted facts and Marge Wyckoff wrote notes. Alice Quinton. Divorced. Lived alone in a good apartment in a good neighborhood in Rockville Centre. Apartment building. No doorman. No elevator man. Alice Quinton, naked, her throat slashed, her breasts mutilated, her wrists bound in leather strips, her ankles bound in leather strips, semen in her mouth, semen on her face, semen on her body. Nothing stolen. No disarray. "Leather Boy," Medford said. In the press he was, sensationally, the Nassau Slasher. To the insiders, because of the thongs, he was Leather Boy. "Jake wants a conference tomorrow. He wants to pick it all up, a full review."

Wyckoff nodded. She consulted her diary, made phone calls, arranged postponements. At long last she said, "Starting at two o'clock tomorrow, I'm free the rest of the day."

"Fine. Jake'll call and tell you what time."

"How's Tom?"

"Wonderful. How's Hugh?"

"Wonderful." Hugh Ramsey, old-line police reporter for *Newsday,* a widower for nine years, and Wyckoff's lover for twelve years. When Pam once asked why they didn't marry, Marge had said,

"Better this way. We're separate, we're distinct, and therefore forever lovers. With us it's always a date, it's always romantic. We always dress up for each other, we touch on the perfume, always try to look good for each other. It doesn't descend to the take-for-granted—the slovenly attitude which seems after a time to become a normal concomitant of marriage."

Pam Medford did not agree. Pam Medford loved being married. And it was a traditional-type marriage. She did not fool around, nor did Tom. People joked about it because Medford and Stockton, young and pretty, certainly had a hell of a lot of time and opportunity in their separate professions. Nothing. Old-fashioned. Strictly monogamous. But there was a little buzzing fly in their ointment—a situation about to be remedied. Tom wanted a child. Pam had her work. Tom had talked with Marge, Marge had talked with Pam, but the fly had stayed right in there in the ointment. Now Pam said, "I'm pregnant."

"I don't believe it." Wyckoff beamed.

"Believe."

There had been many long talks between them. Wyckoff had delivered many long lectures, plumping in Tom Stockton's cause.

"Three months pregnant," Pam was saying. "On March one, I'll take a year's sabbatical. I'll have my baby and stay with it for practically a year. Then I'll take in a governess and go back to work."

"Jake knows?"

"Of course."

"I congratulate you."

"I thank you. Well—got to go back to work."

"Just a minute."

"What?"

"Hugh's taking me out to dinner tonight. I'd love it if you'd join us, you and Tom. Like our treat, in advance of the happy event. Can you make it?"

"I think so. I'm on an eight-to-four tour. No matter this new thing with Leather Boy, Jake won't let me hang out too late. What time, and where?"

"I'll give you a lot of time. Let's say—seven-thirty. La Coquille. You know, Manhasset. We'll meet there. Hugh'll make the reservations. Please don't say no. A bit of relaxation. You've got to get away from some of this grisly—"

"Yes. Thank you. La Coquille. Seven-thirty. Got to run now. See you later."

Wyckoff opened a drawer and took out a long, thin, black, gnarled cigar. She smiled as she lit it. She never smoked these cigars with a patient, or in public. She smoked cigarettes. She smoked her cigars when she was alone, or alone with Hugh, or with McVail, who had introduced her to them—a long time ago. Twenty-two years. They had to go in to New York City to get these *sigari,* to a father-son tobacco shop in Little Italy. Twenty-two years, that's one hell of a long time. He was her closest friend. Hugh was her lover, but McVail was her closest friend and the one person she admired the most in all this world. A stupendous man, this Jake McVail. A high school graduate, never went to college, but the most brilliant police officer on the force, respected by his superiors and venerated by the men and women who worked with him. Brilliant? Why not? The man had an IQ of 180—and she knew because she herself had done the tests. He had joined the cops at age 22 and had quickly made detective with Homicide. And then, with his mind, he had flown up like a kite in a high wind: sergeant, lieutenant, captain.

She smoked the cheroot and closed her eyes, thinking about Jackson Brendan McVail. He had a gravelly voice and that too was as it should be: rivers of Jack Daniel's had passed down his gullet, and it went down straight, not in solution. He did not mix his drink. He knocked back his Jack Daniel's and that was it, knock after knock. When he could have his preference, he liked to have beer to chase down the Jack Daniel's. He was a big man, grizzled, a slow talker. His face was furrowed, wrinkled—hell, he was 59 and fat—but his teeth were all his own, and his eyes were gimlet sharp. He was a thinker, a good cop, a compassionate cop.

But a maverick. Unorthodox. A loner who worked at his trade in his own manner, and his success record was spectacular. Nobody—but nobody—interfered with Captain Jackson Brendan McVail.

She remembered once in her presence what the Police Commissioner had said to the County Executive: "Jake McVail is a law unto himself. Absolutely the guy is a genius, and the doc here can verify that. I am smart enough to know that when you've got a genius on your hands, you let him have his head any way he wants to go. Period, next paragraph.''

"McVail?" the County Executive had said. "You bet."

But he had had his share of personal tragedy. None of us can escape tragedy. Jake McVail's had caught up with him fourteen years ago when his daughter, Jennifer, his one child, had been raped. Age 19. She had left the house—the McVails lived in an excellent neighborhood in Plandome—to walk over to her girl friend's house nearby. It was nine o'clock in the evening; the street in the pleasant little town was quiet. Jenny was suddenly assaulted from behind and pulled to a hedge of bushes. She was beaten unconscious and repeatedly raped. As luck would have it—pure luck—when the attacker left the scene he was spotted by a policeman in a patrol car. The cop sensed something. He stopped the man for routine questions and heard the moans by the bushes. He put his gun to the man and investigated. Then he handcuffed the man and radioed for an ambulance. The man was arrested, but the district attorney had a poor case. Jenny, who had never seen the man, could not identify him, and there was no corroboration of the actual rape. Plea bargaining put the man away for two years, but Jenny was finished for the rest of her life. She never recovered from the rape. She became Dr. Wyckoff's patient, and when Wyckoff could not effect amelioration, she became another psychiatrist's patient. But, as the doctors bitterly know, every patient does not respond to treatment. Jennifer, a gentle girl, a frail sensitive human being, could not climb over the trauma and became a cripple, a psychological cripple. She quit college. She was afraid to leave the house. She would not go out on dates. She was, in a sense, a prisoner in her own home. If she could hold her father's hand, or her mother's hand, she could go out for a walk.

Jake McVail was 45 at the time of Jennifer's rape and even back then, 14 years ago, Captain McVail of Homicide had been advocating a sex crime unit, some of whose superior officers should be women. A man before his time. Back then, women officers were used as decoys, or detention matrons, or glorified office workers. Rape complainants were handled by the same cops who handled normal assault and battery cases, leering cops whose very *macho* was a put-down to women. *You can't thread a moving needle* was pervasive in regard to rape complaints (in police departments all over the country). Jackson Brendan McVail, a man before his time, was advocating a "rape squad" and was of course, 14 years ago, being denied it. When it happened to Jennifer, McVail went to the top—to the Police Commissioner, and with the Commissioner to the County Executive. McVail announced that either he got his "rape squad" (with women officers) or he resigned from the force, picked up his pension and took a job with private security. The County Executive gave his approval and a "rape squad" evolved. It was a special unit called the Sex Crime Squad and its nucleus was four persons.

There was Captain Jackson McVail. There was Detective-lieutenant Pamela Medford, whom he had clipped from the waiting-lieutenant's list. There was Sergeant Mary Caldwell, whom he had transferred to him from the Vice Squad. And there was Sergeant William Emerson, whom he took over with him from Homicide. From this nucleus they could reach out to cops in all the departments, but McVail laid down one cardinal rule: a rape victim's first interview must be with a woman police officer or in the presence of a woman police officer.

Dr. Margaret Wyckoff smoked her cigar, remembering a conversation with Captain Jackson Brendan McVail. They were discussing rage, the animal inside the psyche, the pathological criminal mind—and the gut reaction of the allegedly normal human being, the instinctive reaction to a criminal act. Do they blend? Does one become the other? "Suppose you were the cop who caught the guy who assaulted Jenny. You had the rapist in your hands and there was your daughter. You're a trained police officer. You know what you're *supposed* to do. But in those circumstances, what would you have done?"

"I'm not essentially a violent man, and it's my job to apprehend the perpetrator. But in those circumstances I'd have killed the son of a bitch. I'd have torn him apart, limb from limb."

"The beast resides in all of us, doesn't it? Sometimes hidden deep down, but it's in there, isn't it?"

"You're the doc. You ought to know."

"But you never touched the man. And you *did*

have him right there in your detention pen.''

''The hot moment was over. As you said, I'm a trained policeman, and even back then I was already a cop for twenty-three years. Most of us, cop or civilian, we learn to tamp down the rage, to keep our beast in control. Don't you think?''

''Most, yes. Not all. And not always.''

FOUR

Frank Demarest arrived at six o'clock at his brother's house in Old Westbury. He shook hands with Vic, kissed Lori, lifted little Kathy right off the floor and kissed her on the forehead. Then he made his own drink, a rob roy on the rocks, and listened to the chatter of family excitement. They were buzzing with plans for this weekend in the Adirondacks. The Victor Demarests were bird-watchers, hikers and wildlife photographers, and it was an absolutely marvelous time of year for this type of weekend. And they knew just where they were going: a rustic hotel with an excellent cuisine. And Kathy was simply jumping with delight at the prospect.

"We'll drive up in the station wagon on Friday afternoon and we'll stay through Monday evening," Vic said.

"If you're going on Friday, why not leave in the morning?"

"Because, my dear brother, I've an operation on Friday morning."

Dr. Victor Demarest was a surgeon with offices on Park Avenue in New York City. He shared these offices with a fellow surgeon, Dr. Gary Tennent, and an internist, Dr. Vernon Lyons. He was married to an extremely beautiful woman, Lori Parlin

Demarest, age 36, and they had an extremely beautiful child, Kathy, age seven. All three were blond.

"What about school?" Franklin Demarest inquired. "Seems your dad has figured out a weekend that includes Monday."

"I applied for permission to have Monday off," Kathy said gravely. "It was granted."

"She sounds like her grandfather," Frank said. "On *our* side." That grandfather had been an Episcopalian minister.

"I'm hungry," Kathy said.

"Dinner," said Lori, "is about to be served."

During dinner there was mention, but small mention, of the news that had come through about the Nassau Slasher. The Demarest family had given it scant attention. As Vic said, without interest, in the matter of the Slasher the victim was always a single woman and the murder always occurred in an apartment house. As Frank Demarest knew, that was not quite true. But the general public does not have the time or the inclination or even the opportunity to study closely the facts of modus operandi. Further, no matter how heinous a crime, there is no time for concentrated study; one day it appears in the newspaper and the next day it disappears, superseded by the crimes of the new day.

Now the conversation was back to bird-watching and wildlife and the Adirondacks, and Frank Demarest retreated. He was forty-nine years of age, six years older than his handsome brother. He was twice divorced and both wives had remarried but not he. He was a rich man, as was Vic, hugely rich

by inheritance, each having inherited from their
father, who had been hugely rich by inheritance.
Frank and Vic were the only children; the father and
mother were now deceased. Frank owned an apartment in Washington and a small house here on
Long Island in the town of New Cassel, but he was
dying to trade them in for Moscow, and he was
dying to talk to Vic about it, and lovely Lori was a
damn wise lady. No sooner was the dinner over
when she said to Kathy, "You want to help your
Mom with the dishes, honey? Let's let the
chauvinists go to the study and talk about their big-
deal male matters. One can plainly see your Uncle
Frank is fairly jumping out of his skin."

In the study Frank poured himself a Drambuie
and Vic took a brandy to the desk. "Yep. Plainly
see. Fairly jumping," Vic said. "What's up, Uncle
Frank?"

"Moscow."

"That again?"

"Stop the wise-guy shit, Doctor."

"I deserved that. I'm sorry. How's it going?"

"Look, you know my tale of woe up to now."

"Bill Oradell."

"I'm his Washington specialist and I do damn
good for him and he wants me just where I am. But
that's not where I'm going to be. I'm going to be in
Moscow—foreign correspondent. I've been pulling
strings, but today I really think I hit the piano
wire." He told about his meeting with S. Lloyd Jutland. "He promised to put in a little pressure on my
behalf. With that kind of pressure I'm in the bag

and poor Bill will have to neatly tie the strings and smile bravely.''

"So? What do you want from me?''

"S. Lloyd loves you dearly. You operated on his wife. Hell, a five-hour job. You saved her life; her own personal physician has said so. So—the County Executive owes you. And that guy can turn the trick for me, easily. But he's a busy man and I'm in Washington, D.C. So what I need is somebody here to keep the pressure on him to put in the pressure for me. And you're the man. Do you dig me, brother?''

"Blood is thicker than Burgundy, et cetera.'' Victor chuckled. "We're very similar in that respect, aren't we, Frank? When there's a real need upon us, we positively become obsessed.''

"It's a real need. The cap for my career.''

"I'll stay right on his tail. I promise you.''

They gathered at LaCoquille at seven-thirty and they had *soupe de poisson,* and *croûte Berberac,* and *pompano Grenobloise,* and *pigeon grand-mère,* and fine wine, but the subject of the Slasher kept returning to the conversation because one was a police reporter, and one was a lawyer, and one was the psychiatric consultant of the police department, and one was a cop.

"Look, you people have got to admit that the press has cooperated one hundred percent, and voluntarily,'' Ramsey said. "You guys know that this Leather Boy of yours is dark, tall, young. But we haven't printed one word of that. We're not going to let him know that you people know.''

"Actually, we don't *really* know," Wyckoff said. "We've put a few things together—"

"And the press has cooperated about the thongs. After the beginning, and after McVail talked to us, we wrote 'the victim was bound,' but didn't add 'by leather thongs.' " Hugh Ramsey looked from Marge to Pam. "But I know cops. I've been in this racket for thirty-five years. I'm sure there's stuff you've been holding out on us."

Stockton laughed. "You think she's holding out on me, too?"

"I'd bet on it." Again Ramsey looked to Pam. "Like this business of fingerprints. You mean, in all this time, not a one?"

"Thirty-five years in the business? Then you ought to know. It's not like in the movies or TV. A readable is rare, rather than common. A readable print won't show on cotton or wool or velvet or any fabric. And on hard surfaces you usually get a partial—insufficient ridges for comparison. And if the finger moves at all, forget it—all you have is a smudge. Let me tell you something I wouldn't shout out to the great general public: Anybody with brains who doesn't want to leave fingerprints, won't leave fingerprints."

"Marge," Stockton said. "What's the psychological picture on these kinds of guys? I'd imagine that doctors, the psychiatric doctors, have worked out some kind of composite image, and identity of the modes of action. Possibly a similarity, however nebulous, in family backgrounds. You know?"

"Yes, indeed, counselor. I know. There have been intensive studies done on those who've been apprehended, and during the last fifty years a great deal of this information has been collated. Essentially, these sex murderers exhibit four salient characteristics." Wyckoff pushed away her *fraises romanoff*, sipped her *café filtre*, lit a cigarette. "The first used to be called periodicity."

"Periodicity," Ramsey said. "Sounds like when you have gum trouble and have to go to the dentist."

"When dear Hugh strains for humor, he sounds like an underdeveloped cretin."

"Please." Stockton grinned. "Let's not have a lovers' quarrel."

"Periodicity"—Wyckoff glared at Hugh— "would entail the occurrence at regular intervals, and therefore we no longer use that term. 'Catenation' is now the word. A linkage, a connected series. We will have a continuity, a sequential recurrence, but without regularity. There are interludes, temporary stoppages, fugue periods—but no permanent cessation. They don't stop until they're dead or captured." Wyckoff inhaled cigarette smoke. "The second characteristic: the utilization of a weapon with phallic significance. The Slasher with his knife—"

"Or that shooter in New York," Ramsey said. "That .44-Caliber Killer."

"And there's that son of a bitch in New Jersey," Medford said. "It's two and a half years now . . ."

"Third," Wyckoff said. "The febrile sexual excitement that continues throughout the episode. The victim may already be dead, but for the assailant she is still the primary object of his pleasure.'' She mashed the cigarette in an ashtray.

"Fourth?" Stockton said.

"Fourth—is what makes these people so difficult to apprehend. Fourth—they return to wherever in hell they come from and appear to be perfectly normal human beings. Until their goddamn motor starts churning again.''

"What starts them?" Ramsey asked. "Tom talked about family background. *Is* there any . . . childhood pattern?"

"I think so, although criminologists are no longer in total agreement on that point. The great weight of authority has it that there was deprivation of love in childhood. Or, the other side of the coin—actual parental aggression. Some of our young turks today—preponderantly my young women colleagues—talk about a naturally violent male, infected by fury, attacking females because he's physically stronger and thinks he can get away with it. We all agree on the fury, but the old-timers like myself don't think it's 'natural'. We believe the unconscious cause of that fury is the deprivation of love early on. Of course, no two cases are exactly alike, and of course there are always exceptions.''

"Whatever it is, there's a hell of a lot of it going on,'' Ramsey said. "Rape statistics keep climbing all over the country.''

"Leather Boy—isn't your usual rapist.''

Stockton said, "Marge, do you think those rising

statistics are related to the mores of our times? Do you think permissive sex moves along to kinky sex, and then the kinky sex triggers off the criminal sex?''

''No. I don't think one goes into the other and the other goes into the other, *ad nauseam*. I don't think if you drink wine, you have to go on to whiskey. I don't think if you smoke pot, you have to go on to heroin. Of course you might, depending on your nature. But—no must. No domino theory. There are those who disagree. What I've expressed is my opinion.''

''Pam, your opinion?'' Ramsey asked.

She shrugged. ''I'm not a shrink. I'm only a cop.''

''Won't talk, will you?'' Ramsey chuckled. ''Tom, do you think she talks to you?

''Of course she talks to me.''

''Think she tells you everything?''

''I—think so.''

''Tommy boy, are you wrong! But you're young and I suppose you have to think the way you think. However, let me tell you. From thirty-five years of experience. She's a cop. And cops do *not* tell all— they *cannot* tell all—even to the old man.''

Dr. Margaret Wyckoff lit a new cigarette and smiled small through the smoke at Detective-lieutenant Pamela Medford. Hugh Ramsey had spoken wisdom, and he had spoken truth, although she would not overtly credit him. There was a secret here amidst them to which only two were privy, Wyckoff and Medford, and that secret concerned

Leather Boy's activities long ago in the city of Chicago, and Wyckoff had not told her lover, and Medford had not told her husband.

Captain Jackson Brendan McVail worked all day and into the night. Routine. You must do routine. If you do enough routine you may be ready if and when your perpetrator makes a slip. This bastard, so far, had made no slips, and therefore Captain Jackson Brendan McVail was not sanguine that this particular investigation would bring his prey to bay, but a cop always hopes. He worked. He sent his people out to bring in people. He questioned Newton again, hoping to shake up recollections. He questioned, from Newton's office, Seymour Roebling, Richard Rochelle, Frederick Blackwood. He questioned Roy Allendale of the Allendale Pharmacies. He questioned every person in Alice Quinton's address book, hoping to hear about a new boy friend. He questioned Mr. Gordon Quinton of Wall Street, New York City. He looked over the reports of the autopsy which confirmed what the medical examiner's portable ultraviolet machine had disclosed: semen in the mouth, semen on the face, semen on the body. The autopsy further disclosed that Leather Boy did not veer from modus operandi: an inviolate vagina. Legally, Alice Quinton had not been raped. He distributed duplicate photos of Alice Quinton to 50 plainclothes policemen: they were to fan out, in an ever-widening circle from Quinton's home, to every bar, pub, tavern, restaurant. That had to be a one-night operation—nobody casually remembers on Thursday what one has seen on Tuesday. Unfortunately, as Captain McVail ruefully knew, nobody remembers on Wednesday what one has seen on Tuesday. And photographs just don't look like the people. Further—bartenders, waiters, waitresses, working the job, simply do not pay attention to the features of the people; they are customers that come and go in the haze of the workday (or night). It is only when a customer is a *regular* customer that a photograph brings recognition from a servitor. The captain worked in his office until ten o'clock and then he closed up shop and drove home to Plandome. He ate a late dinner of fresh ham, mashed potatoes and creamed spinach, and then he went out alone to the back porch and sat there in the warm night and smoked a cigar.

FIVE

At three o'clock on Thursday they came in two cars to the house in Cedarhurst: Captain Jackson McVail, Lieutenant Pamela Medford, Sergeant Mary Caldwell, Sergeant William Emerson. In the office Dr. Margaret Wyckoff had her files open on the desk. On a wall, tacked to a corkboard, was a map of Nassau County.

Captain McVail laid a manila envelope on the desk.

"That's duplicates on all the stuff on Quinton. We have nothing. Pam gave you the facts, Doc. A Leather Boy murder. No fingerprint in the Quinton apartment matched any fingerprint in any of the other places where Leather Boy did his thing. Therefore—QED—we still do not have any fingerprints on Leather Boy. Autopsy disclosed no molestation of the vagina. We have no idea how Alice Quinton fell into his hands. We have no idea how they met, or where they met, or if they met at all. Maybe he got into her apartment by some ruse. I personally questioned everybody connected with Ms. Quinton. I got zero. Last night I sent out fifty people with photos. To bars and restaurants. They worked through the night till curfew. I got their reports this morning. Zero. So now we're here, Doc, for a refresher course. We want the whole picture,

55

and then we talk. The last time that bastard pulled off a wingding, it was December. Ten months ago. And a hell of a lot of sex crimes ago. We need the refresher course, Doc.''

Wyckoff, consulting her files and using a pointer at the map, recited the history.

"All of Leather Boy's crimes have been within the perimeter of Nassau County. They have gone on, intermittently, for the past three years. This one now in October, the Quinton murder, is the first in the fourth year.

"In the first year, there were four such murders. A single woman in her apartment, the murder at night. Another single woman in her apartment, again the murder at night. Then the daytime murder of two persons, a mother and her 22-year-old daughter, in their eight-room house.

"Second year. A single woman in her apartment, the murder at night. Then again the daytime murder of two persons, a mother and a 16-year-old daughter, in a private home. Then another single woman in her apartment, the murder at night.

"Third year. Three single women. Each at night. Each in her apartment.

"None of these persons was actually raped in the technical legal definition, which is penetration by the penis into the vagina. All were sodomized, semen in the mouth or over the body, and all were bound, wrists and ankles, in leather thongs. All had their throats cut. All the breasts were ripped, hacked, mutilated. And now, after ten months: Alice Quinton.

"Three years ago, after Leather Boy's second murder in Nassau, we had a definite psychopathic modus operandi. We realized it was not a single crazy-bastard slash murder, the victim bound in leather strips. Therefore Jake McVail put through inquiry to the computers of the FBI, which gather and collate the various crimes in their *Uniform Crime Reports*. The computers returned a report reciting the exact modus operandi of Leather Boy— for a two-year period in Chicago, Illinois. The thongs on the wrists. The thongs on the ankles. The throat slit. The breasts slashed. Semen in the mouth. Semen on the body. No semen in the vagina. No vaginal penetration. A cluster of three such murders occurred the first year in Chicago, each a single woman in her own apartment. Then for a period of seven months—nothing. Then the second year in Chicago, a repeat, three such murders happening again, each a single woman in her own apartment.

"Then—nothing.

"A full year of nothing.

"Then, three years ago, a shift of locale. Three years ago, the first of the Leather Boy murders in Nassau County. *The press has not been informed of the precise similarity of the Nassau murders and the Chicago murders*. The reason: we do not want to tip off Leather Boy that we are aware of his Chicago activities. There are only seven persons who have this information—the four members of the Sex Crime Squad, the Police Commissioner, the County Executive and myself—and all have been sworn to secrecy. On the other hand, the press, voluntarily, has been most cooperative. After the first two Nassau murders, and upon request of the police, there is no longer mention of leather thongs. The press will report "the victim was bound" without further description, because such information would feed fodder to crackpots, eager to confess. Thus the real criminal, if ever apprehended, would be able to tell what the general public no longer knows (or remembers). And if that man would also have knowledge of the Chicago victims, then the cops would know they have their man."

"Dr. Wyckoff," Mary Caldwell said. "It seems he's confined himself to Nassau County. Nowhere else. That can't be sheer coincidence. There must be a reason, don't you think?"

"The reason would be familiarity. It has been found that most criminals prefer to operate within an area with which they're familiar."

"Then what about Chicago?"

"We don't know, Mary. We can only conjecture. He is either a Chicago man who came to Nassau, or a Nassau man who went to Chicago and then returned to Nassau. In the early days, Captain McVail tried to find out."

"I put it up to the FBI computers," McVail said. "But there is no magic in computers. Their magic is speed, but they're only as good as the information fed into them. I tried. I asked. The computers came up with a blank."

Sergeant Emerson said, "In the matter of clues, the Chicago police came up with the same blank. I think in our three years, or this, the fourth year, we've done slightly better. Would you want to review that, Dr. Wyckoff?''

In Nassau County the cops have a sum total of two clues—one ephemeral, one solid. Three years ago, at four o'clock in the morning, a husband and wife had seen a man emerging from an automatic elevator in the lobby of their apartment house. The husband and wife had entered that elevator to go up to their apartment. They had casually glanced at the man, a fleeting glance. The next day a victim of the Nassau Slasher had been discovered in that apartment house, and the husband and wife, good citizens, had apprised the police. Whether or not the man they had seen was in fact the Slasher remained moot: neither they nor the police could say. And their description of the man, no matter the patient urgings of police experts, remained frail. A tall man, dark-haired. No, they could not possibly identify him if they ever saw him again. It had been a momentary, uninterested glance, and absolutely nothing definite had registered.

The solid clue, which thus far had led them nowhere, was a strand of hair under a fingernail of a victim who had apparently struggled with Leather Boy. It was a black hair. Which coincided with the husband-wife description of a tall man, dark-haired. Laboratory examination produced further facts. Leather Boy was Caucasian, between 26 and 32 years old. Margaret Wyckoff's earlier speculation had been 27. After the lab exam Pamela Medford had expressed admiration for Dr. Margaret

Wyckoff's perspicacious on-the-nose guess.

"No credit to me, really," Marge had said. "The credit belongs to the medical examiner. That office informed us, time and again, that Leather Boy has three or four separate and rather copious ejaculations. So, we tuck it together in ratiocination. We know of his Chicago period. We know of a lapse of a year. And we know of this Nassau period. He can't be some callow kid; the women he murdered weren't teenagers. On the other hand, that kind of sexual vigor bespeaks a young man. Therefore my guess, at that time, was twenty-seven."

But they had more. They had Dr. Margaret Wyckoff's composite psychological picture of the guy. A slick, crafty individual—above average intelligence. "No prints. Six murders in Chicago and now, with Quinton, twelve murders here, and we cannot put together a similar pair of fingerprints. And in the apartment houses there is never a doorman, and never an elevator man. And he never takes his intended victim to a motel. It is easy to posit the reasons. He will not expose himself to a doorman, an elevator man or a desk clerk at a motel."

"What about the private houses?" Emerson asked.

"I would say our very careful, cautious son of a bitch cased the joints for a good long time before he made his move."

"Do you think he's some kind of a derelict, or do you think he works for a living?"

"My guess—not a derelict. He's made his way

into some pretty fancy apartments. He met these women on the outside, or he talked his way in. Either way he'd have to have a nice appearance, and he certainly would need a smooth gift of gab.''

''Want to guess what he does for a living?''

''He could be a cop.''

Laughter. Except McVail.

''I'm serious,'' Wyckoff said. ''A sociopath, when not engaged in his criminal endeavors, acts and lives quite normally. He could be a cop. He could be a professional man. I mean I don't think he's limited to a nine-to-five job. He's done his murders at various hours, day and night.''

Captain McVail grunted. ''Sociopath. Let's have the definition.''

''Quick definition: a person who violates the laws of society without a feeling of guilt. No remorse. No pang of conscience.''

''Leather Boy,'' McVail said. ''In the beginning, the one physical clue, repeated without exception in the modus operandi, was the leather strips, the thongs. The FBI studied the thongs and we ourselves did checks. The thongs were thongs, the ordinary thongs. They were the leather laces for high-top hiking boots. There was no way to run them down in sales and purchases. They were sold in department stores, sporting goods stores, camping stores. For a time I put some men on it, but it was impossible. In Nassau, in Suffolk, in New York City, they were sold in the hundreds of thousands. They were sold in pairs. They were sold in bunches. And they were not sold at all but came laced into the high-top boots. And if you were going to use the thongs in murders, you certainly wouldn't be giving your real name and address for the sales slip.''

"The slashing of the throat could be murder to protect yourself after the sexual assault,'' Wyckoff said. "But the mutilation of the breasts—the secondary sex characteristics of all females—that's classic in all studies of psychopaths obsessed with mother hatred, conscious or unconscious. Every such attack upon a female is another attack on the mother; again and again he kills and mutilates the mother and in the process he experiences the ultimate in orgasmic sexual excitement. And it never ends. That compulsive pent-up rage must periodically explode into this frightful type of violence.''

"He seems to work in cycles of three,'' Caldwell said. "Three such crimes a year. And always, at minimum, a few months pass before we have the next crime in the series. Would you say, now, he's starting on a new cycle of three?''

"I would say nothing of the sort. One cannot predict the unpredictable. One cannot tune in on insane rhythms.''

"How in hell do we handle it?'' Emerson said. "How in hell do we ever catch up with him?''

"We stay on the ball and blunder around,'' McVail said. "We keep working, we stay close on it, and then, when the son of a bitch makes his first slip, we pounce!''

"There's no way to lay out plans,'' Wyckoff said. "These persons are not like other offenders. They don't add up. They don't make sense. They march to strange drums. There are no logical victims, no logical reasons, no patterns, no cycles, no motivations to pursue. Remember the Boston Strangler. He used a nylon stocking as a garrote, stabbed and bit his victims' breasts, rammed wine bottles into vaginas. He was not brought down by police investigation. He was in Bridgewater State Hospital for observation on a nonrelated crime when his ego-need pressed him to boast that he was in fact the Boston Strangler. And the archetype of them all, the infamous Jack the Ripper who slashed, cut, dismembered, disemboweled, had *never* been apprehended.''

"How does it end?" Emerson said. "I mean, like Leather Boy—how does it *end?*''

"He is killed, or he kills himself, or he dies of natural causes, or you people catch up with him and put him away.''

"May God have mercy," said Mary Caldwell.

McVail scowled. The meeting ended.

On Friday the Volvo station wagon tooled upward into the Adirondacks along roads festooned in the glorious colors of the autumn foliage. Yesterday Vic had called home and told Lori that in view of Friday's early morning operation he had decided to stay over in the city.

"Right," Lori had said. "We'll be all packed and waiting for you tomorrow afternoon.''

Now in the lovely October afternoon, Kathy between them, the equipment in the rear, they continued to chat lightly, frequently interrupted by the volatile Kathy. Victor had spoken briefly of his morning operation, quite successful, and about Gary Tennent, who would attend the patient while Vic was away. They were close associates, Dr. Tennent and Dr. Demarest, and one would spell the other during vacations. Lori had spoken of their close friends, Leon and Elaine Weinstein, who yesterday had dropped in unexpectedly and had been disappointed to learn that Victor, in physician's exigency, was staying over in New York. But Lori was quite certain that it was more a pretty nurse than physician's exigency that had kept him over.

Neither was a youngster when they were married eight years ago and from the beginning they were exponents of open marriage (at a time when the term was not yet a part of the language). They loved one another and understood one another and were secure in their sexual psychology. By instinct and education these two comprehended that at least for them there could be a demarcation between sex and love, and that desultory extramural sex could be a form of recreation to be enjoyed like a game of tennis with a worthy partner, and so on occasion Lori would stray, and on occasion Victor, but neither ever became involved, and always they were deeply in love with each other, and sometimes they would talk about an extramarital adventure, and sometimes they would not, and this time they did not.

The Hotel Zrinyi proclaimed its name on an ancient wooden sign, but Laszlo (Papa) Zrinyi did not call it a hotel, and neither did Magda (Mama)

Zrinyi. Papa Zrinyi called it The Lodge, and Mama Zrinyi called it The Farm, and it had grown by wing, annex, adjunct and ell until now it could accommodate 100 guests. The Zrinyi was staffed exclusively by family: sons and daughters and brothers and sisters and aunts and uncles. But Papa Zrinyi, of the walrus mustaches, was the boss of bosses, and Mama Zrinyi, his well-endowed wife, was the best Hungarian cook in the western hemisphere, and all The Lodge was supplied by The Farm. The vegetables were organically grown in the Zrinyi gardens, the eggs were fresh-laid, the chickens were fresh-killed, the pigs lived in salutary pens, the cattle grazed in luxurious pastures, and there were barns and slaughterhouses and icehouses and smokehouses. Papa Zrinyi, an indefatigable sportsman, added fish from the streams to Mama's tables, and rabbit from the woods, and venison, and sometimes bear, partridge, woodchuck, grouse and canvasback. When the Demarests arrived, they were effusively greeted by assorted Zrinyis. They were kissed, embraced, enclasped and virtually convoyed to their rooms. Mama herself brought schnapps for the grownups, a taste of sweet Hungarian wine for Kathy and a platter of hors d'oeuvres for all. After the Demarests had showered, rested and changed, it was again Mama herself who served them a sumptuous dinner on a butcher-block table in the kitchen.

It was glorious October: high skies and hot sun and cool evenings. They hiked, they climbed, they backpacked picnic lunches. They observed bitterns, siskins, a hermit thrush, a fly-catching warbler, a red-winged blackbird. One afternoon Kathy spotted a bear cub and Victor got it in a full-frame photo. But it was Lori who triumphed with three zoom-lensed trophies: a golden-winged woodpecker, a red-shafted flicker and a deer drinking from a stream. The whole weekend was joyful and invigorating, and then on Monday they packed and were kissed by the exuberant Zrinyis and Kathy was given a gift of a beautiful doll. Then the Demarests climbed into the station wagon and rode home to their great house in the best section of the richest part of Old Westbury.

SIX

November. A weird month, November. A strange month in the northeastern United States. November had been different when Donald Wharton Cranford was a child. November had been white, and bitter cold. And a hell of a lot of snow. But gradually November had changed and now it was different. Maybe it was the Gulf Stream or something. Or them atom bombs they were always testing somewhere. These days in November, different from his childhood, the sun still had heat, and there wasn't much snow, and when it did snow it would rain pretty soon after and wash the snow away. Gulf Stream. Cranford was proud that he knew about the Gulf Stream. Well, look, he said to himself, why not? Nobody ever said I was dumb. I did all right in Nassau Community; got my diploma, didn't I? I stunk in English and grammar and crap like that, but I was great in science and chemistry and I was a whiz in electronic engineering, right? And I've done all right for myself, right or wrong? I'm a good businessman and I'm a goddamn great salesman. I got a nice house and a nice wife and two nice kids. And dough in the bank. Plenty of bread in the bank. How many of them English majors own Delanco's Sporting Goods Store? How many of them got my kind of bread spread out

67

in the banks? How many of them got a nice little house, free and clear, and a good obedient wife and two nice kids? But he was unhappy. Vaguely unhappy. And he knew why. Because he was out hunting again, and it was too damn soon. Used to be, after he pulled one, he would lay back for months. Just thinking about it, playing it over in his head, would give him crazy pleasure. And he knew. He was not dumb. When you go out too often, you multiply the risks. Up to now he had always prided himself on his cool, and how he handled himself, and all the tricks to outsmart the cops. Not cool to be out hunting this fast after the Quinton shindig. On the other hand, he did know that nothing could pop real quick. First of all, he didn't go out every night; he wouldn't leave the wife and kids alone night after night. And second, the rules he laid out for the right broad. It takes a hell of a long time to catch up with one that meets with all the special rules. But he was unhappy. Vaguely. Because he was pressing too soon. He was changing. Like the climate in November. Gradually he was changing.

On this Thursday in the middle of November, Franklin Demarest sat impatiently in the reception room of the County Executive's office in Mineola. He was here in direct response to the County Executive's summons, and the guy had said four o'clock. He had come promptly at four, and now it was four-thirty, and finally he blurted to Jutland's beautiful Puerto Rican receptionist: "What the hell is holding him up? Did he die in there?"

"The accountant. The accountant's in there. Haskell. Ralph Haskell. You know?"

"I don't know. I know *about* him. I know he's got some damn important clients in this county."

"Must be a pretty good accountant, no?"

"Yes. But I wish—"

His wish was granted. A tall bald man came through. He smiled at the receptionist, nodded to Demarest, and marched out. In minutes there was a buzz on her desk. She picked up the receiver, listened, put down the receiver.

"You may go in now, Mr. Demarest."

"Thank you."

He pushed through the swinging doors, greeted the outer secretary, greeted the inner secretary, opened the heavy oak door and closed it behind him, and there was S. Lloyd Jutland, standing, his hands clasped behind him, looking out a window, his back to his visitor.

Was this some kind of politician trick? What now? "Hoo hah," Demarest called. "This here's your newspaper boy from *Newsday*. You sent for me, Imperial Majesty?"

Jutland turned. "Accountants," he said. "They depress me. How about you, Frank? What's your reaction to accountants?"

"They depress me."

"Why? Ever thought about it?"

"I'm a newspaper fella, Your Highness. I've enough to think about without thinking about why accountants depress me. Jesus!"

Jutland grinned. It cracked his doleful expression. He was back among his people. "I have news for you, Franklin, and I wanted to be the first to tell you."

"Yessir?"

"You've got the job. Moscow correspondent. Your visa's already being processed. You'll be going over the first of the new year, January one. Tomorrow you'll be hearing about it from your office."

"Jesus, Lloyd, I thank you."

"Not at all." Graciously Jutland took his bow but then, good politician, he turned humble. "Hell, man, if anybody deserved that job, it's you. It needed a little squeeze and I gave it that squeeze, but the real squeeze was on *me!* From my dear friend, Dr. Victor Demarest. Lord, that man has the tenacity of a bulldog."

Frank Demarest got to his brother's house at six-thirty that evening. He parked his car, walked up the long pathway, rang the bell and Lori opened the door. "Frank!"

"Hi, you beautiful thing."

"Why didn't you call? You could have had dinner with us."

"Had a previous dinner engagement. I do hope our surgeon is home."

"He is. And we have guests. The Weinsteins."

"Oh, Christ, I *love* it."

And then inside the house there were handshakes and kisses and little blonde Kathy flew about like the youngest cherub at a meeting of happy angels.

The Weinsteins, the dear Weinsteins. The Weinsteins, who had the kind of money that made the rich Demarests seem poor, were their oldest friends, in both meanings of that word. Leon Weinstein was 72, and his jaunty Elaine was 69, and Leon knew the Demarest boys from the time they were born; Leon had grown up with a boyhood pal, Freeman Holt Demarest, who was destined to be an Episcopalian minister and the father of Franklin and Victor.

Frank shook up some whiskey sours and drank most of them. He told about his meeting with Jutland. He thanked Jutland, he thanked Victor, he thanked God. "Moscow!" he shouted and grabbed Elaine Weinstein and danced with her.

"Moscow," grumbled Leon Weinstein. "What the hell's that to be so happy about?"

On Thursdays Ralph Haskell always stayed at home in Hewlett, sort of as the caretaker, the house-sitter, because on Thursdays Francine went out with her friends—and why not? Didn't he on every Wednesday attend the poker game at Lloyd Jutland's house? Smoking his cigar in the living room, Ralph chuckled. Many a Wednesday night they played poker all the way through to Thursday morning.

He smoked his cigar. He thought of Fran dressing upstairs and felt an urge for her, but did not dare move. That's all he'd need. Heck, she'd bite his head off. He chuckled again, puffed his cigar. Married folks are entitled to a night out once a week

away from each other. Best thing in the world for a
marriage. He nodded. He was getting sleepy. Last
night had been late at Lloyd's and today had been
frightfully busy.

Ralph Haskell. Tall and bald and very rich and he
had married late in life. He was an accountant, a tax
expert. He was 55 years of age, his office was in
Freeport, his home was in fashionable Hewlett, his
wife was 20 years his junior, and they were married, happily married, for 11 years. At age 24 she
had of course married him for his money, for a life
of ease and leisure; he had wanted her and had been
aware that in a sense he was purchasing her; but this
marriage had developed in extraordinary measure.
He was mad about her, of course; heck, by now he
wouldn't want to *live* without her; but the wonderful
development was, she loved him. She had a fear of
bearing children; it was one of the reasons she had
married an older man. They had no children but
they had each other; they had grown *into* each other;
each somehow satisfying a need one to the other.
She was now a *lady!* She was the wife of the esti-
mable Ralph Haskell. She was a member of the best
clubs, moved in the highest spheres of their community, and knew and appreciated that it was Ralph
Haskell who had elevated her to that echelon. She
was the best of all possible wives. She doted on
him, stroked him, pleased him in every way; it was
11 years and they were really enfolded one to the
other like clasped hands.

He was a quiet man, aggressively sexual, but
only with his wife. He loved his wife and he knew

that she loved him. It was possible, quite possible, that she may have had another man—or other men—during their 11-year marriage, but it could not be anything serious because they, Ralph and Fran, were so perfectly compatible that anything she might risk on the side would have to be momentary, esoteric. Quite simply, she had it too good to hazard throwing it away. They had a very good marriage despite their difference in age and were damn good friends. And he—he was a faithful spouse. He had no need of any other, no desire for any other. Actually, he was a shy man, and he made no passes at any woman other than his wife. But he did make frequent passes at his wife, many of which she ducked. He sighed, grunted, chortled again. His eyes were closed when she entered the room but he smelled her perfume and opened his eyes.

"Like that," she said, "you set the house on fire. I mean anybody falls asleep with a lit cigar—"

"When you're right, you're right." He extinguished the cigar. "Honey, if I may say," he said, "you look perfectly gorgeous."

"Well, thank you, lover." She was a vibrant woman, dark, attractive, brimming. "If I were you, Ralphie, I'd go up to bed. Put on the TV—" Outside, a horn beeped three times. "Good night, lover."

"Have fun," he said.

She waved and went out to Ellen's green Cadillac. Paula was sitting beside Ellen. Fran opened the rear door and got in and the Caddy pulled away and made the first turn on the journey from Hewlett to East Meadow.

They were cheaters and cheaters do not cheat close to home. They were Mrs. Ellen Laurel, and Mrs. Paula Sewell, and Mrs. Francine Haskell, who on Thursday nights screwed their husbands by fucking their lovers. All except Fran, who had recently broken up with her guy. Which was why, after the initial smattering of small talk, it had grown so silent in the car. The two up front felt sorry for the one in back and they hoped, in the good charity of cheaters, that she would discover somebody interesting tonight. So, of course, did she.

She lit a cigarette. She felt no guilt, nothing even akin to it. Ralph was a good man, a fine man, and she did love the old boy, but he bored the shit out of her. Dear God, he was dull! She was a damn good wife to him, but without a little action on the side she'd have gone absolutely mad.

Cheaters find cheaters; water seeks its own level. Five years ago Fran had found Ellen in a beauty salon. They had tested one another over afternoon cocktails and had practically fallen into each other's arms. Ellen had brought Paula and their triad was established. They were esteemed citizens in the town of Hewlett, their husbands were wealthy (but tired) and they were young and needed that outside action. They found it in a cheaters' joint called Dino's. For their husbands, it was "girls' night out." They would go off together, three in one car. They alternated as to who would drive. Three together, a group, it gave off an aura of innocent fun.

For the husbands, the "girls" were going to have dinner somewhere, and then perhaps to a jazz joint, or to a tavern that features a comic, or maybe even to a pub where "we'll drink up a storm and flirt with all the men." In fact they drove directly to Dino's Blue Grotto in East Meadow: *Piano Bar and Cocktail Lounge. Music and Gracious Relaxation Till 4 A.M. Try Our Prime Steaks and Chops.* In Dino's they met their lovers (when they had specific lovers) and separately went their ways, inevitably to a motel. At two o'clock they would gather again in Dino's and drive home, and on the way they would concoct the story they would tell in the event a curious husband should inquire.

In East Meadow Ellen parked and locked the car; the men had their own cars. In Dino's they met their guys and stayed for a drink and then took off, leaving Fran alone, alert and looking. She knew her way around. She was extremely particular. She liked her men handsome; she liked them tall. If they were fat, forget it. She drank at the bar. She flirted, she danced. If there were vibes, if a man attracted her sufficiently, she might take him off for a casual jump in the feathers. If he proved interesting, it might develop into a relationship. If not, it's a one-night gig, and see you around some time. If the guy was shy, she could be the aggressor. And if she liked him and they didn't make it that first time, she would arrange a date for the next week, or arrange for them to be in touch during the week. When necessary, she could take over. She had laughing eyes, an ironic sense of humor, a cynical view of life and an innocent heart. She could be sweet, but she could be tough. She had nerve, intelligence, an adventurous sensuality and warm good looks.

Paula came back to Dino's at ten to two.

Ellen came at two o'clock.

In the green Caddy Ellen inquired, "How'd you do, Francie?"

"Nothing," Fran said. "This was my night for creeps."

SEVEN

The Sex Crime Squad was a task force constantly engaged. Carnal malefaction is ceaseless, inexorable. The human beast displays its sexual claws in a variety of means: sadism, sodomy, incest, gang bangs, harassment, humiliation (urinating or defecating on the victim after a rape), straight rape, screwy rape (the violent interjection of a foreign object into the vagina), statutory rape and on and on, including peeping toms and gropers and dirty-word whisperers. Most of these are written up as routine assaults by the weary cops. Then they go out and round up the neighborhood kaysos (known sex offenders) and frequently it is one of them who is repeating. Or, simply, the woman knows the man and if she has the courage to ride out the indignities, she will lodge her complaint at the precinct house and a cop will accompany her back to the site in an effort to pick up the offender.

They were only four in the Sex Crime Squad but in important matters they could (and often did) multiply themselves tenfold; and it would be Medford or Caldwell or Emerson in charge of a covey of plainclothes people from other detective squads. Rarely McVail. He preferred to work alone; he worked best alone. He was not a ''brass'' captain chained to a desk. He was out there on the job, and the job was his life, and he often worked a 16-hour day (but never put in for overtime). His *bête noire*, of course, was Leather Boy. Leather Boy never left him. Leather Boy itched in his scalp like sweat, burned in his stomach like an ulcer; and since Leather Boy was exclusively a Nassau County phenomenon, he was a calumny upon Captain Jackson Brendan McVail, a personal affront. The bastard was a savage murderer, a killer animal on the loose, and they had no lead on him; they had nothing. The Alice Quinton investigation was done; it was in there in the records as another open case. Everybody Quinton had ever known had been questioned and every lead had been run down and up and sideways. Nothing! Now Quinton was another part of the Leather Boy file and many a night the lights burned late in McVail's office as he drank his Jack Daniel's and smoked his cigars and studied and sifted and collated his papers and pondered the aspects of the meager information and sought without success to find a cross hair to put him on target.

Donald Cranford did not go out every night because he would not leave Diana and the children every night; but he was out there many nights, shaved and shined and neat and clean. He never went back to a tavern from which he took a woman out—even if nothing happened between them. He always played it cool and careful; hell, it wasn't easy to find the special chick who fit in with his special needs. He was not a street rapist. Not a flasher, exposing himself. Not a grabber of strangers. He had to feel something from the other, a kind of love, an affection, something flowing between them. A mutuality.

Or else—entirely different—the other thing. No meeting, no flirtation, no mutuality. Just, you saw a woman and got caught by the balls, and she became that other thing, a whole different thing, an enterprise, a watching and waiting and tracking down. That was way out, rare. It didn't happen often but when it did it could provide that extra benefit: a second one to please him; a combination of two! But it required a stalker's skill; it required watching and waiting and tracking and planning; he wasn't a street rapist indiscriminately busting up a dame he'd never even seen before.

Seeking in the bars was another matter, and therefore the care and the caution and all the special rules. He was the hunter, but he was also the hunted, and it made for one hell of a great game— because the odds were all against him. The whole damn world against Donald Wharton Cranford. No opportunity for a comeback, no second chance. *If you lose once, you lose forever!* But he could win and continue to win and win, as long as he played by his rules, exercised every possible caution. Which he did. Hell, he was cautious to the point of frustration, but he never broke a rule, never made a brainless move as others had done. Oh, he had read about the crazies. He knew all about the crazies. He was aware that he was a crazy (may God have mercy on my soul). God? He laughed out loud.

It was not easy to find the proper companion, to leave the tavern with the proper lady in hand. The nights could spread into weeks, and the weeks into many months. Most of them ran in packs, and right away that was finished for Donald Cranford. Or they were friends with the bartender, who, naturally, took a good look at you—and that meant finish. Or the one you happened to dig did not happen to dig you. Or she lived with her folks, or a girl friend, or a lover, or a husband, and therefore wanted to make it in a motel. Or lived alone in an apartment house, but there was a doorman. Or an elevator man. When you wanted it *all* strictly by your rules—then you had to wait. And wait. It took a long time, unless you got very lucky, to get it all together, matched up perfect.

Tonight he was drinking Canadian Club, and he had drunk up a hell of a lot of it. He had been to four fucking pubs: nothing. But here in this last one he thought he had a goodie. Very pretty. Nice big tits. She was drinking red wine and talked him into drinking red wine and the room began to spin. In Chicago his old boss had once told him: *"Never mix the grain with the grape."* You were correct, old boss. Time to go home. One of his strictest rules: you don't make moves when you are drunk. And he was drunk as a goddamn lord. So he paid the check and left the girl sitting there in amazement.

At home he didn't even look in on the kids. In bed he touched naked Diana but he was too drunk. He lay on his back. His eyes were closed but he was not sleeping. His mind was rolling. Rolling back. Like a movie.

Donald Wharton Cranford. His mother's name was Martha Belmar Cranford. His father was Jeffrey Jay Cranford. He had no memory of a father. His mother had told him his father had died when he, Donny, was two years old. Donny! He hated it. He never let anybody call him Donny.

They lived in a five-room apartment in Hicksville, and Donny had his own bedroom. His mother was a cocktail waitress. When she went to work, she left him with a baby-sitter. There were many baby-sitters, but he remembered none of them. Often, in the evening, his mother would bring a man home. Different men. He must have been about four years old when he became aware of the groaning, moaning, growling sounds of fucking. As he grew older the sounds grew clearer and he tried to shut them out by pulling the blanket over his head.

When they were alone in the apartment, Donny's mother always walked around in a pair of briefs and nothing else. She had a big pair of tits and she was proud of them. She walked around like that even when he was grown. He hated it, but that's the way it had been from the time he was a little kid.

She used to hit him a lot. She drank gin, and when she got drunk she would find excuses to hit him and she used a strange instrument. He had heard of fathers taking sons out to the barn and using a paddle on their asses. He had heard of parents beating children with a strap, or a ruler, or with their fists. His mother used a cat-o'-nine-tails. She had stolen it from her father (who had whipped *her* with it). She had taken it, along with other crazy items, when she had packed up to leave home. Long ago, she told Donny, in the cities in the South they sold these cat-o'-nine-tails in the hardware stores. It had a round wooden handle about two feet long. Attached to one end of the handle were six (not nine) thin strips of leather, each about two feet long. Attached to the other end of the handle was a leather loop, and the "cat" hung by the loop on a nail inside one of the closet doors. When she wielded it, it hurt like hell.

He had never seen any of his grandparents. His dear mother, born in Asheville, North Carolina, had run away from home at age 17. (Maybe she used the handle of that whip to play with herself or something.) She never once wrote to her folks; she did not know if they were dead or alive (and did not care). He knew nothing whatever about his father's parents, where they lived or where they came from. He grew up in the five rooms in Hicksville. He went to high school in Hicksville. He lived with his mother because his mother supported him. He hated her and her big naked tits. He knew where she got most of the money to pay the rent and buy the food and clothes for them. But as he got older, she stopped bringing the men home. Now the men took *her* somewhere. Many a night she did not come home at all.

He went to Nassau Community College, took up electronic engineering and electrical engineering. He graduated and went to work for the phone company as a repairman and he traveled all over Nassau County and got to know it like a book. He used to steal things. Sometimes crazy things (like his mother stole the cat-o'-nine-tails from her father). He did not steal from the houses where he went to repair, because he was shrewd and he knew that if there were enough complaints, they would home in on him. He stole from the company and the men who worked for the company. Anything the men happened to leave around that appealed to him, he took. From the company he stole all kinds of tools. He stole two coverall uniforms. (He still had them and used them.) He continued to live at home because he was able to save money. He did not pay rent to his mother, nor did he chip in for food.

She still walked around in her panties, her naked bazooms bouncing around, and the dark triangle of her pubic hair showing through her tight briefs. The way she looked at him from time to time, he knew just what was on her twisted mind. He had grown up to be one hell of a good-looking guy. He often got laid in the homes to which he went to make phone repairs, and he thought about getting laid in his own home. All he had to do was push her over—she was begging for it—but he wouldn't give her the satisfaction. He hated her too much. He was 22 years old, working his second year with the telephone company, when his mother got married to a guy named John Glasser, who moved into the apartment. And that was when Donny finally moved out. And he moved all the way. He quit his job, he pulled his savings, he packed his stuff, and he went to Chicago.

In Chicago, kind of vacationing but looking around, he got a job, of all things, as a salesman in a sporting goods store. He had answered an ad, just for the hell of it, and then he told the man he had no experience at all. It made the man laugh. The man said that Don was a nice-looking kid and had a nice voice and a nice manner. The man said that if Don Cranford was not a natural-born salesman, then the man did not know buckshot from bullshit. The man's name was John. The name of the man's business was John's Sportsman's Store. He sold everything from guns to backpacks to camping gear to bowling balls. John said he would break Don into the business. At the beginning he would pay Don less than an experienced salesman, but he was sure that Don in due time would come up to snuff. Don took the job, wrote to tell his mother, and corresponded intermittently with her over the next couple of years.

It happened to Donald Wharton Cranford when a shipment of laces arrived at John's Sportsman's Store: leather laces for hiking boots. When Don opened the box and saw all those leather thongs, he had a quick flash of that old cat-o'-nine-tails. And then another flash happened. He saw himself tying his mother into those goddamn leather thongs. And then something else happened. His cock stood up, an erection like a lunatic. And it kept standing; it wouldn't let up. He had to go into the bathroom and jerk himself off. And starting from that day, that was when the fantasies began. He would be out at a bar, on the make for some girl, talking real nice, when something got hot in his belly and the heat spread all through him as he imagined tying her up, the fucking cunt, the cheap bitch, the barfly broad, and he would leave her and go home to his furnished room, and the other things would come into his mind, the crazy bloody things, and he would grab his prick and jerk off and hold onto his prick and keep jerking off. It was weird. It was crazy. Wild!

He stole a couple of switchblade knives from John's Sportsman's Store, and he stole a hell of a lot of those leather thongs. He wrote them up as sales, and John didn't know from nothing. John was happy with Don Cranford: the guy had lived up to expectations. John's business was never better. Don received a substantial raise in pay plus a hefty bonus. John was a good man.

Donald Wharton Cranford carried a switchblade and thongs when he went out to the bars, but he was careful. He was smart. Like they told him back there in school, he had native intelligence. He had a fine IQ. His big trouble was lack of interest. When you lack interest, you don't apply yourself. When you don't apply yourself, you don't do good. In school, at whatever he applied himself, he did great. Like electrical engineering. In electrical engineering, he graduated number one. In the other stuff, hell, like music appreciation, he was down on bottom. Well, now he was interested. He goddamn applied himself, because if he didn't apply himself he could lose his life. In the bar it had to be a girl alone, no friends. It had to be a girl who was not cozy with the bartender. It had to be a girl without a roommate. It had to be a girl who did not live at home with her parents. No motels. It had to be a girl who lived alone in an apartment. And there could not be a doorman in the apartment house. And no elevator man. And the girl had to like him enough to want to take him with her, and he had to like her enough to want to go. He sure specified a hell of a lot of strict rules, and it all had to work out perfect, and that took time, and it took patience, but if you gave it enough time and patience it would happen, and when it finally happened, it was marvelous, it was the greatest, it was fantastic. Lying in bed alone, just thinking about it, he would come without even touching himself.

That was when the first of the grisly slasher-murders, the first of that modus operandi series, occurred in Chicago and was listed in the *Uniform Crime Reports* by the Federal Bureau of Investigation. The woman was found in her own apartment. There had been no burglary, no breaking and entering. Nothing was stolen. The woman was naked. Her throat was cut. Her breasts were slashed. Her wrists were bound behind her by leather thongs. Her ankles were bound by leather thongs. There was semen in her mouth. There was semen on her body. There was no semen in her vagina. There were six such murders using that precise modus operandi over a period of two years, and then Donald Wharton Cranford in Chicago received a phone call from John Glasser of Hicksville, Long Island, who informed him that Mrs. John Glasser lay ill in Meadowbrook Hospital, a serious illness, cirrhosis of the liver. The doctors were planning an operation—it was called a portacaval shunt—which possibly could help, but the doctors did not hold out much hope. Her condition was critical. Donald Wharton Cranford quit his job. He packed and flew home. He was through with Chicago. The reason was six murders. He knew it would not end. He knew he was driven, compelled. It could stop temporarily, but it would never cease. Self-protection. Survival. The territorial imperative. Chicago was not home base; after two years it was still a strange city. Better to be where you know it all. If you stay smart, if you play smart, if you don't lose your head, if you keep to all the rules, nobody will ever catch up with you. But go home; it's better to be home.

He came home to Hicksville; he visited his mother in Meadowbrook Hospital. She died ten days later. They buried her in a plot she owned in Plain Lawn Cemetery. John Glasser moved out of the apartment in Hicksville, and Don never saw him again. He didn't even know what the guy did for a living, and he didn't care. A lawyer called him and he went to the lawyer's office and the lawyer showed him a copy of his mother's will. (''A courtesy,'' the lawyer said.) She left everything to John

Glasser. Everything, the lawyer told him, consisted of her savings account of $4497 and her life insurance policy of $5000. She left nothing to Donald Wharton Cranford, and he didn't give a good goddamn. He never went back to Plain Lawn Cemetery. His only reason to go to Plain Lawn would have been to piss on her grave.

He watched the want ads. He got a job at Delanco's Sporting Goods Store opposite Bloomingdale's in Garden City. The old man questioned him and shook his head in approval. Don was now an experienced man: he knew the business backward and forward. The old man was Giuseppe Delanco (called Joe). It was a two-man store. Joe's assistant had quit and moved to Arizona because his wife had lung trouble. Joe was an old guy, his wife was dead. He lived with his only child, a daughter, in a nice little house in West Hempstead. He got dizzy spells. He was not a well man. He suffered from arteriosclerosis. He suffered from high blood pressure. He was crazy about Don Cranford. ("It is like God has sent you.")

Joe would invite Don to the house for a good, healthy, Italian home-cooked meal prepared by his *figlia,* Diana. She was a year younger than Don. Joe was worried about Diana. Joe was old, he was sick, he was going to die, and the *figlia* was not married. She was not a beautiful girl. But she was not ugly. She was shy. She did not go out on dates. A good girl, a decent girl, taught by the nuns in convent school. She went to church every Sunday. The young man, the Don Cranford, it was as if he was sent by God. The *figlia* told the father that Don was pleasant to her eyes and pleased her heart.

One day the old man took Don to a *ristorante* alone. They ate and they drank Chianti wine and Giuseppe Delanco laid his cards on the table. "I am an old man, a sick man, and soon I will die. I am worried to leave Diana alone. I am sure you know that Diana is very pleased with you. I am very pleased with you. I have watched you. You are a good boy. You are a good worker. You are educated. You are an American born in Hicksville. I am from the old country, and I should like to do like in the old country. I should like to make a match for my *figlia*. You are a young man. It is not good for you to live alone. So. If you take my *figlia* to be the wife, I will transfer the house, it is free and clear, to you and Diana. Also the business I will transfer to the husband and wife, to you and Diana. And so all will be in order when it comes my time to die, and I will go in peace."

Don liked Diana Delanco. He liked her because she was not aggressive. He liked her because she was not a cunt (like all the girls at the bars who were always after him). He liked her because she would never walk around in her panties with her legs bare and her belly bare and her tits sticking out in the wind. She was a fine girl, a good girl, a religious girl, respectable, dutiful, quiet, and obedient. They got married, and Joe transferred the house to them, and then transferred the business to them. Diana became pregnant the very first month of the marriage, and Joe Delanco was happy at the prospect of being a grandfather, but he did not live to see the twins. He died of a cerebral hemorrhage four months before the twins were born.

Don hired an assistant for the business, Paul Mercer, a lifelong bachelor, a charming old guy, who lived in a small apartment in Hempstead. Paul, white-haired, tall, gallant, experienced in the business, really wanted a part-time job and that was perfectly all right with Donald Wharton Cranford. It was a small store with a splendid show window, and Don did the window dressing. For Paul Mercer, Don split up the day at the store. Paul would open and would work five hours, from nine to two. That gave Don the time to be home with Diana during the latter weeks of the pregnancy. Then he would go to the store at two o'clock, and Paul would go home, and Don would work until seven. The mornings were slow: two to seven were the busiest hours.

Sometimes, of course, he would come in early, to shape up the windows, to see salesmen, to do the ordering, to see to the books, to unpack and distribute new goods from the wholesalers. Sometimes, mornings, he himself delivered goods that were ordered by customers, and for that purpose he purchased a van. It was olive-green. It had *nothing* printed on it. The license plates were always too dirty for their numbers to be discerned. Diana had her own car, a Ford. Don had the van, and a Mercury which he traded in every two years, but the license plates were permanently just dirty enough not to be able to read. He thought about leather thongs and knives and blood and slashed breasts, but he held back. He held himself in check until the twins were born. Then, on occasional evenings, showering and shaving and redressing in the store, he went out to the pubs. Sometimes he drove the Merc. Sometimes he drove the van. In the beginning of that year he killed two girls in their apartments, and then he had his first experience with *two* females, but not in an apartment. In a house.

He had gone shopping for Diana at a supermarket. He had put the stuff into the car—it was a summer morning—when he saw the woman. Carrying a package, she was coming toward him. She was not a young woman, but terribly good-looking. She was wearing a white blouse, and there was no bra under the blouse, and she had big stickout bosoms like his mother. She drove away and he drove after, his cock throbbing, his heart pounding. He saw where she lived, and he went by.

Thereafter, morning after morning, sitting a distance away in the van, he checked her out, he learned all about her. The husband left the house at eight o'clock and the wife drove him to the train. Sometimes the daughter drove him to the train. The daughter worked in a beauty parlor, went to work at one o'clock in the afternoon. Before he made his move, he had the scam all angled out; his plan was precision perfect.

He came there in the shiny olive-green van at ten-thirty one sunny morning. He was wearing his New York Telephone coveralls. He went around to a side of the house and used a clipper to cut the phone wire. He left the tool in the van, went to the house, rang the doorbell. The daughter came and looked through the screen door. She saw the telephone man in his coveralls, saw the olive-green van in the background. He told her, in his pleasant voice, that the phones were out of order. It was either the main cable, or individual wires. He had to check, house by house. It was gentle, rapid gibberish, but he was a good-looking, clean-cut guy, with a soft voice and a nice smile. She left him there outside the locked screen door, and he knew of course where she went. To check the phone. She came back, smiling, and opened the door. She was still smiling when he killed her. And the mother with those gorgeous tits was still in bed when he came in upon her!

He came out to the van and drove home and into the garage. He dressed in back of the van in his normal clothes and folded away the repairman's coveralls. He looked in on Diana. He played with the kids. He drove the Merc to the store. He greeted Paul. He pretended to work. But he was still jumping, holding down excitement. No question it was wild to do two, to do two like that, but terribly dangerous. Much easier to do a girl from a bar who took him to her apartment in the middle of the night. No doorman, no elevator man, no nothing, nobody. But a house in the daytime! Jeez, you have got to be crazy. He grinned in his store opposite Bloomingdale's in Garden City. Hell, he had not looked for her. *She* had found *him*. He had been *struck* by that goddamn woman. Hit in the pit of the stomach. Jeez, how that bitch had knocked him out.

Dangerous, but good. It had been good. Christ, good. Two! God, it was wild. The wildest!

EIGHT

Newsday issued the official word on the last Friday in November. As of January 1, Franklin Demarest was their Moscow correspondent. And on the first Sunday in December Mrs. Lori Parlin Demarest gave a little luncheon in his honor; just the immediate family and of course the Weinsteins. They were six: Frank, Vic, Elaine, Leon, Lori and Kathy—who, like Amy of the White House, was always at table with the adults.

"Moscow," Leon Weinstein said. "That's one place we don't visit on our cruise."

"They skip the Soviet Union," Elaine said.

"When do you leave?" Lori asked.

"March fifteenth," Weinstein said. "The Ides of March."

"For a year," Lori said to Kathy. "A year's cruise all around the world, and many stops at many ports. They spend days, maybe weeks, away from the ship, and then, bang, all aboard and they're sailing again."

"Boy, would I love that!" Kathy said.

"Now, would you?" Victor said. "Would you give up the skiing? Would you give up the Christmas vacation in Sun Valley?"

The little blonde girl grinned. "No, I don't think so."

95

"Where in Sun Valley?" Elaine asked.

"Garwood's. Phil Garwood. He was my commanding officer in 'Nam."

"You know, Vic, it's the first time you ever mentioned the war," Elaine said.

"That's the pose of all the patriots," Frank said. "A posture. Mum is the word, and I don't mean the champagne."

"I hated that goddamn war," Vic said.

"So why did you go? You didn't *have* to go, you know," Weinstein said. "You enlisted."

"A doctor. I didn't think we belonged in Vietnam, but we were there, and there were guys wounded and guys dying and they needed doctors; always there's a shortage of doctors. I was young and strong. We couldn't expect our elderly medics to go over, though a hell of a lot of them did. Those kids were out there fighting for their country. Sounds corny? Not to me. I was a surgeon, and I could help, and I felt they were damned entitled to two years of my life."

"You know Victor," Frank said. "When he really gets onto something, nobody—but *nobody*—can stop him."

"Very stubborn," Leon said. "Even as a little boy."

"He got medals," Kathy said. "Mommy says he got medals."

"Shush," Victor said.

"Medals?" Elaine said.

Frank chuckled. "If he won't talk about his war, would he talk about his medals?"

"Purple Heart," Lori said. "And the Distinguished Service Medal."

"Oh, cut it out," Vic said.

"That's my Pop," Kathy said.

Elaine asked, "Did you save your medals, Doctor?"

"What the hell for?"

"Any idea where they are?"

"Not the faintest."

Lori stood up and walked away.

Watching her go, Weinstein clucked. "Victor, that's one heck of a beautiful woman. Victor, if there's one thing I envy you—"

"A lecher," Elaine said sternly. "I don't know what it is with this man. People are supposed to slow up, right? Not my Leon the lion. The older he gets, the more lecherous."

"What's lecherous?" Kathy asked. Her question produced laughter and little Kathy frowned. "What the heck's funny?" she said.

Lori returned with two medals on a flat tray.

"I don't believe it," Victor said.

"Purple Heart," said Frank Demarest. "And the Distinguished Service Medal."

"I do not believe it," Victor said.

"She saves everything," Kathy said. "Daddy says she saves every *thing!*"

"One of the squirrel people," Victor said.

"Like our mother," Frank said.

"Everything and anything," Victor said. "In the bedroom she has drawers full of—everything. Bank statements that are eight years old. The hospital bills from when Kathy was born. Old keys, paper clips, rubber bands, old bills, new bills, single earrings, warranties, guarantees, pencil stubs, broken crayons. She does not throw anything away.''

''Well, please, these *are* medals,'' Elaine said, defending Lori.

''What our mother used to call herself,'' Frank said. '' 'A string saver'.''

''Everything and anything,'' Victor said.

''Daddy,'' Kathy said enthusiastically, ''tell about how she spends money.'' The child frowned. ''Like water?'' she inquired.

''Oh, shush,'' Victor said and laughed.

''My dear little girl,'' Elaine said, ''when you have it, you're *supposed* to spend it. It's a patriotic duty. Money must circulate.''

''Daddy, tell how she buys two of everything.''

''Now that's a fact,'' Victor said. ''Sort of, I would say, a kind of neurosis. If she loves it, she'll buy two. The second is a backup for the first, in a manner of speaking. Because if it turns out she *really* loves it and would then want another, by that time it may no longer be available.''

Lori cast a deprecating glance at her husband and with her medals turned from him and swung away.

''An absolutely delicious woman,'' Leon Weinstein declared.

''Incorrigible,'' said Elaine Weinstein. ''My spouse, the sybarite. An incorrigible old cocker.''

Frank took off for the office. ''There are no Sunday holidays for a reporter who wants to straighten things out before he flies away to the land of Lenin and Trotsky and all those guys. Even Catherine the Great.'' Elaine Weinstein helped Lori and Kathy with the dishes, and Leon and Victor gathered in the study, Leon with a Grand Marnier and Victor with a cognac.

"Victor, you shall be my caretaker."

"For what, my friend?"

"Here are the keys. They're duplicate keys. You know my house, you know where I live."

The Weinsteins owned an estate in Brookville, Long Island. An estate. Many acres. And within the many acres, two buildings. One was a split-level, spacious, rosewood ranch house. The other building was a large barn in which there once had been many horses. The Weinsteins no longer rode and no longer owned horses, and they utilized the barn to store furniture and other items that over the years they had removed from the ranch house.

"Every so often you will please check out my house, starting in March when we go for the cruise. Just to see there's no broken windows and such. Next winter please turn off the water so that we will not have busted pipes. You won't have to turn on the water because we'll be back next spring. You will please do the normal checkups—like no roof has been blown off by a storm. I'll give your name to the gardeners who come to trim and prune in the summer, and they will send you the bills, and you will please pay them. If you want to look in on the barn—not really necessary—then look. We have no worry about thieves. We have the silent alarm sys-

tem which is hooked in directly to the police station. That goes for the house and it goes for the
barn. I know you know how to switch off the system and how to switch it on.''

''I do.''

''Both the house and the barn.''

''Both.''

''How do you get into the barn?''

''A big key. In the middle drawer of the antique
desk in your beautiful downstairs drawing room.''

''Very good, Doctor.''

''Thank you.''

''So. I think that's everything. I have given you
the keys. You will take care of my house?''

''To the best of my ability. Now, may I ask a
question?''

''Ask,'' Leon said.

''Aren't you a bit premature? You're not leaving
until March fifteen. We'll certainly see each other
before then.''

''Victor, by now I would think you would know
my nature. Simply, I want it settled. Out of the way
and off my mind, if you know what I mean.''

Demarest nodded. ''I know what you mean.''

''And I thank you in advance for your trouble.''

''Not at all, dear friend. No trouble at all.''

In December, Don Cranford would stay home a
few nights and then there would be a night out and,
of course, Diana understood. She encouraged him,
even sympathized with him. It was necessary for
him to entertain ''the boys.'' They were the cus-

tomers, and they recommended the new customers, and then he would have to go out with the new customers. It was a sporting goods business and they were sporting-type men. She understood; she even hoped it gave him some relaxation, because he was a hard worker, even harder than her father had been. Many a morning Don would go in to help Paul, a nice old man, a real gentleman. And many a morning Don would go out with the van—to make deliveries, or to pick up new stock. He worked hard, and the store had certainly shown improvement. It was still called Delanco's Sporting Goods Store (to keep up the long-established goodwill) but it was producing much more money than in Papa's time. Don had added new stock to the inventory, and now there were even attractive items for the ladies, and Don knew how to draw them into the store. He put beautiful things into the windows facing the street. He knew how to dress up that window really artistic. And he was a terrific salesman, a crackerjack; old Paul said he was the best.

They were rich, the Donald Cranfords. They had a heck of a lot of money. Papa had left $60,000 in cash, and he had given them the house and the business. Papa was dead four years now, and Don had added much more money to the family. He did not hog the money. He had his own checking account, but their savings were in joint accounts and she was in charge of the bankbooks. He did not believe in investments. The savings banks had plans for very good interest. The Cranfords had $40,000 in one savings bank, and $40,000 in another savings bank, and $30,000 in another savings bank. When the last one got up to 40, they would start a new account in another bank. Don explained the reason: the federal government insured each separate savings account, but only up to $40,000. Don was very smart. And a good husband, a shrewd businessman, a hard worker. He was a boss type: he was a strong man on whom you could lean. Papa had made a good choice. *Grazie, Giuseppe.*

Nothing went right. Nothing wanted to happen. They all had roommates, or they had their girl friends with them (a girl friend could always identify you), or they were chummy with the bartender who kept smiling at you (and would remember your face), or their apartment houses had doormen or elevator men. November had seeped away, and here it was early December, a Thursday evening. He had hit a few bars and moved on. He was driving the Merc. He had stopped off at a diner for hamburgers and coffee. He had been drinking Scotch tonight and he was feeling good, coffee and hamburger and Scotch whisky flowing through him, and suddenly there in the beanery he thought about Dino's Blue Grotto. Yeah. They drew a nice crowd and he had not been there in a long time and it was safe ground because he had never gotten lucky in Dino's.

He drove to East Meadow, parked, strolled into the Grotto. A real chic joint, this Dino's, soft lights and a long bar, and also a circular piano bar, and neat little tables in the cocktail lounge. And a cute little dance floor, and a nice little four-piece combo playing easy music, slow and sexy, for romantic couples.

He checked his coat and by the wall clock inside the check room he saw it was five minutes to eleven. There were thongs in a pocket of his coat—so what? Why shouldn't he have thongs if anybody asked; he was in the business. But who the hell would ask; who would go looking in his coat pocket? The knife; that's a different story. But the knife was not in his coat; the knife was in his pants pocket and he had not checked his pants, right? Yeah, man, right. He walked tall in the soft lights toward the bar and female eyes flashed like summer lightning, but suddenly, astonishingly, he saw the woman coming toward him, from the lounge, the ladies' powder room, and he was hit in the balls with the magnum force of a Colt .45. Oh, sweet Jesus! Dear Jesus Christ Almighty! Here out of nowhere was a bitch who dropped into that whole other category. He felt her instantly, in the legs, the groin, the cock, the belly, the heart. Oh, motherfucker, this one he will tail, trail, sit, wait, observe, watch, and make plans like a general of the fucking army. But danger. This one is what I know to be the danger of my sickness. With this one there will be no matter of roommates, doormen, elevator men. This bitch I must have. Oh, I wish to fucking God she hates me; I wish she spits on me; I wish she is here with some guy and I cannot even start to get to first base with her.

The woman was dark, with dark shiny eyes; she

was wearing a sleek, simple, expensive dress, cut deep in front, and she had a great pair of gorgeous breasts. She passed him and he turned to watch. Oh, man. A nice tight waist, a bulgy ass, a sexy walk. She went all the way to the bar and only then, when she was all the way there, did she turn around and flash a quick smile, like the beam of a searchlight, directly at him. And then at the bar she joined *two* guys.

At the piano bar there was only one empty seat, but it faced the long bar. He sat and ordered a J&B with soda, drank, tapped a foot to the piano music, and watched the back of the bitch at the long bar, and then quite suddenly she swung around and she found him and their eyes met and from all that distance there was a bang like the crash of cymbals, and he smiled. He did it big, a wide smile, and she stood up and left the two guys at the long bar and, carrying her glass, she came to the piano bar and stood before him. Christ, he could feel the heat of her. He turned, looked up, stood up, but she said, "We can't both sit in that one seat, can we?"

"You're so right," he said and pointed toward the rear, toward an unoccupied cocktail table. "Okay?"

"Love it," she said.

The waiter was old with a bald head and glasses with lenses like the bottoms of inkwells. "Yes, please?"

She was drinking his drink, J&B. They ordered two new J&Bs, his with soda, hers with water.

"I'm Fran," she said.

"Don." He gave her the small shy smile.

"You're a very striking man."

"You're a very striking woman."

"Thank you."

"What's to thank when it's a fact?"

"Where you from, Don?"

"Los Angeles."

"Los Angeles? My goodness, what brings you to Dino's?"

"No. What I meant was I originally was from Los Angeles. Born there. Now I live here on the Island."

The waiter brought their drinks.

The combo began to play *Fascination*.

A soft glow came to her eyes. "I love that song."

"That's a great tune. I melt everytime I hear it," he said. "With the violins and all. I stay up to watch the movie, *Love in the Afternoon*, any time it's on the late show.

"Will you dance with me?"

"I'd be fascinated to."

"Oh dearest God, our handsome devil also has the gift of subtle gab."

"That music really sends me. I'll be Gary. You'll be Audrey. So? Shall we dance, madame?"

"We shall dance, monsieur."

She shoved it into him real good. She breathed in his ear. His cock stood up and he pushed it to her and she pushed right back. Wordlessly, they made their points. They declared themselves. They danced closely, quite gracefully, and then *Fascina-*

tion ended and another tune began and they returned to the table.

"Fran Haskell," she said.

"Don Corbin."

"You came along just in time. Creeps. The whole world inhabited by creeps. That couldn't be, could it? It had to be me. Sick in the head or something." She sipped her drink. "Donald, you have saved my sanity."

Donald. Not Donny.

"Me too," he said.

She squinted. "You too . . .?"

"Inhabited by creeps. The whole world. Like for months. You have saved my sanity."

She laughed. Gleaming, expensively capped, large teeth. "You know how to say all the right things."

"Honest, I mean it."

"Well, it's finally ended. At least for me. I think you're darling."

"Ended for me too. I—I—"—so hesitantly—"I'm in love."

"Wow, you're a fast one."

A deep earnest whispery voice. "I really think these things happen. I mean—just like that."

"Don't let it go too far, Donald. I'm a married lady."

"I'm a married man." Sadly.

She finished her drink. He drank his and ordered another round. The waiter took away the old glasses and brought fresh drinks. She stirred her drink.

"You don't come here often, do you, Don?"

"How do you know?"

"I've never seen you before."

"Is this kind of your candy store?"

"We come here once a week. On Thursdays. Two girl friends and me."

His heart sank. Girl friends. If they saw him—forget it. Finished. He couldn't let it go on. That crazy he was not! He smiled genially. He looked about.

"Girl friends?"

"They're not here."

"But didn't you just say . . ."

The teeth gleamed, small now, in a tight impish grin. "Don, you're a married man and I'm a married woman, so we don't have to kid each other. I'm a cheater." A pause. "Are you?"

"Well, I suppose—"

"Hard to put it into words, isn't it? Hard to say it straight out. Well, let me give you my picture. My girl friends and me. We're family women, love our husbands, but we like a little extracurricular excitement, if you know what I mean. We don't want to break up our happy homes, you know? Have your cake and eat it. It can be done. With the right person, it can be done."

She had a sexy mouth. He imagined his prick in her mouth. "Where are your girl friends?" he asked.

"I'd say, right now, in bed somewhere with their lovers. Here in Dino's, it's sort of the meeting place. They met their people and they're gone. We meet back here, the three ladies, at about two, and off we go. Home.''

''Lovers,'' he said musingly. ''What about you?''

''I broke up with my guy some time ago. Since then there've been a couple of silly little episodes, and then this whole long negative period of creeps—and then suddenly Don Corbin.''

These cunts. These broads. All alike, except for so very few. Here's this gorgeous bitch, obviously rich as fucking hell. A cunt like all the rest of them. Not like Diana. Not like the nuns who used to be Diana's teachers. There must be other broads who are real decent people. But there aren't many. There are very few. He looked into her eyes. She made a kiss of her mouth. He knew—he knew!—that right now, this minute, if he said to this very rich, very fancy lady, let's you and me blow this joint and grab a fast fuck in the nearest motel, she would fly.

''A once-a-week thing,'' he said. He knew how to do a put-down.

''We have responsibilities,'' she said. ''Don't you have responsibilities, Don?''

''A once-a-week lover. Can't be too much love.''

''Responsibilities. Don, I know you know!''

''Damn right I know.''

''You have a family?''

''Three kids. A blind wife.''

''Oh, I'm sorry.''

''Blind. A smash-up, auto accident. Left her blind. We don't really get along. What I mean, in bed. Cold. A cold woman, you know? But I can't leave her. I mean you can pay alimony and child support and all, but you can't walk out on a blind woman.''

''You sound like a damn nice guy.''

''Thank you,'' he said. Humbly.

''What do you do?''

''About my wife?''

''No. Your business. Please, you don't have to say. I mean—I don't want to be presumptuous.''

''Pilot. I'm an airline pilot.''

Long ago he had thought it over, figured it out. It was romantic, the women went for it: airline pilot. There were other romantic items like a doctor, a psychiatrist (not a dentist). But he knew his English was lousy, and also he certainly didn't have the knowledge to play those roles, so, most of the time, he was a goddamn airline pilot. The education, the electronic and the electrical engineering in Nassau Community College, and a boyhood interest in planes and aeronautics, had given him a smattering, and who was there to question him? He was an airline pilot when a woman at a bar asked him what he did for a living. It was a romantic answer and there could not be too many in-depth questions. Who in hell could quiz him? A cunt looking to make out with a good-looking guy in a bar? Sometimes he thought, fleetingly and laughingly, if one of these cunts should decide to go shopping in Delanco's Sporting Goods Store? Didn't figure to happen. The odds were a million-and-a-half to one, or so. But suppose it did happen. So what? One of these cunts walks into Delanco's and there is Don Corbin—or whatever the hell his name is—as storekeeper and salesman. So what? So he was lying. A con man. A bullshitter. So what? If they were alive, and they happened to drop into Delanco's Sporting Goods Store opposite Bloomingdale's in Garden City, and there was the great airplane pilot politely trying to sell them a pair of ski pants or a tennis racket or a badminton bird or a Ping-Pong table—so what? If they were alive, then he had never done anything wrong with them. He had seen them in a bar, flirted, and bullshitted that he was an airline pilot—and had never seen them again after that first encounter at the bar. If he *had* seen them again, then they were dead.

"A pilot," she was saying. "That's so very interesting. From where to where?"

"Los Angeles to New York, and then right back again. How about you? I mean, family. Children?"

"None. Just me and my husband."

"What does he do?" He grinned. "Heck, you asked *me*."

"An accountant. In Freeport."

"Let's dance."

"Love it."

Their bodies caressed. They flirted. He held her closely, but he was more careful now. He had her—but he had to go away. He had to leave before her girl friends returned. The dance ended. At the table, he looked at his watch. "I—really gotta go." He smiled. "I really don't make this scene too often. I'd have to arrange it. Prepare at home, you know? And meet you, sort of, earlier."

"We're here every Thursday night."

"Not good. I may not be in town for many Thursdays. And when I am, I don't know when I can get away. No. I'd have to be in touch with you. May I—call you?"

"Anywhere I can call you?"

He shook his head. "No good. Look, I got a blind wife. You can't call me at home, and on the outside any strange calls coming through and right away I'm the heavy."

"All right." The dark eyes glittered. "It won't be the first time. Good thing you didn't lie to me, tell me you're single. Then I wouldn't do it. Single guys take too many chances. Now I'm not going to give you my number because I don't want you writing it down. I don't want anybody finding my number in one of your pockets. What you'll do, you'll look it up in the book. We live in Hewlett. Ralph Haskell. Got it?"

He took her hand to his mouth, touched the tip of his tongue to the palm, kissed it, released her hand.

"Donald, I swear to God, you're giving me palpitations."

"Sweetie, what do you think you're doing to me?"

"You'll call after nine and before five. And of course," she laughed, "not Saturdays, Sundays or holidays."

"Got to go." He called for the check and paid. "I'll be in touch."

"Soon, I hope."

"You bet."

He retrieved his coat and went out to the car. All the way home he thought about the woman Fran Haskell. In the house he did not look in on the children, and in bed he pulled Diana to him before she was awake.

Many mornings, early, from the discreetly parked van, he watched the house in Hewlett. The husband left at about eight-thirty. Fran served his breakfast in the kitchen. The bald guy ate like a horse, the same breakfast every morning: juice, bacon and eggs, toast and coffee. After he was gone, she also had coffee there in the kitchen (with buttered toast and jelly). They kept the light on in the kitchen and he could see clearly through the window. He knew where the bedrooms were, the bathrooms, he knew it all, but he bided his time, savoring the anticipation. Several times from home, when Diana and the kids were out of the house, he undressed and called Fran, telling her he was calling from Los Angeles, and turned on the conversation sexily and always her voice grew husky in response, and he would come several times before he hung up, and then he would get a towel and water to clean up his mess before his wife and kids came home.

NINE

At Christmas the Victor Demarest family flew away to Sun Valley. In advance by air freight they had sent their skis and poles and heavy shoes and thick bright clothing, and then on Friday, December 23, they left LaGuardia in New York to fly to Garwood's in Sun Valley, Idaho.

Christmas fell on Sunday and the Demarests would celebrate in the snows of Sun Valley. They would come home to Old Westbury on Monday, January 2, which was still a holiday, because New Year's Day, like Christmas Day, fell on a Sunday. On Tuesday, January 3, Dr. Vic would go back to work and Kathy would go back to school and Lori would go back to her role of homemaker. But in between, Lori would shop. For necessities, but also for items of absolute nonsense. Such as flimsy black underwear that she would never wear, or a trinket that might catch her eye, or an antique chest of drawers that they would have to store in the attic because there was no place for it in the house. Somewhere in the recesses of her mind she understood the reason for these bursts of profligacy and sometimes in their serious talks she tried to explain it to Victor. In an insane world that seemed to be devoted to the mass murders of war, to bombings, assassinations, explosions, terrorist killings, street killings, rapes, assaults, homicides and suicides, there are those particularly sentient who must develop their own crazy system of therapy to keep holding on and not slip over the edge into the safe refuge of madness.

At Christmastime a man named Irwin Waldwick flew with his wife and three small children to the new home he had purchased for his wife's parents in Palm Beach. It would be a short vacation for Irwin, a longer vacation for his wife, and a real long vacation for the children.

"You know what?" his mother-in-law said. "Right next door there's a nice old couple, the Parlins, and they got a daughter married to a doctor lives right where you live, Irwin."

"Where?"

"Old Westbury."

"We live in Woodbury."

"Well, it's Nassau County."

"Nassau County, Mama, is an area of three hundred square miles. Three hundred times three hundred equals ninety thousand. And in the aforesaid area there's a population of a million five. And Woodbury is not Old Westbury and vice versa."

"His name is Demarest."

"Jesus, get her off my back."

"A doctor. Demarest. Could be you heard of him. It's always possible. Nassau County."

"Never heard of him. Why should I hear of him?"

"Look, Irwin, what do I know about Nassau County? I am proud to say we were born and raised in Schenectady."

"Get her off my back," Irwin said to his wife and Irwin's wife surrounded her mother with the grandchildren, and Irwin made himself a large drink.

He was president of Waldwick Plastics. On Tuesday he would fly up to Chicago for the industry convention. It had been *his* suggestion that the convention be held in a central city, Chicago, and it had also been his unconventional suggestion that the period of the convention be from Tuesday, December 27, to Friday, January 7—a solid 12 days. Waldwick, although a young man, was a power in the industry and he took pride in the fact that he frequently came up with innovative ideas. He contended that for this convention the business leaders would lose only five days. It was an accepted fact that during Christmas week the wholesale in plastics was at a standstill. Therefore out of the twelve days of the convention, only the five business days in January would entail any pragmatic sacrifice. And naturally the retailers would have to fall in with the plans of the manufacturers or they would fall behind in their knowledge of the new creations for the coming season. It was a beautiful deal all around. The men would spend Christmas with their families, and then for New Year's Eve the wives of the married men would fly out to them, while the single men would roister with the girls of the Windy City.

* * *

The Cranfords had a tall tree with spangles and streamers and rosy balls, and there were wonderful Christmas gifts under the tree. They went to church on Christmas Sunday and stuffed themselves with meats and wine on Sunday and Monday, but on Tuesday morning, very early and despite the fact it was Paul who opened the store, Don was off to work.

At eight-fifteen he sat in the van under a tree near the Hewlett house. He saw the man eating his breakfast in the kitchen and saw the man drive off to work. You bet. The guy was an accountant, and if you're an accountant, like if you own a sporting goods store, you take off the three days of the Christmas holiday, but on Tuesday you go back to work, is what you do.

He was ready. It was time. He could contain himself no longer.

On Wednesday morning, at ten minutes to nine, he parked the Merc out of the way and briskly walked the distance to the house in Hewlett. He was immaculately attired—shirt, tie, conservative suit, conservative topcoat—and he was carrying a slender attaché case. He rang the bell, a light touch, a short ring.

Fran, in a long housecoat, peered through the round glass porthole of the wooden door. She saw him, and he saw her amazed expression. He waved his left hand. She opened the wooden door but the screen door was still between them.

"Are you crazy?" she whispered.

"Impulsive," he said. "I was here. I had to be here. I have to see somebody here in this neighborhood at ten o'clock." He gave her the boyish grin, disarming. "Figured it'd be fun to drop in on you before, just for the heck of it. But I won't be able to stay long." He pointed to the attaché case. "This here, it's like protection. Like I'm a salesman, you know. Madam, perhaps I can interest you in an encyclopedia?"

She had to laugh. She shook her head. She admired the daring of the handsome son of a bitch. "But, God, what I look like," she said.

"Are you kidding? You look beautiful. The belle of the ball. Sweetie, this is for laughs. We're not going to do anything. I'm a salesman. Maybe, even, you could offer the salesman a cup of coffee."

She was still chuckling, shaking her head, as she opened the screen door. "Honey, you really shouldn't be here."

She closed the screen door, closed the wooden door. He followed her to the kitchen. He put down the attaché case, removed his topcoat. "Real nice place you got here," he said and measured her, swung his fist, hit her jaw, and she toppled.

He pulled down the blinds. He opened the attaché case, took out the thongs, tied her wrists behind her, tied her ankles. He tore off the housecoat and she was naked. He unzipped his trousers. He produced his knife, touched the button, and the blade sprang free. He pulled her up to her knees and began gently slapping her. When her eyes opened, the point of the knife was at her chin.

"Don't scream. If you scream I'll have to kill you. Don't make me kill you."

The dark eyes looked up imploringly. "What? Don, what, why—"

He smiled. "I'm a little nuts that way. I dig it like that, when somebody's tied up. I won't hurt you, I swear. You'll give me a little blow job, and then I'll untie you, and then, well, if you'll forgive me, and if you want, we'll make a little real love."

He put his rigid penis to her mouth, forced her to open, and she did him. "Good girl," he said. "Yeah. Nice and easy. You're doing it real good. Yeah, baby, that's it, you're a real great cocksucker, sweetie." And then finally he exploded in her mouth and pulled out. "Okay, okay," he said. "Don't talk. Nothing. Not yet. I'm gonna undress, and then I'll untie you, and *then* we'll talk. We'll kinda discuss this, and then if you want, we'll make a little love, a little real love, you and me, sweetie."

He placed the knife on the edge of the kitchen table. Her eyes, glazed with fear, stared as though hypnotized at the blade of the knife.

"Smart," he said. "Smart girl. You don't holler, you don't scream, because why should you go and get yourself killed, right?"

He undressed quickly. He took the knife to her. "Okay, I'll get you out of them strips of leather and then we'll get nice and comfy and we'll talk and maybe you'll understand."

He cut her throat and the blood shot out over him. Now he stooped and pushed at her shoulders and pulled at her ankles until she was lying supine. Oh, man, look at them big bombs. He hacked at her breasts, stabbing, slashing. He heard himself gasping; he felt the blobs of spittle forming at the corners of his mouth. He stood up and his ejaculate squirted out of him and onto her. He wanted more. He stood astride of her and then he heard the sound—a hoarse howling, a wailing, the deep baying of some large dog—from far away. He squinted, angled his face, listened, and heard it again—far away. A warning. An omen. He picked up his clues in his own ways; it was time to split. He wiped the knife on the torn housecoat, closed it, dropped it into the attaché case. He ran up to the bathroom and quickly, carefully, touching no hard surfaces, he washed and toweled, cleansing himself. Downstairs in the kitchen he dressed, shrugged into the topcoat, shut the attaché case. He used a handkerchief on the knob of the wooden door and the handle of the screen door. He strolled to the parked Mercury and laid in the attaché case and commenced the drive to Delanco's Sporting Goods Store in Garden City. And on the way he opened his fly and took out his penis, and with his left hand he directed the steering wheel and with his right hand he masturbated.

Ralph Haskell discovered her at quarter to six. At six o'clock the house was swarming with the people from the Homicide Squad. At ten after six Captain

McVail arrived with Lieutenant Medford and five minutes later the medical examiner appeared. McVail questioned Haskell briefly; then McVail went out and examined the telephone wires attached to the house; then, on returning, he questioned Haskell more rigorously. Haskell maintained that he had left the house at about eight-thirty, that she had then been alive and well, and then at a quarter to six he had found her on the kitchen floor and had immediately called the police. The medical examiner, before autopsy, approximated the time of death between nine and eleven. Lieutenant Medford frowned as McVail kept pressing Haskell for alibi information. Haskell stated that he had come to his office at about nine o'clock and had remained there all day except for a lunch date with a client. McVail elicited names and addresses—of Haskell's secretary, of other employees of the office, the client with whom Haskell allegedly had lunched, and he dispatched a group of detectives to talk to these persons for verification. He returned to his interrogation of Haskell, but Haskell stood up, commenced to shake violently, and fell against McVail in a dead faint.

The medical examiner revived him.

"Got to give him a jab of sedation."

"But make it a small one, Doc. I don't want him out of the ball park. I still need to talk to him."

Two policemen, under the supervision of the medical examiner, carried Haskell to a bedroom.

"Now, Jake, please," Medford said. "You don't really think that guy is Leather Boy, do you?"

"My dear lieutenant, I know that file better than I know the palm of my hand. In all these years, this is only the third time Leather Boy does a daytime job. The daytime jobs—contrary to the nighttime jobs—are in private houses. Now on those other two private-house jobs, he cut an outside phone wire. I assume he *first* cut the wire, because what sense to cut the phone after the people are dead? You don't have to be a genius to figure that he cut those wires so that nobody would call the cops if they managed to know that he sneaked in. *But in this house no outside wire was cut.* No outside wire, no inside wire, no nothing. What does that suggest to you?"

"That he was pretty certain he'd be admitted."

"And what does *that* suggest to you?"

"That he was acquainted with the deceased."

"In such case—rule of thumb—the first suspect is the husband."

"Now you really don't think this guy is Leather Boy."

"No, but he could be an imitation."

"Now, what—?"

"A guy gets a hate for his wife, but good. He kills her and then to cover up he uses an M.O. that figures to throw us off. Does it the way the Nassau Slasher would have done it."

"How would he know about thongs?"

"Could have a retentive memory. At the beginning the newspapers did mention the thongs." McVail shrugged. "I'm only talking. I don't know. But I do know, in my bones, that Mrs. Haskell and

Leather Boy weren't strangers to each other.'' And at that moment a uniformed policeman arrived with the two other surviving relatives: Francine Haskell's widowed mother, Mrs. Yetta Millburn, hysterically crying, and Francine Haskell's brother, Mr. Eric Millburn, staunch and stoic.

The body was taken to the morgue, and the reporters had their stories. The group of detectives returned with indisputable confirmation of Haskell's alibi period. McVail talked with Haskell again, and then with the Millburns, and learned nothing that could help. Fran had been a good wife, a happy extroverted human being. She loved people, she loved to laugh, she enjoyed life. He learned that in the Haskell household Wednesday was boy's night out: on Wednesday evenings Ralph Haskell played poker with the boys in S. Lloyd Jutland's house. That rang a little bell, unheeded, in the mind of Jake McVail. Careful with this Haskell. He was simply not another rich guy. He was a friend and poker crony of the County Executive. He learned that Thursday was girl's night out. On Thursdays Fran Haskell went out with the girls, who were two, Mrs. Ellen Laurel and Mrs. Paula Sewell, and who were in fact Francine Haskell's only friends. McVail turned them over to Lieutenant Pamela Medford. She was to take with her a couple of uniformed policemen and she was to collect Laurel and Sewell and deliver them to him at his office at Headquarters. It was enough here in this house of death in Hewlett.

"Take care of this guy," McVail said to Eric Millburn. "I'm an old hand. He's not in good shape. Get him to his doctor, or get his doctor to him. He's shook. Of course he has every reason to be, but I can tell, I know the signs. He's more shook than most. He can hurt himself. I'd stay with him. I wouldn't leave him alone. I'd be careful of him."

The weeping woman said, "You're very kind, Captain McVail."

"I'm in a lousy business," he said. "Sir," he said to Eric Millburn. "Your business, if I may ask?"

"Mortician."

"Beg pardon?"

"Funeral director."

"Oh," McVail said. He smiled a crooked smile, the creases of his face deepening. He bowed to Yetta. He shook hands with Eric. "Do take care of the guy," he said and went out of the house and into his car.

He drove directly to a saloon where they knew him. It was a dark saloon with a long dark mahogany bar without music, no juke box, no entertainment. The bartender, whom McVail knew for 20 years but only as O'Hara, said, "Hi, Cap," but did not need to ask what the captain wished. He placed a shot glass on the bar in front of the captain, and a bottle of Jack Daniel's, and a tall beer. The captain did not rush to drink. In ten minutes he polished off four Jack Daniel's, finished his beer, paid, laid down a dollar for O'Hara (mostly in appreciation of silence), ambled out into the cool night air and drove to Headquarters.

They were pretty women. They had wise eyes, naive smiles, and tender, innocent, deeply concerned voices. Whatever they said, he did not believe a word they said. He admitted to himself that that was extreme, but his instinct and his experience told him that if his disbelief fogged over some facts of truth, he would nevertheless be out in front. They were rich ladies, as every outer garment conservatively proclaimed. They talked for a time, the ladies and the detectives, politely, the hidden tape recorder registering every word, until the wrinkle-suited paunchy old man felt it was time to shake them up.

"And so on Thursday nights, where did you shack, ladies?"

"How *dare* you?" said Ellen Laurel, a shimmering blonde with a darkness showing at the roots of her hair. She had been unprepared. She had been yanked precipitately by a woman detective and a male policeman out of her home and into a squad car and up to the captain's office in Headquarters.

"How dare you?" echoed Paula Sewell, red-haired all the way to the roots.

McVail cleared his throat. It was time to frighten indignant ladies. "Francine's throat was cut wide open. Her breasts were hacked by a knife, one of them practically severed from the chest. We have evidence of semen in the oral cavity, in the esophagus, and there was semen splattered on her nude body. We have reason to believe that Francine Haskell was acquainted with the man who murdered her.''

Now the fabrication, the cop's trick, the threat. ''We also have reason to believe that he knows you, Ms. Laurel, and you, Ms. Sewell, and that both of you are on his list. So—let's have some real information on the Thursday nights. I assure you it stays with me. I guarantee to you—confidential.''

Hoping against hope, he knew it wouldn't work. He had been a cop for 37 years. He knew the type, very rich, and therefore as obstructive as a high wall. They would rather risk possible death than the notoriety of open scandal and the subsequent loss of husband, hearth and munificent support.

''On Thursdays we were the girls,'' Paula Sewell said. ''We'd go out to dinner. Maybe a movie. Maybe a show in New York.''

''Guys?'' he said.

''Sometimes we might go to a jazz place, or even a pub. For laughs, for some crazy but innocent excitement.'' Ellen Laurel lit a cigarette. ''Yes, guys,'' she said.

''Tell me,'' he said.

''Captain, there's nothing to tell,'' Ellen said. ''At a bar we might talk to an attractive man, for the hell of it, for fun on a night out. But that would be it. Maybe even a little sexy talk, but that would be it—talk. Then off we'd go, home, to the husband and to the kids. Gosh, we'd have to be crazy, Captain McVail.''

"Francine?"

"What?" Paula asked.

"Innocent? Always innocent? I feel in my gut that she met a guy. I feel in my gut that she let this guy into her house. I tell you this son of a bitch killed her. I tell you, I feel in my gut, that you ladies can help me. I plead with you. I'm begging you. I promise—confidential. For chrissake, your friend is dead. You, either one of you, may be next. Talk! Tell me. For chrissake, I swear to you, you may be saving your own lives. Will you tell me?"

"I wish there was something to tell," Ellen said.

"So do I," Paula said.

They were lying. Thirty-seven years. He goddamn knew they were lying but he also knew—thirty-seven years—that for now it was done. You cannot squeeze blood from a turnip. The phone rang and he seized it in relief, angrily. "I left specific instructions I was not to be disturbed."

"This is Mel Burns on the board, sir."

"Specific instructions."

"Captain McVail, you ever hear of a dude name of Morton Maurice Clayton?"

"Mr. Money?"

"That's the one. Financial tycoon."

"So?"

"So that's the dude on the phone. He wants to talk to Captain McVail, and first he mentions Commissioner Dumont. Leaves me in what you call a quandary. If I turn this guy down, you might bawl the balls off me. On the other hand, if I disobey your instructions, you might put me out to pasture like in Sands Point, right? Quandary, right? Had to make the decision. So I disturbed you. How'm I doing with Sands Point, Captain?''

''You're doing all right.''

''Thank you, sir.''

''Put the guy through, please.''

''Yessir.''

A short wait. The captain smiled at the ladies. Then the voice at his ear said, ''Captain McVail?''

''McVail.''

''Maurice Clayton here.''

''What can I do for you?''

''I believe I have some information that should interest you.''

''About what?''

''Francine Haskell.''

''Oh?'' McVail sat up straight.

''Just heard the horrible news over the radio. Immediately called my friend Arthur Dumont. He told me Captain Jackson McVail was in charge of the case. I should like to see you, sir. I can be there in twenty minutes, if that's all right with you.''

''Yessir. Excellent. I'll be waiting. Appreciate it.''

McVail hung up. He called in Medford to take the ladies home. He told the ladies he would probably talk with them again. He called downstairs and informed them that he was expecting a Mr. Clayton; that Clayton should be shown up immediately when he arrived. He lit one of his black cheroots, rested the nape of his neck against the leather of his high-back swivel chair. Morton Maurice Clayton was the

M. M. Clayton Corporation, a conglomerate that owned banks, businesses, ships, restaurants, factories, oil wells, publishing houses and newspapers. Who in hell *were* these Haskells? The husband was a poker partner to the County Executive, and the wife was a friend, or at least an acquaintance, of one of the richest men in the world. McVail smoked his cigar and rocked in his swivel chair.

The buzzer sounded. It was Burns again, this time on the intercom. "Guy's on his way up, Captain McVail."

"Thank you."

Clayton was small, splendidly dressed. He had a pink face, a receding hairline, a mouthful of shiny teeth and a quiet cultivated voice. "Pleasure to meet you, Captain. May I sit down?"

"Please."

He sat. He produced a cigar different from the one McVail was smoking. He lit it with a gold lighter. In the blue air he said, "Irwin Waldwick. Have you ever heard of Waldwick Plastics, Captain?"

"Who hasn't?"

"Irwin. He's president of Waldwick Plastics. Irwin's a friend of mine, kind of a neighbor. I have a house in Woodbury, and so does Irwin. Kind of devil-may-care fellow, Irwin, and well, sort of a ladies' man. About six months ago Irwin became immersed in a problem and he consulted with me about it. He was in love. Francine Haskell. This very same woman, Captain. Wife of Ralph Haskell. He was taken with this woman, fascinated, enraptured. Now Irwin himself is a married man. A fine wife, three children. He was ready to break up his marriage. I'm an older man; naturally, I advised against it. A love affair is one thing. Tearing apart a family—in this case, actually two families—is another thing. Fortunately for Irwin, Mrs. Haskell was sensible and practical. It was an affair. Two married people. Pleasurable, sexual, a secret affair, the very secrecy punctuating the pleasure, if you follow me.''

''I follow you.''

''For Mrs. Haskell it was not at all a serious *amour de coeur*. It was a sexual frolic, but not a cause for divorce, and certainly not for remarriage. I believe she grew frightened, because bit by bit, she withdrew from Irwin, and about, well, I'd say, three months ago their romance terminated, and by then Irwin himself had come to his senses. Today he's the devil-may-care fellow again, bouncing about, having fun with the ladies.'' Clayton put the cigar to his mouth and puffed delicately. ''The point of all of this, Captain, is Irwin Waldwick. I'm quite certain he can help you in your investigation. What I mean, here's a person who has had a long-term, intimate, secret affair with the victim of this terrible tragedy. I'm quite certain he can help you. I'm quite certain he can acquaint you with—well, hints—pertinent characteristics of her personality that you simply couldn't obtain from any other source. Don't you think, Captain?''

''I do.''

''I've already talked with him, Captain. I'm certain he'll do whatever he can to help you."

"Good." McVail laid away his cigar and stood up. "You said that he's in Woodbury?"

"Chicago."

Chicago! A thin shiver like a cold wind coursed through McVail's big body. Chicago was where Leather Boy had begun. Chicago was the shibboleth, the secret word in connection with the Nassau Slasher. "You talked to him in Chicago? When?"

"The moment I heard about Haskell. He was my first call."

"What's this guy look like, Mr. Clayton?"

Clayton smiled. "Tall, dark and handsome. Naturally."

McVail paced. "Young?"

"Yes."

McVail paced. Leather Boy, to the best of their knowledge, was tall, dark, young. The phone wire in the Hewlett house had not been cut. McVail had the gut feeling that Leather Boy had been acquainted with Francine Haskell. A guy can come in from Chicago and kill a person in Nassau County at nine or ten in the morning and be back in Chicago in a couple of hours.

"What's with Chicago?" he asked.

"They're having their convention. He's staying at the Continental Plaza."

McVail pointed at the phone. "You think you can reach him now?"

"Certainly. He's either in his suite, or at the convention, or at a restaurant, but he's Irwin

Waldwick, and there'd be word at the hotel desk where he could be reached."

"Would you call him, please? Would you tell him I'm coming out to talk with him?"

"Yessir. When would you go, Captain?"

"Now. I'll grab the first flight available as soon as I get to the airport. We're the Police Department. For cops they find room, Mr. Clayton, even if they have to bump a stewie. Please call the guy. Please tell him to be at the hotel, or leave a number where I can reach him when I get there."

Captain Jackson Brendan McVail, the loner. McVail, the eccentric. The genius cop, 37 years with the force. A strange man, a law unto himself, but with his long success record nobody dared criticize and nobody ever was moved to criticize. Jake McVail, a legend in his own lifetime. McVail paced. He was not going to make any written record of this, nor was he going to take anyone with him. People talk, even cops, and the word spreads, and a guy gets marked lousy. He would not do this to the man in Chicago. If the guy was Leather Boy, or even if there was a suspicion that he was Leather Boy, that's a whole other story. But if he was not, then his relationship with the dead Francine would remain exactly where it was; it would not spiral up into the newspapers (from an unimpeachable source) and thereby wreck a man's life, wife and his family.

M. M. Clayton laid the receiver in the cradle.

"Starting one hour from now," he said, "Mr. Waldwick will be in his suite in the Continental

Plaza and he won't budge out of there until you get there.''

"Thank you, sir. You're a damn good citizen.''

"My car and chauffeur are downstairs, Captain.'' The shiny teeth flashed. "We can get you to the airport real quick.''

"Thank you, but no. Got to do this through channels. I repeat, Mr. Clayton, you're a damn good citizen.''

The small man shrugged. "We do what we think is right.''

"Yes, most of us do,'' McVail said seriously. "But there have been times in my life when I've done things, perhaps unorthodox, which I believed to be right, but which others condemned as terribly wrong.''

"Captain McVail, I've arrived at a time in my life when I don't give a damn what others think. The establishment, and the established thinking, is not always necessarily right. I have done things which, if clinically examined, could be called criminal because in fact I broke a law. But I did not harm anyone, and in fact I helped. My conscience was as clear as the driven slush, ha ha. I'd say we're approximately the same age, Captain. If we're evil men, by now there's no help for us. But if we're good men and we do an act that may be considered evil in the strictest sense but is nevertheless an act of kindness, an act of compassion, an act that helps a fellow man no matter whether it transgresses a legal law—then, in my philosophy, we have done right, we have done a good work.''

They shook hands. McVail grinned broadly.

"We are one," he said. "We must get together sometime, socially. I love you. You have said my say perfectly, and far better than I could ever express it. You have said my sentiments exactly. I thank you, sir. For now and for the future."

TEN

He called the house and told Eileen he had to go to Chicago and he would probably be home tomorrow. He provided himself with money from the petty cash drawer. He talked urgently with Communications, and Communications got back to him promptly. They had a seat for him at La Guardia, but he had to move his ass fast. They went in a squad car, the siren blaring all the way, and he was in the seat, *Esquire* on his lap, with 15 minutes to spare. It was a quick flight, La Guardia to O'Hare, without turbulence; and the cab was clean and the driver silent on the ride to the Continental Plaza. He inquired at the desk and then called from the housephone in the lobby.

Irwin Waldwick was simply too young to be the Waldwick who was president of Waldwick Plastics. The guy looked like about 27 but confessed to 34. He was quick, voluble, dapper, handsome, sophisticated. He had grown up in the business and, eight years ago, when his father had died, he had succeeded to his father's stock and to the presidency of the firm. "Irwin," McVail said, "you know from Clayton what happened to Francine Haskell."

"Yes."

"It happened this morning between nine and

135

eleven, Eastern time. Can you tell me where you were this morning between nine and eleven?''

''Now, look here. You don't think that I—''

''Irwin, in my business we have to cover every stoop on the block. I'd appreciate some straight answers.''

''We had a breakfast seminar. I'd say fifty people. From nine to twelve, Chicago time. That would completely cover the time period you're talking about. I was at that seminar. I was one of the principal speakers. It didn't break up until about one. I'll give you the names of fifty witnesses.''

It was already good enough, but he pushed it a little further to cover it all the way. ''Could you tell me what you did after the seminar?''

''Went up to my suite for some drinks and a little recreation.''

''Recreation?''

''A lady. She stayed with me until four o'clock.''

''I can check all of this out?''

''Absolutely.''

''Right. In due time, we'll attend to that. Now then. Please tell me about your relationship with Francine Haskell. You can start as far back as you like. This is confidential information. I have no personal interest. I'm not a reporter. This is not for the newspapers. We're simply trying to solve a horrible murder.''

''You'll be able to keep my name out of it?''

''I'm quite sure of that. What I'm trying to get from you is background on Francine. Our investigation thus far seems to point to the fact that she was acquainted with her murderer. If we dig deep enough, through you, through others, we may—we may!—get a line on the guy.''

''Irwin Waldwick married when he was 21. Started running around when he was about 26. All kinds of women; even call girls like the lady who was with him in the suite today.''

''Let's get to Francine, please,'' McVail said.

''Occasionally, on free evenings, he'd drop into a class-type pub, looking for a bit of fun, a bit of action. About a year ago, in a place in East Meadow, Dino's Blue Grotto, he met Francine Haskell and he flipped, first time in his life he really tilted over. These things happen. There simply is no rationale when you talk about love.''

''Right,'' McVail said.

''She was pretty, she was vivacious, she was fun out of bed, and in bed she was absolutely sensational. And also he had to admire her because she was a damn good woman. Took care of her husband, took care of her home. She went out on the town once a week, never more. Perhaps that added to the romance. When you see a woman only once a week, you see only the best; you don't get to see the warts on the hog, if you know what I mean. Anyway, after six months, Irwin Waldwick proposed marriage and Francine got scared. That was when Waldwick talked with Clayton, and Clayton did help, and then Francine, a once-a-week cheater, began to get cooler and cooler to Irwin Waldwick, and finally the tilt went out of his machine—he had a good wife and three great kids—and about three months ago they broke it up, Francine and Irwin, and he sure recovered fast, and maybe it was the best thing that ever happened to him, because you learn by experience, and it's good to have a good wife and good kids and still be able to run around and have your fun.''

''The once a week was Thursday night?''

''Correct.''

''What about her cheating on *you*?''

''Impossible. She simply wouldn't have had the chance. It was Thursday night, period. And every Thursday night she was with me. We'd meet in Dino's, maybe have a drink, maybe go out for a bite, and go to bed.''

''What about Ellen Laurel and Paula Sewell?''

''You know it all, don't you, Captain?''

''No, I don't. Believe me, Irwin.''

''The Thursday night trio. When three respectable married ladies go out together once a week, they can stay respectable with friends and acquaintances, because they each are the cover for the other. Do you know about Marty Hampton? About Doug Bartley?''

''No.''

''Are you kidding me, Captain?''

''Why would I kid you, Irwin?''

''I mean you guys know everything.''

''The way we get to know is by asking a lot of questions.''

''And sometimes double-questioning, right?''

McVail let it remain like that, mysterious. ''Who's Hampton?'' he asked. ''Who's Bartley?''

"Marty Hampton, Ellen is crazy about. Doug Bartley, Paula is crazy about. Both married guys, naturally. That puts the titillation on it, you know? Each one has a kind of fear, a sexual frenzy, when both sides are cheating."

"You know them all? I mean the women *and* the men?"

"Of course. The Thursday night special. We'd all meet in Dino's. The guys would get there maybe seven, seven-thirty, and start drinking. The gals, maybe eight, nine o'clock. Sometimes the six of us would go for some crazy food or something, but not always. Sometimes, each pair would break away right away. No orgies, no group sex, none of that. Matter of fact, always separate motels. Then about two o'clock, we'd get the ladies back to Dino's, and they'd take off, in one car, for home. The men, we might stick around, talk, drink a little, but no fooling around with any dames at the bar. Not at Dino's. We were doing all right with our own ladies at Dino's. You don't screw up your action by fooling around at the place where you meet every week, week after week."

"Hampton. Bartley. What do they do?"

"Marty's an executive vice-president over at Grumman's. Doug Bartley's a dentist in Syosset."

That was it. McVail knew he had all he could get from Irwin Waldwick. The rest were pretend-questions to flatter Irwin's ego; and then the easing-out process. Waldwick provided verification of his presence at the breakfast seminar, and he reached the call girl and she answered McVail's questions without any prompting from Waldwick. Her name was Lois. She was quite beautiful, Waldwick said.

"Where you staying, Captain?"

"Don't know yet."

"I'll send Lois over. She'll massage your back. Compliments of Waldwick Plastics." He grinned. "I mean wherever you stay."

"Thank you, no."

"Then at least you must let me arrange a room for you here at the Continental."

"Yes. But I pay my own way, Irwin."

McVail returned on Thursday morning, December 29. A squad car was waiting for him at La Guardia. Before he got into it, he called Detective-lieutenant Pamela Medford. She was to pick up Martin Hampton, an executive at Grumman's. She was to pick up Douglas Bartley, a dentist in Syosset. She was to use an unmarked car, she was to be assisted by a plainclothes officer, and the siren must remain mute. It must not look like an arrest: there must not be any uniformed police. She must handle it quietly, subtly. But he wanted both these guys in his office at 12 o'clock noon. She was to mention two names to them: Francine Haskell and Irwin Waldwick, but quietly. McVail was certain that the gentlemen would arrange to go along with Ms. Medford without noise, fanfare or furor. On the other hand, should either gentleman give her trouble—McVail doubted they would—then Medford was empowered to pull the stops, to open up the siren, to flash badges and engage in whatever was necessary. He wanted these guys in his office, without fail, at 12 o'clock noon.

He was driven home in a squad car. He kissed his daughter, shaved, showered, dressed in fresh clothes and grabbed a fast bacon and eggs with an English muffin well buttered. The squad car, siren open, drove him to Headquarters. At eleven-thirty he engaged in an earnest off-the-record conference with Nassau Police Commissioner Arthur Dumont. At eleven-forty, in his office, he had a hamburger on a sesame roll with coffee. At ten minutes to twelve Pam Medford delivered Mr. Martin Hampton and Dr. Douglas Bartley. Pam introduced them by name, bowed to her captain and managed a small, imperceptible wink.

"Please remain available, Lieutenant," McVail said.

"Yessir," the lieutenant said and bowed herself out.

They were in their early 40s, good-looking men who looked similarly ill—pale yellow as though afflicted by jaundice. McVail knew the color. The affliction was fear.

"Gentlemen, we shall endeavor not to involve you in any scandal. We are police here. We are not gossip mongers. As both of you must goddamn know, Francine Haskell was the victim of a brutal murder. My job is to run down the murderer. Like it's your job, Doctor, to fill a cavity. Like it's your job, Mr. Vice-President, to ass-lick your superiors and browbeat your inferiors, which is how the corporate business is run in the good old USA. You are both outside fuckers. Thursday-night cheaters. What bugs me is why I had to find *you*. What bugs me is why you didn't come forward. Your friend Francine was a victim of the Nassau Slasher. She was the victim of a dreadful sexual crime. Christ, the local papers were full of it. Explain it to me, Dr. Dentist Bartley. And you too, Mr. Vice-President. What kind of shit are you people? What kind of tripe *are* you? You did not come forward. I had to find you. What I'm asking you is why?''

The dentist said it all in four words.

''Sir, we were terrified.''

McVail looked to the vice-president.

The vice-president amplified. ''We neither of us knew anything at all that could possibly help you.''

McVail lit a black cheroot. ''Mr. Vice-President, you might, possibly, have a knowledge of airplanes. You, Mr. Dentist, might, possibly, have a knowledge of teeth. Would you say, either of you, that you have a knowledge of crime, of criminals, of police work?''

No answer.

McVail, rough now: ''How in hell could you know, either of you, what might help?''

No answer.

''Sit down,'' McVail said. They sat. They lit cigarettes, both of them, the fingers of the vice-president trembling more than the fingers of the dentist. ''Thursday-night cheaters, fucking around,'' McVail said. ''You'd rather let a murderer stay loose, a guy who might kill one of *your* wives. You would rather let that goddamn fiend run free, rather than come in and talk to the cops—because you don't want the scandal, you don't want your wife biting off your ass, you don't want your kids taunted in school.'' McVail stood up and pointed his finger down. ''Now you listen to me, both of you. I don't want you to lose your practice, Mr. Dentist, and I don't want you to get fired out on your butt, Mr. Vice-President, so you had better, both of you, right now make up your minds to cooperate with me. Ms. Ellen and Ms. Paula have bullshitted me right up to my ears. Like you, they're afraid of scandal. Well, just remember, both of you, I'm not in the scandal business. You noticed, I hope, that you were brought in discreetly. If you cooperate, that's the way it'll remain. But if you play games with me, then I'll call in the news boys and throw you to the wolves, so help me. Do you read me clear, gentlemen?''

They nodded. They cooperated. McVail pumped them dry, but whatever they gave him he already had from Irwin Waldwick. The captain sighed. He touched a lever on the intercom and talked to Medford. ''Bring in Mrs. Laurel and Mrs. Sewell. No fuss. Unmarked car. Nice and easy. Except if they get snippy. If they give you any touch of trouble, then you can let out all the stops. I don't think they'll be any trouble.'' He clicked off the lever. ''While we wait, gentlemen, would you like some coffee or muffins or something?''

The gentlemen wanted nothing.

* * *

They were better prepared today. Ellen Laurel's roots were blonde and Paula Sewell was wearing an exciting pantsuit, but they were not prepared for Dr. Bartley and Mr. Hampton smoking cigarettes in Captain McVail's office at Headquarters. They opened their mouths, revealing their surprise. Ellen Laurel sank into a hard chair. Paula Sewell stood as though petrified. There was no greeting. Nobody spoke. Until McVail said, "Lieutenant, please see to it that these fine gentlemen are returned to wherever they came from. Unmarked car. No police uniforms. All pleasant and proper." Impatiently he waved at the men. "Out. Crawl back under your rocks." If I need you again, you'll hear from me."

Medford herded them out.

McVail said, "Sit down, Paula, before you fall down."

Paula Sewell sat. She looked toward Ellen Laurel. Then they both looked at Captain McVail, rocking in his swivel chair. "Today, ladies," McVail said, "you are both going to do your darndest to be of assistance to the Nassau County Police. The fact that your dear friend Francie was criminally butchered was insufficient to bring about your cooperation. Even the fact that either of you could be the next victim on the Slasher's agenda could not move you out of the closet, could it? Okay. You've seen the dentist from Syosset and the executive from Grumman's. I'm sure that's instilled a little respect in you. Cops ain't quite as dumb as people would like to think, especially rich people.

I'll drop two more names, and then I'm sure you're going to do a hell of a lot more talking than you did yesterday. Dino's Blue Grotto. Mr. Irwin Waldwick. How we doing, ladies?''

Laurel lit a cigarette. ''You couldn't be doing better, Captain.''

McVail clasped his hands on the high part of his stomach.

''There's nothing to hide now, ladies, and nobody to protect, not yourselves, not Francine. But it all stays right here. It's all confidential. We think that son of a bitch of a murderer was known to Francine. He didn't break into the house, he was *let* in. You're out of the closet now, ladies. What's your opinion?''

''She knew him,'' Laurel said.

''Thank you, Ellen. Did you know him?''

''No.''

''You, Paula?''

''No.''

''Ladies, are you back to playing games with me?''

''No,'' Sewell said.

''Listen,'' Laurel said. She took a deep drag of the cigarette. ''Francie, she fell for a guy. Really flipped. It was the Thursday—December eight. In Dino's. First time in a long time—after Irwin—she really flipped out.'' She ground out her cigarette.

''Yes.'' McVail's hands were off his stomach. He was making notes on a pad on his desk.

''Flipped,'' Sewell said. ''She couldn't stop talking about him.''

"We were already out of Dino's," Laurel said.

"When she met him," Sewell said.

"Let's keep it clear and simple," McVail said. "No bushwhacking. You mean you two had already met your lovers and had already taken off from the Dino joint."

"Right," Laurel said.

"And Francie, she no longer had Irwin."

"Right," Laurel said.

"And in Dino's on Thursdays she would keep hoping she'd meet another Irwin."

"That's right, exactly," Sewell said.

"And for a long time nothing really happened," Laurel said. "Until this man on this Thursday, December eight. She really went overboard. Told him how to find her in the phone book. Told him to call her."

"When did she see him again?"

"She didn't see him again."

McVail looked up from the pad. "Didn't see him again?"

"No," Laurel said.

"Ever?"

"I would say yesterday morning in her house." Sewell shuddered.

McVail sighed. "But she did talk to you about him."

"Couldn't *stop* talking," Laurel said.

"She gave you a description?"

"Everything. Said he was the sexiest man she'd ever run up against in her life."

"That's not a description, Ellen."

"Six feet tall," Laurel said. "Black hair. Dark eyes. A soft voice. Talked quite well. Made a few little mistakes in grammar, but who doesn't? Vibes. They had vibes. She was terribly taken with him. Beautifully dressed. Expensive. Francie knew a good deal about men's clothes. This guy was wearing a tailor-made suit, with handstitching on the lapels."

"She gave him her phone number and address?"

"In a manner of speaking," Laurel said.

"If he was to call, then he must have given her his name."

"Don Corbin."

"Did he say his business?"

"Airline pilot. On the New York-to-LA run."

"Married," Sewell said. "Said his wife was blind. Said he had three kids."

"How old a guy? Did Francine mention?"

"Thirtyish. Early thirties."

"Did he say where he lived?"

"Here on the Island," Sewell said.

"Did he say where?"

"No. She didn't ask."

McVail lit a cigar, chewed it. "She didn't see him again since that night of December eight, right? But she did give him her phone number."

"She told him to look it up in the phone book," Laurel said. "Ralph Haskell in Hewlett. That would give him the number *and* the address."

"Do you know if he called her?"

"Yes. Several times. He said that because of his work, traveling and the blind wife, he'd have to work out when to see her, since she did limit him to a Thursday night.''

Sewell, biting down on her lip, began to cry. She touched at her eyes with a handkerchief from her purse. "He saw her," she sobbed. "That fucking bastard saw her. Yesterday morning he saw her. I *know* it.''

"You know?'' McVail said.

"No. I mean in my heart I know it. He has to be the guy. It wouldn't be anyone else. Francie wasn't stupid. She wouldn't open the door to a stranger. But to this one, to this guy, my God, would she open the door!''

McVail, an expert, asked many more questions, but the replies were now repetitious. He had gleaned from them whatever pertinent information they knew. It was time now, in appreciation, to tender a kindness. "Ladies, just as yesterday you lied to me, so did I lie to you. I gave you the impression—and today too—that you were putative candidates for the Nassau Slasher's attentions. Not true. Francie probably didn't mention your names to the alleged Don Corbin.''

"Definitely she didn't,'' Laurel said. "She told us she didn't.''

"And even if she did, he would keep far away from you. This bastard has been making his moves for four years. He's careful, he's cautious, he doesn't ever double-track. So, you two, as friends of his latest victim, would be the safest of all people.'' He clamped his teeth on the cigar. He puffed acrid smoke. He brought his bulk out of the swivel chair and onto his feet. He smiled around the cigar. His furrows deepened. "Ladies, even though you were coerced, I do appreciate your cooperation. I will say that I understand the reason for yesterday's reticence. I don't approve, but I understand. I should like to add, from a policeman's point of view, some words of caution. In my profession I've learned that cheating is an incurable disease. Despite what happened to Francine, you girls are going to keep on doing it even after your Marty and your Dougie. But you can't do it alone. As St. Jerome said, 'Adultery without two persons to commit it is not possible.' What Jake McVail is trying to tell you—*check that person out*. Pick your spots. We have homicides all the time between guys and gals that meet at bars. There are all kinds of nuts around, both male and female, and they look normal and they talk normal. Before you get intimate with somebody, before you go to bed with him, I tell you to get the background on him and check that background out. Don't hand out your names, addresses and phone numbers to strangers." He turned from them and went toward the intercom on the desk. "I'll arrange to have you driven home. Good day to you, ladies. Please wait outside in the anteroom."

It was their first real lead in four years. McVail conferred with the Commissioner; then 30 men were put on the phones in a rapid mass-action investigation. The police communicated with all the airlines, the airline programmers fed information into the computers, and the airline executives relayed the readouts to the Nassau County Police Department. In two hours the 30 men were off the phones and back at their normal duties, and Commissioner Dumont and Captain McVail knew what they could do with their first real lead in four years. The Commissioner's secretary typed up the report and Xeroxes were made for McVail's office and a Xerox was made for Dr. Margaret Wyckoff.

There were four Don Corbins who were airline pilots. Donald Xavier Corbin was a pilot for National Airlines. Donald Bertram Alfred Corbin was a pilot for Trans World Airlines. Donald Corbin was a pilot for United Airlines. Donald Horace Corbin was a pilot for Pan Am. On Wednesday, December 28, Donald Xavier Corbin was in London, England. On Wednesday, December 28, Donald Bertram Alfred Corbin was in Rome, Italy. On Wednesday, December 28, Donald Corbin of United Airlines was on vacation with his mother, father, wife and children in Jerusalem, Israel. On Wednesday, December 28, Donald Horace Corbin was in a hospital in New Orleans recuperating from an operation for a ruptured appendix.

Two airline pilots had the combination of a blind wife and three children. One was Eugene Manchester of British Airways. The other was Heinz Allamuchy of Swissair. On Wednesday, December 28, Eugene Manchester was in Vancouver, British Columbia. On Wednesday, December 28, Heinz Allamuchy was in Oslo, Norway.

* * *

In the evening, at seven o'clock, they were in Dr. Margaret Wyckoff's office—McVail, Medford, Caldwell and Emerson. But at this meeting Commissioner Dumont himself was also present, and he was in charge. He read the reports to them, he played back the tapes of the interviews in McVail's office. Wyckoff, at her desk, smoking a cigarette, observed him. Arthur Dumont was tall, a large man, corpulent, but different from McVail. Dumont liked the out-of-doors; he was a golfer. His hair was white, his face was florid, and his belly was thick and hard, like a beach ball. McVail was as large as Dumont, but McVail was tousled, wrinkled, rumpled; his fat hung loose, his belly was a paunch. He did not like golf, he did not jog, he did not like to swim, he did not walk if he could ride. Wyckoff remembered McVail's reply when the County Executive asked him what was his favorite form of exercise. "I like a good sit in a chair," McVail said.

The last tape was finished. "We do have some stuff on the Slasher," Dumont said. "We have a lot of his crap, but we do have, in my opinion, for the first time, some definite material. What do you think, Marge?"

"I think so."

"Jake?"

"Yes."

"We have to assume that this Don Corbin *is* the Slasher, but I think we have sufficient basis for that assumption. Once again, what do *you* think, Dr. Wyckoff?"

"I believe that we can go along with that hypothesis."

"Okay. This is the description of the man we're after. Six feet tall. Black hair. Dark eyes. A soft voice. She said he was a good talker. She said he made some grammatical errors, but, what the hell, nobody says he's a college professor."

"Not some kind of bum. Not an illiterate," McVail said. "She was Mrs. Ralph Haskell. She simply wouldn't take up with an illiterate. I make grammatical errors. Hell, I never went to college. But I know plenty of college people who don't talk in great grammar. We got to give him high school, and we can't rule out college."

"And a money guy," Caldwell said. "Expensive clothes. Tailor-made suit, the lady said."

"A young man," Wyckoff said. "Thirtyish."

"Sexy." Medford laughed; then shook her head, grimaced. "This killer bastard must be something. The quote, verbatim, from a woman who's been around. The quote is Ellen Laurel's, what Francine told her. 'Said he was the sexiest man she'd ever run up against in her life'."

"All the rest is con," McVail growled. "A smooth talker, the son of a bitch. Don Corbin, the airline pilot. That gives him glamour. Then a blind wife and three kids; that would rouse sympathy in a woman, wouldn't it? The son of a bitch plays his con on all the strings."

"Think he always uses the airline-pilot bit?" Emerson asked. "What do you think, Captain? Or the same phony name, Don Corbin?"

McVail looked toward Wyckoff.

"Probably yes," Wyckoff said. "Of course I'm not sure. But if a certain pattern works—and he's had two years in Chicago and four here—I imagine you keep working the same pattern."

McVail shook his head. "But we don't know it's been a pattern."

"But it *might* be," Wyckoff insisted.

"Do we now tackle Leather Boy on what might be?"

Dumont intervened. He raised his hands. "Hold up, you two. Now, Jake, you would have to agree that we give it a whirl."

"Like what?"

"We've assumed all along that he works the bars. Now we know that at least he's worked that Dino's bar. He's too smart to go back there, but—M.O.—he's going to keep on working the bars. He *might* again use the name Don Corbin. He *might* again be a pilot. So, I say we tip off some of the bartenders in the good pubs all over the Island. If a guy says his name is Corbin, if this Corbin says he's an airline pilot, if he's tall, dark, good-looking—then the bartender, quietly, is to call it in to Headquarters. And we get a guy there fast."

"Don't let your hopes run away with you, Arthur. Let's—for the hell of it—go along with the Corbin and the pilot crap. It's one thing to be conning a woman you're on the make for, but guys don't sit at bars—especially a shrewd killer type—and give their names to the bartender and give their line of airline crap to the bartender."

"Jake, we've got to do it."

"But very goddamn careful or we tip the whole mitt. The order can't come from you, Mr. Commissioner, or from me, Captain McVail, another half-ass big shot. We can't get our barkeeps excited. The word has got to go through to them from our street people. This guy by the name of Corbin who is a bullshit airplane pilot is a narco dealer, and the call has to go through our narco department, and then upstairs to me or you. That's the way to handle it, and I wouldn't hang out any flags of hope."

"Whether or not we think he'd skip Dino's," Medford said, "we would *have* to include the bartenders at Dino's."

"Of course," Dumont said.

"You know, I think we're finally getting somewhere," Emerson said.

"Nowhere," McVail rasped. "The Commissioner is practicing on us how he's going to bullshit the County Executive. Now listen, people, and listen hard. This is a guy who for two years stymied the Chicago police, and for almost four years has stymied the Nassau police. Now that's not some simple little prick—no matter how much the Commissioner would like it—who sits around in bars and babbles to bartenders. He hasn't left us a clue, anywhere. In the Haskell house on physical evidence, the report has been the same zero-nothing as always. Now for the files we do have a fairly clear description, and we know he's a good con merchant, and we know he's a sexy guy, and we know that at least this once he used the name Don Corbin, and we know that at least this once he was an airline pilot, and we know he's tall and dark and handsome and, he's young. But we don't have any eyewitness, do we? We don't have anybody who can point him out in a lineup and say, 'Yeah, he's the guy who was talking to my friend Francine that Thursday night in Dino's'."

McVail dug in for a cigar. He bit it, lit it, took it out of his mouth. "We've got some nice new material that will pretty up the file, but what we really got is nothing!" The whiskey voice rasped. The forehead wrinkled. The eyebrows were ledges over the deep-set eyes. "Mr. Commissioner, this stuff will help you butter up the County Executive, but we, us, here on the inside, we must not kid ourselves. There's a madman out there on the loose—a slasher, a murderer, a necrophiliac, a hacker, a ripper, a stabber—and I tell you we're no nearer today to this animal than we were four years ago, and that is the fact of the matter, and we must not permit ourselves to think otherwise. Mr. Commissioner, I think we've had it here for today. I suggest we close this meeting and pack up and go out and buy ourselves a drink or something."

ELEVEN

On Friday, December 30, the coffin of Francine Haskell was lowered into the ground. Eulogies had been uttered in the chapel of the Millburn Funeral Home and dignified services had been vouchsafed in the wintry air at the graveside. Without exception the mourners had remarked upon the fortitude of the widowed husband who had stood straight and true and unwincing from the very inception of the ceremonies. Hatless in the cold blasts of December, he remained in tight control until the last thump of earth sounded over the wood of the coffin.

Now the funeral was over and the mourners turned away from the grave and moved to the cars, but Ralph Haskell stood rigid between Mrs. Yetta Millburn and Mr. Eric Millburn, each of whom, on either side of him, was firmly holding an arm. Yetta pulled and Ralph responded and they walked toward Eric Millburn's car. Then Ralph stopped and tilted his head and looked up at the gray, sunless sky. Yetta pulled again and they walked and Yetta reminded him that he was to come to her house tonight for dinner. Seven o'clock. Yes, he knew, he remembered, and Eric Millburn, the funeral director, was pleased. A good sign. When they remember, it is a good sign. But in the car Ralph evidenced even a better sign. He looked at his watch and mentioned that a client was coming. He mentioned that he must not be late for the appointment.

Eric drove quickly and skillfully and delivered Ralph to his office in time for his appointment, and Ralph Haskell served his client competently, and when his client was gone, Haskell continued to comport himself well. He worked and accepted with quiet grace the condolences of his office staff. At five o'clock most of his people had departed, and at five-thirty his secretary looked in on him. She asked if there was anything he needed done, anything at all. Nothing, he said. She said she would be home all evening. If there was anything he needed, please would he call her. He promised he would.

He sat alone in his office. It was too early to go to his mother-in-law's for the dinner she was cooking or had cooked. He sighed. He folded his hands on the desk, rested his weight on his elbows, leaned his body forward, and lowered his forehead to his folded hands. He closed his eyes. Resting like that, he thought about his automatic pistol, a legally owned instrument locked in the lower left-hand drawer of the desk. He was an accountant. Frequently on behalf of clients he was obliged to carry large sums of cash money, and therefore upon the advice of persons in authority he had procured a permit and purchased the pistol and had gone to gun school to learn how to use it. Now he opened his eyes and raised his head and unfolded his hands. He unlocked the lower left-hand drawer, took out the automatic, gazed at it, smiled at it gratefully, touched the muzzle to his right temple and blew his brains out.

On Monday, January 2, the Demarests returned from their vacation in Sun Valley. Brimming with health, bursting with energy, they were home at one o'clock in the afternoon, and they were unpacked and ready when the chauffeured limousine came for them at three o'clock.

It had been Leon Weinstein's idea and four days ago he had called it through to them. The Demarests' first day at home would be on Monday. Then on Tuesday Kathy would be going back to school and the doc to the office, and Lori would need time to set her house in order and resume the patterns for the care and feeding of the family. That Monday of course would be an impossible day for her, and therefore Leon suggested that on Monday they come out to Brookville for a midday catered dinner at the Weinsteins' house. Leon would rent a car and chauffeur to pick them up and take them home. It would be an easy, pleasant, restful day for the Demarests, and thus in a sense a gradual return to their workaday world. At first Lori had gently remonstrated, but then she had succumbed to Leon's reasonable persuasions. She had thanked him and accepted. He had asked to talk with Victor, and after their amiable exchange of news and views, he had informed Victor of the new Slasher murder which had occurred the day before. There had been no mention in the Sun Valley newspapers.

Now there was no longer any mention of the Haskell tragedy in the Long Island newspapers. The new sensations crowd out the old and, as the philosophers and reporters keep telling us, yesterday's news is as dead as a doornail. There is a constant succession of muggings, murders and various forms of demise by violence. The new crimes overlap the old, and if the human crimes are momentarily quiescent, the crimes of nature—earthquake, flood, fire, avalanche, hurricane—are always somewhere available for a front-page headline.

The discussion waxed warm in the Weinstein drawing room after Leon had informed them of the aftermath of the latest Slasher murders, the suicide of the husband, Ralph Haskell. They were all interested and apprehensive, except of course the seven-year-old Kathy. The old man approved of the interest but deprecated the apprehensions.

"The human being must roll with the punches or else you're down for the count. My dear ladies, if you yield to fear you are in retreat and that kind of retreat is a withdrawal from life. That won't do. The healthy must face up and fight. Certainly, one must not be foolhardy, but one *must* remember that there are more than two hundred million people in this country and really it's a *small* percentage that die through crime or catastrophe. Most of us live to a good old age, as witness me and my beloved Elaine. That Slasher can't kill all of us, and each day his risk factor grows; the authorities are going to catch up with him and put him away. What I'm saying—leave him to them, the authorities. What

I'm saying—the healthy mind finds the cudgels to fight off fear and panic. What say, Victor?''

"I say you're a wise and profound gentleman.''

"*Qué sera sera,*" said Elaine Weinstein. "It's kind of my philosophy. It's sort of the rule I live by.''

"Isn't that a song?'' Victor said.

"It is a song,'' Elaine said.

"She lives by a song,'' Leon said.

"Providence,'' Elaine said. "I'm a fatalist.''

"What's a fatalist?'' Kathy asked.

Everybody laughed. Elaine kissed Kathy and then talked past her. "*Qué sera sera.* A fatalism. It translates to, 'what will be, will be.' ''

"A steal from Aeschylus,'' Leon said. "A hell of a long time ago. Around 500 B.C. And the way Mr. Aeschylus put it—'What is to come, will come.' ''

"When will dinner come?'' Kathy asked.

Once again everybody laughed and once again Elaine kissed the child's blonde head. "Right now,'' Elaine said. "Come on, people. Dining room. As they used to say when I was a little girl—it's time for the eats.''

He stayed home these nights, a family man. Night after night he stayed at home. A cooling-off period. You got to be smart, you got to keep your head. That was a big one in Hewlett, bigger than he had expected. Fran Haskell's husband had not been just an accountant. The motherfucker had also been some kind of big-ass politician, and the papers gave it a big play, and then the cocksucker had to go and shoot himself. So now you got to wait your turn. Got to wait till a hot one like this cools off. Got to wait till the cops get aggravated by a whole other deal. So you stay home and you watch the football games on the big-screen color TV and you watch the basketball games. And you tend to the business. You go in early to help Paul and you stay all the way till seven o'clock. And then maybe you pick up your favorite ice cream from that store that makes it homemade, or a pizza with hot sausage, or some of that new kind of Chinese food that they cook up to burn your tongue like Mexican chili, and Diana she just melts.

"It's like a whole new honeymoon, Don."

"You don't like it?"

"You kidding? I love it, my husband home all the time."

"What you got to remember, babe, that's the way I would like it forever. But I'm not old man Delanco. I got to keep perking up the business and we been doing pretty good, right? I got to take out a lot of them guys, the customers, buy them maybe a meal, maybe some beers, on the expense account, and then take out the guys they recommend, deer hunters and all, who they can spend a hell of a lot of money once they know they got a guy they can depend on for the best of equipment, and a guy that won't rob them like the department stores. But when I don't have to, I don't. Lately, I don't have to. Maybe it's been the Christmas, maybe the money got tight now in January, but my guys they ain't pressing me, and when they don't press me I like it much better to stay home with my missus and my kids. But it's gonna change, it's gotta change. If they don't press me, I'll start pressing them. You got to work the business. You got to go out and drum up the bread to take care of your wife and your kids and their future, if you know what I mean.''

He went to the fancy tailor in Cedarhurst and had some new suits made up. He went shopping in New York to Tripler's and Brooks and Shields: he knew where to get the best for himself. January passed but in February he could no longer restrain himself; his blood was beginning to heat up. He went out, a night here, a night there, the best of the saloons but never the same joint from which he had ever hooked out a broad. He was a well-dressed man, quiet at a bar, uncommunicative. He talked to the broads that attracted him, but he was always aware, sharp, cautious, careful. He never gave out information about himself until the chick figured to be a possible, and they were very few. It figured almost a hundred percent that if a girl was out without a guy, then she was with a girl friend or girl friends. Most broads just don't do the single-o, out in the night by themselves. So right away, for what you're looking for, the odds are way against you, and you have got to figure it for a long period of time before you hook up with a possible. And then that's only the beginning, because she has got to be living out of the house, away from Mama and Papa, and she cannot have a roommate, male or female, and if she wants to go to a motel, you have suddenly got to have an attack of hemorrhoids or something, and all the time you have got to play it cool and mysterious, not even giving a name if you can help it, and then she has to wind up living alone in an apartment house, and no doorman, and no elevator man— jeez! It always figured for a long haul, but he was out there looking now, a night here, a night there, the well-dressed, tall, dark gentleman, quiet, polite, reserved, reticent.

The first week in March, the Weinsteins were ready. All was in order. Their preparations were complete for the year-long cruise. So, naturally, Elaine decided on some last-minute shopping. Nothing important. Small personal things. And she called Lori Demarest and of course Lori agreed to accompany her, and Elaine picked her up at ten-thirty. Kathy was at school.

They drove to Bloomingdale's in Garden City and there Elaine picked up her last-minute things (and more) and Lori purchased some charming gimcracks on the charge account (to be sent). They had a bite of lunch and then at one o'clock they emerged into the sunshine and Lori spotted the high-laced hiking boots in the gleaming window across the street.

"Boy! Don't they look beautiful—at least from here. Do you mind, Elaine?"

"Of course not."

They crossed and from up close the boots were even more beautiful, a rich grained leather in a style that, although sturdy was nonetheless feminine and graceful. There were two pairs on display in the window, one pair beige, the other mahogany. "They're as lovely as I've ever seen, and I really can use some new boots. I do hope you don't mind."

"Not at all."

They entered the shop and a slender white-haired man came toward them. "Ladies, may I help you?" he asked courteously.

"The boots," Lori said. "The high boots in the window."

"Aren't they exquisite?" the old man said. "Imports. From Yugoslavia. Which color would you prefer? The beige, or the mahogany. Actually, that's the only two colors they sent us."

"Both, please," Lori said and gave him her foot size.

In the rear Don Cranford stood rigid. Slightly bent forward, taut as though in muscle spasm. Oh, Christ. Oh, Jesus fucking Christ! Not again. Jesus, not again. Jesus, not so quick.

He had been at the desk. He had been working on the books. When he had heard the customers enter, he had stood up for a look. Not usual. Not a usual procedure. Christ, like God had willed it. Jesus, how that blonde knocked him for a loop. Man, he had seen plenty of blondes in his life, maybe even prettier than this bitch, but for him this one had it. His heart pounded. His blood raced. His penis swelled. Vibes. Jesus holy Christ, the vibes! Look at her, a lady, the tall blonde bitch. Look at them stuck-up tits, that stick-out ass, the flawless white skin, the well-shaped long legs.

"Would you care to try them on, Madame?"

"Yes, please."

"Please sit right here, Madame." Paul laced the thongs into the lower eyelets. "Yes, now. Let's give it a try."

Christ, the shape of them legs. Paul is pushing on the boot. Her skirt is up, over her knees. Jesus Christ, that thigh! With both hands Don Cranford is holding his prick as though clutching an animal to restrain it from escaping. Shit. This is no good. He is entrapped again. That is not the way he wants it. He wants to be boss. He wants to be out there in the bars, picking his spots, no matter how long it takes. Mr. Boss, making sure, figuring out each and every angle. Not this way. This way the bitch is the boss.

"How much?"

"Fifty-five dollars a pair, Madame. Which pair would you prefer?"

"I'll take them both."

"Yes, ma'am."

"Do you honor American Express, Diners, Carte—"

"No, ma'am. No credit cards. But we can arrange for a charge account here if you wish—"

"Not necessary. If you'll please make out the bill, I'll pay in cash."

Paul writes down her name on the original of the duplicate sales slip, and her address, and adds up the amount, including tax, and the bitch dips into her bag and produces a couple of hundred-dollar bills like she's producing a couple of coins to drop in the slot in the bus. Paul makes change, and he wraps up a real nice package. Why not? That's what I pay him for. The ladies blow and Paul looks like the cat that swallowed the bird. Don Cranford returns to his desk, but he sits there doodling.

At two o'clock Paul Mercer washes up, says good afternoon, and goes home to his dinner of organic foods. Immediately Don Cranford pulls the duplicate sales slip from the records. Mrs. Lori Demarest. Old Westbury. He memorizes the address; destroys the slip. He waits on customers but his mind is not with them; his mind is with that big-titted long-legged blonde who tosses around hundred-dollar bills like toilet paper. Money? Who cares about her money. Fuck her money. I hate her. I hate the cool smart-looking bitch. I must be going nuts. I mean real fucking crazy. Because no more bars; finished with bars. Jesus, this is the first time there's been two in a row. Haskell. Now this Demarest bitch. They're gonna catch up with me. If I go this route, I tell you they're gonna catch up with me. But it's not always gonna be this route. Happens. Anything can happen. Two in a row can happen. Never happened before and it don't figure to happen again. But when it does happen, baby, you cannot deny it, you got to go.

The first week in March, Detective-lieutenant Pamela Medford took her pregnancy leave of absence. They gave her a little party—McVail,

Caldwell, Emerson, Wyckoff, Ramsey and Tom
Stockton—and then she was gone, out for a year.
McVail talked to Arthur Dumont about a replace-
ment, but Dumont had to refuse him. Money was
tight, the county was trimming the budget, and in
the Police Department the Commissioner was
struggling to hold the line.

Cranford, up early these mornings, was out in the
van on watch in Old Westbury. It was a fine house,
rich, with year-round-type greenery, and a long
pathway leading up to the entrance door, and there
were three of them in the family and he began to
know about them, which room was whose, and
what were their habits. Three. There was the Mama
Bear: his big beautiful blonde. And there was the
Baby Bear: a daughter who looked to be about six
or seven. And there was the Papa Bear: he drove a
car with an MD license plate. A bus from a private
school picked up the blonde little girl at about a
quarter to nine; Dr. Papa Bear took off about nine
o'clock. And that left Mama Bear all alone. But he
did not want Mama Bear all alone. He wanted that
pretty little one too. God, his balls got hot and his
heart pumped. Man, he had never had anything like
that, so small, so cute, and with all that long blonde
hair. Man, I gotta have that. Man, for once in my
life I have got to *have* that. But, how? You have got
to plan it real careful, pal. No. Hell, nothing to
plan. Easy. This was the season, right? Easter. For
the kids it's like about ten days: the spring vacation
from school. So that's when we pull it off, Eastertime. That's no great big holiday, like Christmas, or

the goddamn Fourth of July or something. At Eastertime Dr. Papa Bear will go to work and Mama Bear and Baby Bear will be all alone in their nice rich house.

On March 15 the Demarests brought in Mrs. Dora Somerset as baby-sitter for Kathy. Mrs. Somerset would serve as cook and companion and housekeeper for the day. She was a widow and an old friend.

And then the Demarests picked up the Weinsteins and drove them to New York for the bon voyage party aboard the enormous ship, the S.S. *Kungsholm,* which would carry them to many ports all over the world. "Scares me to death," Elaine said.

"Yeah, she scares real easy," Leon scoffed.

"You'll love every minute of it," Lori said.

Leon said, "I trust you'll take care of my house, Doctor."

"Punctiliously, I assure you."

"Punctiliously." Leon looked at Lori and laughed.

"That's my Victor," Lori said.

TWELVE

In April during the Easter vacation the kid sleeps late after the Papa Bear leaves for the office. Don Cranford, who has watched, waited, reckoned, observed, knows precisely what he will do and how he will do it. His course is calculated, his plan is mapped. He wants the Mama Bear, the blonde with the vibes, but he wants the little one more: he has never had one that young. It is a warm, muggy, cloudy Tuesday morning and he is dressed in his New York Telephone Company coveralls as he sits waiting in the olive-green van. He is naked beneath the repairman's coveralls, the pockets of which contain the thongs and the switchblade knife. Also, this time, there is a roll of adhesive tape.

At five minutes to nine, the doctor drives away. The wife is in the kitchen. The little girl is in her room. At nine o'clock at the side of the house Don Cranford snips the outside telephone wire. He returns the wire cutter to the van; then he trudges up the long lane to the house and rings the bell.

The blonde woman, peering through the glass window of the wooden door, sees the smiling, tall, pleasant young man. She sees *New York Telephone Company* embroidered on the coveralls on the left side over the heart. She opens the wooden door. She keeps the screen door locked. She sees

171

the official-looking van down there in the roadway.

"Yes?"

"Phone company, ma'am. We been getting a lot of complaints from this area. The dampness is rotting away the wires, and the phone suddenly conks. We're doing a check, house to house."

"It was all right the last time I used it."

"That's fine, ma'am. Save us both a lot of trouble." He starts to leave, stops. "When was that, ma'am?"

"Beg pardon?"

"The phone."

"Last night."

"Last night?" Smiling, he shakes his head. "Please take a look now, ma'am. So's I can make out my report proper, y'know? Otherwise I'll have my foreman chewing me out."

"Just a minute." She goes away. When she returns, there's a frown between her eyes. "It's dead."

"I better have a look."

"Yes."

She opens the door. He follows her into the living room.

"We have a number of extensions," she says and turns and sees the knife.

"Don't scream! You hear? I'm not gonna hurt you. Don't make me. I'm not here to hurt you. I'm here to rob, to steal. Do you understand?

Pale. But she holds her head high. She nods.

"If you try to get smart, I'll kill you dead. Clear?"

She nods. She is wearing a flowery dressing gown.

"I'll also kill your kid."

"I won't scream, I promise you. I won't do anything. Take whatever you want and get out of here."

"Gotta tie you up, you know?"

He ties her wrists in thongs behind her and he ties her ankles. He winds the adhesive tape around her face as a gag against her mouth. He drags her to a closet and lays her in. "If you kick, if you scuffle, if you make any noise at all, I will kill your kid, I swear to God."

He uses his handkerchief to wipe the knob and closes the closet door. He goes to the foyer in front and locks the screen door and the wooden door. In the living room he replaces the handkerchief in a pocket of the coveralls. He takes out more thongs and the knife. He kicks out of his shoes and removes the coveralls. He is not wearing socks.

He trots up to the child's room. In pajamas, she is playing with a group of dolls on the bedroom floor. She looks up and sees the nude man, strips of leather in one hand, a knife in the other. She jumps up and tries to run past him. He blocks her way. She screams. He hits her backhand across the face. "Shut up! Quiet!"

She screams. He drops the knife, clenches his right hand, hits her jaw. She falls to the carpeted floor; either from the blow or from fright she has passed out. He is not worried about her screams. This rich house is far away from the other rich houses. They need space, these rich bastards. But, always possible, there could be somebody out there nearby. He moves the venetian blind. The window is open. He peeps out. Nobody. The child's dress is on a chair. He crumples it and uses it to close the window. He is experienced. He knows how not to leave fingerprints.

He lifts the blonde little girl and lays her on her back on the bed. His blood is pounding; he is gasping, drooling. He ties one wrist to one bedpost, and the other wrist to the other bedpost. He ties both of her ankles in the same manner. The unconscious child is spread-eagled. He leaps to the bed and on his knees he straddles her face.

He takes up the unused thongs and his knife and he leaves the room, pulling the door closed with the crumpled dress. He drops the dress in the corridor and runs down to the living room, to the woman in the closet. He pulls her out. He pulls off the adhesive. He rips the dressing gown from her body. He grasps her hair in his left hand and raises her to a kneeling position. He stands over her, a naked man brandishing a knife, his penis at full erection. "Suck. You suck me, bitch, or I go up there and kill your kid. You musta heard her scream. She saw me. She got scared. But I didn't do nothing to her. Tied her up like I tied you up. Now you eat me, bitch. You eat me nice and good and I promise I won't bother your kid. I'll take some of your jewels and stuff and I'll get out of here."

She does it good. Nice and good. He retains his

come till he's damn ready and then he shoots his load and makes her lick off every drop and then he grabs her hair and cuts her throat. He kicks her over, bends to her, hacks at her breasts, but the child upstairs on the bed floats in his mind. He kicks again at the woman and pads up to the little girl's room, his knife at the ready, but—no need. She is dead. Flat on her back she has vomited and then has suffocated on the vomit induced by his semen. He pulls open her pajamas, but there are no breasts to slash. Flat. Like a boy. He stands there, heart thumping, confused, undecided. For the first time ever, he is rattled. *Enough! Get out of here before they come and get you, man.* He wipes the knife on the child's pajamas, closes his knife. He cleans up in the bathroom, with care, no hard surfaces. He runs down to the living room, dresses in the coveralls and shoes. He picks up the adhesive. He pockets the knife, thongs, adhesive, and leaves the house using his handkerchief on the knob of the wooden door and the handle of the screen door. In his telephone-company coveralls he walks slowly down the long pathway, enters the van and drives off. He looks at the clock on the dashboard. He had been in the house for 35 minutes.

Demarest came home at seven o'clock. He was tired; a long day. He did not garage the Mercedes; he parked it out front. First—a nice long shower. He would ask Lori to make him an ice-cold martini, a double, and have it waiting when he came out. Then he would talk her into letting him take them out to dinner. He wanted, needed, a change of scene. Out of the house. Relax in a fine restaurant. If Lori had cooked, they'd save it for tomorrow. Kathy? She loved eating out and it was vacation time and she went to bed late and got up late.

He let himself in and strode through the foyer and then he saw her on the living-room floor. *Oh, God! Oh, my God!* Bound, naked, throat gaping, breasts mutilated, she lay twisted in thick pools of coagulated blood. Dead. He stood there for moments, riveted, looking at her. Then he looked up.

"Kathy!"

He ran up the stairs and into her room and for a moment he thought she could be alive—no blood except on the pajamas—but as he came nearer he saw by her color that she was gone. He touched her for a pulse. Dead. Long gone. Cold. His child, lashed to the bed, spread-eagled, was dead by suffocation. Little blonde Kathy, her face blue, her open mouth filled with vomit, had choked to death on her own regurgitation.

He was a doctor, he knew the rules, he knew what he had to do. You touch nothing and you call in the police as quickly as possible. A thin sharp pain stabbed through his head. He staggered but righted himself. He went down the stairs, slowly, and in the living room he crossed to the phone. No dial tone. No sound. He went to another phone. The same. He tried the phone in his study. Dead.

He left the house and trotted to the nearest neighbor, and made the call, and trotted back, and now, recovered from that first absolute shock, he moved about, viewing, looking at the butchered Lori, and at the body of the asphyxiated child lying with her arms spread as though in supplication. They were bound, each of them, in thongs, leather thongs. *Thongs!* He ran up to the masterbedroom and flung open the door of one of the closets, the deep walk-in closet that contained all their hiking gear. *Thongs!* Had the murderer used the thongs from their boots in the closet? He examined swiftly. No. All the thongs were where they belonged, in the eyelets of the boots. Many boots, but all untouched.

He heard the wailing sirens of the squad cars.

He slammed the closet door and ran down the stairs.

The bell was ringing. He opened up for the many policemen.

Finally the bodies were gone, removed to the morgue for autopsy. Finally the telephone people discovered the severed wire and did the repair. And finally they were all gone except the old man, the man in charge, Captain Jackson Brendan McVail. Old. Demarest had never seen a cop that looked quite that old. A big man with a lot of loose fat, he looked a perfect candidate for a coronary. A tousled, grizzled man. Leather-faced. He was paunchy, wrinkled, jowly. He had a raspy-tone gravel voice, but his questions had been succinct, pertinent, right on target. He was obviously a very skillful cop, Demarest had decided. A bright mind. And now deep into the evening they were alone in the house, the doctor and the detective.

"Would you like a drink, Captain McVail?"

"Yes. I am, in fact, off duty. I am, in fact, almost at my bedtime."

"What do you drink, sir?"

"Jack Daniel's. I drink it straight and like to chase it down with beer. If you don't have Jack Daniel's, I'll take whatever bourbon you have. If you don't have beer, I'll take soda, Coke, water—"

"I have Jack Daniel's. I have beer."

The doctor went out of the study and McVail sat down in the biggest chair in the room, a commodious, red, morocco-leather, tough-cushioned wing chair. He had stayed behind out of sheer pity for the poor bastard. Haskell had had a mother-in-law and a brother-in-law right in there with him. This guy had nobody near, no relatives. This guy had an empty house, and that ain't good.

On the other hand, in McVail's opinion, this guy, unlike Haskell, was not a guy to kill himself. Somehow, the contrary. No question the poor bastard was shook. Riddled all over like he'd been hit by a shotgun blast. But in McVail's opinion—often correct but not infallible—this guy was a strong one, a stalwart, and when he got himself together he could reverse his field and create a hell of a lot of trouble. Leather Boy, however unknowingly, had hit at two VIPs in succession. Haskell had been a wheel in the county, and so certainly was the distinguished Dr. Victor Demarest. A lot of heads could get chopped, including that of Captain Jackson Brendan McVail.

The doc had been working pretty good on the Scotch all the while, and McVail appreciated that the doc had finally bethought himself of McVail's possible thirst. Now the doc came back with a loaded tray. On the side table by McVail's wing chair he placed a bottle of Jack Daniel's, a shot glass, and three pull-top cans of beer. And on his desk the doc placed a bottle of Pinch, a tall glass, a bucket of ice and a pitcher of water. He sat in his black-leather swivel chair behind the desk and made himself a highball and sipped.

McVail knocked back a Jack Daniel's. "There are a couple of personal questions, Dr. Demarest. I waited with them till we'd be alone because they're the kind of stuff I believe should be off the record." McVail knocked back another Jack. "The Slasher. Our information has it that he makes his contacts—at least we think so—at bars, at taverns, you know, where people kind of gather for booze, music, a little fun, maybe a little sexual conviviality. Any help along that line, possibly?"

"Nothing. Nothing at all. My wife detested saloons, singles bars, gaudy pubs, all of that. Please don't misunderstand. I'm not trying to give you a picture of a saint. But absolutely—she was not for the bars."

"Forgive me for asking, Doctor—but was it a good marriage?"

"Yes. I don't have to elaborate. Definitely yes."

"Did you confide in one another?"

"In important matters—yes."

"Suppose she met someone—an attractive young

man—do you think she would tell you?''

''My best answer to that—yes.''

''Did she—perhaps—mention anybody?''

''No.''

McVail lit a black cigar. He drank Jack Daniel's. The doc drank Pinch. The doc could handle his liquor and that gave him a merit mark in McVail's book.

''All right, Doctor. I think, now, you've got to make some calls.'' The early investigation had revealed that the wife had parents in Palm Beach, Florida, and had a sister married to a State Department guy in London. The doctor's parents were dead, but there was a brother, a correspondent in Moscow for *Newsday*.

''What sense to disturb them now?'' Demarest said. ''I'll call in the morning.''

''No good. This is two murders in one family and it figures to go out over the wires. At least for the parents, it would be much better if they heard it first from you. And that time is now, Doctor.''

Demarest drank his whisky. ''Yes,'' he said.

McVail would stall. He would give the man time to make his calls alone. ''Where's the bathroom, Doctor?''

Demarest told him where and McVail got up heavily and left the study. He went to the bathroom. He prowled the house. He had a beer in the kitchen. He stayed away a good long time and when he came back, Demarest said, ''Thank you.''

''Welcome.''

McVail sat in the big leather wing chair.

"Tomorrow," Demarest said. "Her folks will be here tomorrow and so will her sister. Then, the day after, my brother."

"Look, Doc, for tonight you don't have to stay in the house alone. I can arrange to have somebody here with you."

"Thank you, no. I'll manage."

This was no Haskell. This guy was a stalwart.

The guy had pale blue eyes. Cold. Eyes like ice. McVail's antennae sensed him. This guy could be trouble. Suddenly the blue-eyed guy pulled open a drawer. He wrote a check and brought it to McVail. It was made out to the Nassau County Police Department in the sum of $50,000.

"I want you people to hold this money in escrow and I would like you to announce, as quickly as possible, that there's a fifty-thousand-dollar reward for whoever will furnish information that'll lead to the arrest and conviction of this killer."

McVail looked at the check. He looked up at Demarest.

The doctor understood. "That check is as good as gold."

McVail grunted. He folded the check and put it away. He smoked his cigar. There were people, not in *his* world, who did have fifty thousand dollars and more merely in their checking accounts.

"About the photographs," McVail said. "My people took away quite a number of photos of your wife and kid. At least for a while they're going to be in all the papers. You're kinda going to have to brace yourself for that—or don't look in the newspapers. Now, in connection with the reward, we're also going to have to flash those photos on the TV news shows.''

"Yes, I understand." Demarest went back to his desk. He poured Pinch in his glass and he added ice and water. "Please tell me more about this Slasher."

McVail talked, roundabout. He talked for a long time, but his information was general. He divulged no more than should be divulged to a "civilian." At the end he said, "A Jack the Ripper, a crazy son of a bitch, like that Manson, like that Starkweather, like Richard Speck, like the Boston Strangler. But we don't let up, Doc. We keep working, we keep plugging, and we hope, we *know*, sooner or later we will catch up with the bastard."

"And then what?" Demarest slammed down his glass. It broke, but he was not cut. The liquid spread out over the tray, over the desk, but he made no move to wipe it. McVail sat motionless. "Hell," Demarest said, "you know as well as I do, Captain. If they're not shot down resisting arrest, then they get away with their murders. Their lawyers plea-bargain with the prosecutors, and thus the prosecutors get another conviction on their tally sheet, but the criminal, the fucking heinous criminal, he gets his release in a few years and he's out there to assault again, to rape and maim and defile and murder."

McVail smoked his cigar. He had no rebuttal.

On Wednesday morning there was an urgent conference in the offices of the County Executive. Jutland had called in Police Commissioner Arthur Dumont, Captain Jackson Brendan McVail and Dr. Margaret Wyckoff.

". . . and for some reason this son of a bitch of a bastard has limited himself to Nassau County," Jutland stormed. "And it's gotten beyond bounds and the newspapers are after me and my constituents are after me and that is as it *should* be. In the end the people have a right to look to the top. Because when there's blame to lay, that's where in hell the blame *should* lie—at the top. And in Nassau County I'm the top and they're piling it in on me and I'm getting worried, real worried. I am getting real goddamned worried!"

"Especially when there's ambition for governor," Dumont said.

Jutland waved a finger at him. "And in the Police Department, *you* are the top."

"Is it kissing time?" Dumont asked. "Do you have the need? You want me to take down your pants and kiss?"

"Cut that out," Jutland said.

Dumont smiled at the company. "A congressman from Queens once laid it out right on the button. 'Politics', the congressman said, 'is about men who kiss your ass and women who kiss your prick'."

"Sexist," Wyckoff said.

"Hell, Marge, we can turn it around. Any better if the men kiss prick and the women kiss ass?"

"I wouldn't vote for that congressman," Wyckoff said.

"We're not here for this kind of expostulation."
Jutland slammed his palm on the desk. "It's time
for explanations. Nassau Slasher. I want to know
what in hell has been done in four long years."

"Everything possible," Dumont said. "Nothing
has been ignored. Every lead, no matter how tenu-
ous, has been investigated right down to the bottom
line."

"Even the nuts," McVail said. "The guys who
come in and confess. When we questioned them,
we didn't trust ourselves. We'd have Dr. Wyckoff
present." He lit a cigar. "And the crank letters, I
myself followed them up, every one of them."

"Crank letters?"

"Crank letters, Mr. County Executive. In the
four years I'd say we got at least a thousand. And I,
personally, whenever and wherever possible, I ran
them down to the source."

"You must press every angle, explore every possibility," Wyckoff said. "But no matter, when
you're dealing with a psychopath, you simply, also,
have to get lucky."

"Insufficient," Jutland said. "And in a duration
period of four years—unsatisfactory!"

Dumont said, "I'm beginning to see the light.
And in the light of that light, I see my head on the
chopping block."

"Quite a trick if you can turn it," Wyckoff said.

"It's the County Executive who's turning the
tricks this morning. Okay, Lloyd. But before your
Commissioner retires on his pension, he's going to
make a speech."

Dumont pointed a long finger. "It's you people who've screwed it up. Politicians hanging on to the old ways because that's where they think the votes are. But I think, finally, even you guys are coming around to what I've been yelling about for years. It used to be the penologists believed that the prisons could produce rehabilitation. But, simply, the prisons haven't done it. Eighty percent of our criminals are repeaters. The criminal is coddled, and the criminal's victims are ignored and the bleeding hearts cry crocodile tears about the death penalty being cruel and inhuman punishment. And the goddamn Supreme Court, they've kept swinging up and back, like baboons in trees, on the question of capital punishment. When a guy dehumanizes, sodomizes, cuts throats, slashes breasts, bloodily murders; hell, we still have states that say: no death penalty. You just put him away for a few years and then you turn him out on the streets again.

"Starkweather. Just for the hell of it, let me give you the Starkweather story. Here was a guy and a gal, Charles Starkweather and Caril Fugate. Went on a two-day rampage. They killed Caril's mother and father and two-year-old sister. They killed a seventy-year-old farmer; they killed a teenage couple; they killed a businessman and his wife and maid; they killed a traveling salesman. Ten bloody murders.

"They were tried separately. Starkweather was found guilty and executed. Fugate, for the exact same crimes, was found guilty and given life imprisonment. Are you ready, folks? Fugate is out.

Paroled. At age thirty-two—no more life imprisonment. At age thirty-two—she is out on the streets again. Forgotten are the ten innocent people savaged to death by those vicious murderers. Forgotten are the victims and the kith and kin of the victims. One of these marauders was extinguished by the death penalty. But the other, sentenced to imprisonment for life, is out on the streets again, paroled at age thirty-two. I am a cop. My entire adult life has been spent as a police officer. There may be criminals who *may* be subject to rehabilitation, but they are few and far between. I say a murderer should be put to death. I say a professional killer should be put to death. I say an organization hit-man should be put to death. I say any deliberate murderer should be removed from society by execution. I say that if the do-gooders don't believe in the death penalty—if they're against murder by the state as punishment for murder by the individual—then let them guarantee to me that a sentence of life imprisonment means to be in prison for the rest of your life, and does *not* mean that you're out in seven years. I say it's time to give thought to the victims, and to the families of the victims, and to stop coddling the criminal aggressors. I say if these bastards knew they'd be executed, or they'd be put away for the rest of their lives, there wouldn't be all that killing in the streets as if there's a goddamn war going on.''

''I'm afraid I have to disagree,'' Wyckoff said.

''Always at least two sides to a question,'' Dumont said. ''I respect your right to your opinion, and I ask, at least, that you respect my right." He smiled toward the County Executive. "I have said my say to the Court. I am ready for the execution. Bring on the guillotine."

"Artie, I do hope you understand."

"Nobody better than I, Mr. County Executive."

"Politics is public relations."

"Yessir."

"A game. Hell, like baseball."

"Yessir."

"You have got to make a grandstand play to please the crowd."

"Yep."

"If a team has lousy players, you blame the manager. You fire the manager, and you're out from under. At least for the time being, you're out from under. I need that time."

"I dig you all the way, Mr. County Executive."

"And I'm going to have to make a stink about it. Statements to the press and all that crap."

"Yessir, Mr. County Executive."

"I've checked out your status. You get your full pension. And I've had some of my confidential people make inquiries and one of the big department stores needs a chief of security at sixty-five thousand a year and confidentially within this group here—that job is yours. You know I don't hate you, Arthur. I love you. But for my own survival I have to get rid of you, and with a stink. I hope you understand."

"I do."

"I'm sorry."

"I know."

"I really am."

"Come on, man. Say it and let's get it over with."

"You're fired. As of right now, Mr. Police Commissioner—you're fired!"

THIRTEEN

On Wednesday afternoon Donald Cranford realized that another murder, quickly, was now essential. No compulsion here, no joy of sex. This was strictly common sense. Necessary. An act of self-protection. He came to the store at twelve o'clock noon. He had read the newspapers and he had seen the photographs of Mrs. Lori Demarest and her child and he had read about the $50,000 reward. He did not know whether Paul Mercer had as yet read the papers, but Paul did know about the murders because no sooner had Cranford entered the store than Paul said, "That weirdo's at it again."

"Who? What?"

"Nassau Slasher."

"Oh, yes, I heard."

Paul Mercer was an old man. His memory was not the best. His eyesight was not the best. Could he remember that back in March he had sold a couple of pairs of boots to a customer named Lori Demarest? Would the name ring a bell in Paul's old head? Or if he saw her picture in the papers or on the TV, would that jog his memory about that short encounter—the sale of a couple of pairs of boots—back in March? Don Cranford doubted it, but he could not risk it. There was a reward out there of

50,000 bucks. Therefore, suppose old Paul did rec-
ollect, it wouldn't be: "Cripes, Don, I think that
was the lady who was in here like a month ago and
bought herself some of them boots from Yugoslavia." When there's a $50,000 reward, you don't
talk to the boss, you don't talk to nobody; you go
straight to the cops with any bit of information that
could maybe land you a slice of the reward. Then
the coppers would come here with all the right and
proper and normal questions, but Donald Wharton
Cranford simply could not risk the police that close
up to him and asking them kind of questions. And if
Paul Mercer did not remember right now, who says
he wouldn't remember tomorrow, or the day after,
or the day after that? Or whenever?

Therefore, while Paul was upstairs taking care of
the store, Don Cranford was downstairs in the dank
basement digging into crannies and pulling out old
cartons encrusted with dust and covered with cob-
webs. And then he found what he hoped he would;
in a carton there were a couple of sealed boxes and
when he broke them open they contained pistols—
in perfect working order. The pistols were perfectly
wadded in the box, perfectly wrapped and covered,
and perfectly sealed. They were gleaming, unrusted
.38-caliber Smith & Wesson revolvers. He hefted
one, slid the safety catch, tested. The trigger responded as though the pistol had just come off the
assembly line. He searched in the carton and found
the sales slip. This was a purchase made 27 years
ago from a jobber in Jersey he had never heard of;
nobody in the world could ever dig up the records

on this merchandise. He destroyed the sales slip and shoved the gun into his pocket. He smiled. There were still items in this old basement that he had never checked out. He put everything back and returned the carton to the gloomy dust and the spinning spiders.

At two o'clock Paul Mercer washed up, waved, and went out to his fender-bent old Chevy parked in the alley behind the store. At five minutes after two Don Cranford was ready to go after him. He closed the store. He debated whether to print a sign for the door: OUT TO LUNCH. BACK AT FOUR. He decided against. He did not want any proof out there that he had left the store at any time this afternoon. If somebody tried the door and the door was locked—he had a reason. The reason would be that Donald Wharton Cranford, the proprietor, working hard, had felt dirty and sweaty, and, after all, he *was* the boss. So he had closed up, temporarily, and had gone back for a shower and a change, and then he had opened up again.

Don Cranford knew Paul Mercer's habits. When Paul left the store he went home to Hempstead for a little nap, and then he cooked his dinner of organic food. Then he went out for a walk for exercise while it was still light, and then back to the apartment to listen to phone-in-talk-back radio or to watch the sit-coms on the TV.

Don Cranford opened drawers until he found a pair of his good, thin, kid gloves. He put on the gloves, inserted cartridges into the chambers of the revolver, straightened the pistol and adjusted the safety catch. He locked up shop and went out to the Mercury. He drove slowly out of the alley and continued to drive slowly because he knew that Paul was a very slow driver.

He came to Paul's neighborhood in Hempstead, not the greatest, and found a place to park. Paul lived on the fourth floor of a walk-up apartment house, an old house where the walls of the rooms were thick concrete. He did not ring the downstairs bell because the door was wide open. He walked up to the fourth floor and pushed the button at 4-A.

The shield of the peephole moved and Cranford saw the eye.

He heard the locks turn, three locks, and then the scrape of the chain latch. The door opened. Paul looked at his visitor in astonishment. Cranford stepped through. Paul closed the door and only one lock snapped shut.

"Mr. Cranford, what the heck—"

"Trouble."

"I mean you, here—"

"I told you. Trouble. My goddamn missus. That bitch is suddenly out of her skull. We been fighting, and now she called and was coming down to the store. With a couple of her brothers."

"Brothers?"

"I closed up, and I lit out."

"I—I don't understand."

"Could be I'll have to stay with you for a couple of days. If you'll have me."

"I'd be flattered, but—" The old man frowned,

and was somewhat perplexed by the situation.

"Her brothers happen to be very tough apples."

"You never even mentioned she had any brothers."

"You never asked."

"True. Yes. I'm not one to pry."

"Tough apples." Cranford dipped into a pocket and his gloved hand brought out the pistol. He smiled at it, and then at Mercer. "A matter of protection in the event of necessity."

"Looks like a Smith & Wesson," Mercer said. "My guess a thirty-eight."

"Very good. You sure know your business."

He shot the man through the bridge of the nose. Mercer spun around. He did a complete rotation before he fell, face down. Cranford discharged four more bullets into the back of Mercer's head. He confiscated his wallet, took his wristwatch. He moved about the small apartment, opened drawers, strewed the contents, pocketed anything of value. Then he stopped, stood quite still, looked about carefully. He saw what he knew the police had seen countless times in countless lousy little apartments: an old man done in during the commission of a cheap shitass burglary. He took one last look around, and then he got out of there. As he drove to the Meadowbrook Parkway, he dismantled the pistol. He threw away the wristwatch and whatever trinkets he had picked up in Mercer's flat. He emptied Mercer's wallet, retained the contents, threw away the wallet, and then along the tree-lined parkway he disposed of the revolver, piece by piece, at intervals. He came back to Delanco's Sporting Goods Store at twenty minutes after four. He kept the money and burned everything else from the wallet and flushed the ashes down the toilet.

On Thursday morning Donald Cranford, as usual, called his store in Garden City. There was no answer. It was ten o'clock. He hung up and looked querulously across the breakfast table at Diana. "What the fuck?" he said.

"Watch your language," she said.

"I'm sorry."

"What's the matter?"

"The store. Nobody home."

"You must have dialed the wrong number. Try again."

He tried again. No answer. "Nobody home," he said to Diana.

"The old man. Maybe he's sick. Maybe—Don, call him in his house quick. The apartment. Where he lives."

"Right."

But there was no answer in Mercer's apartment.

"I got to get down to the store," Cranford said. "That's first. From there I'll try him again, and if there's still no answer, I'll call the cops. I gotta run now. Either way, I'll let you know."

He drove to the store in Garden City. He did make the call to Mercer's apartment, just for the record, just in case it would show on the computers. Then he called the police. He explained the situation. He stressed the fact that Paul Mercer was an old man, but dependable, and it was the first time anything like this had ever occurred. He gave the man Mercer's address and phone number, and his own name and the address and phone number at Delanco's Sporting Goods Store. Twenty minutes passed and he received a call from Mercer's apartment and a policeman informed him what they had found there.

"Jesus," Cranford said. Then he called home to Diana.

Two hours later a car double-parked outside the store and a beefy man came in. He identified himself as Detective Robert Sperling and produced a notebook. "Hate to bother you, Mr. Cranford. Paul Mercer. We got to finish the file on the guy. We'll start—when'd you see him last?"

"He left the store here at two o'clock yesterday afternoon."

The cop asked questions and Cranford answered the questions and then the cop put the notebook away. "Another poor old geezer gone. We tell them all the time not to resist an intruder. What the hell did he get out of it?" The cop shrugged his thick shoulders. "He saved his radio and TV and lost his life. That ain't smart, is it? Hell, while I'm here, lemme give you the same advice. A burglar at night in your home, lay there and let him take what he wants. He's not there to do no killing, unless he's forced. He's there to steal and get the hell out. Here in the store, a stick-up guy or something, don't show no resistance, don't put up no force. One simple rule—your life is worth more than your property. Well, sir, thank you for your cooperation, Mr. Cranford.''

No policeman ever inquired again. Cranford placed an ad in *Newsday* and eventually hired a new assistant, again an old man, courteous, experienced, on a part-time basis, nine in the morning till two in the afternoon.

Lori's parents came up from Florida and her sister flew over from London. One day later Frank Demarest arrived from Moscow.

Victor Demarest had named the funeral home and McVail had promised to phone promptly when the bodies were transferred from the morgue. But that had to wait until the autopsies were concluded. Dr. Demarest kept calling each day, but the autopsies were performed in order and the deceased Demarests had to await their sequential turn. Finally, on Monday morning, Dr. Victor Demarest received a telephone call from Captain Jackson McVail.

''The transfer is being effected right now. You'll probably hear from the funeral home within the hour.''

''The autopsies are completed?''

''Yessir, they are.''

''Would you give me a quick briefing, please?''

Silence. Demarest could feel the hesitation on the other end.

''Captain McVail, I'm certain I don't have to remind you I'm a physician.''

''Hang on a moment. I've got a summary here somewhere.'' Again a silence. Then McVail was back. He cleared his throat. "Mrs. Loreen Demarest. Thirty-six. Cause of death: severance of the larynx. Unusual marks: severe lacerations of both breasts. There is evidence of sexual assault by sodomy. Human semen within the oral cavity and pharynx. No evidence of spermatozoa in vagina. Katherine Demarest. Seven. Cause of death: asphyxiation. Unusual marks: contusions along left mandible. There is evidence of sexual assault by sodomy. Human semen within oral cavity, pharynx and larynx. No evidence of spermatozoa in vagina. Remarks: subject was discovered bound in supine position. It is the opinion of the medical examiner that the intromission of quantities of spurting semen at the pharynx engendered the reflex of regurgitation. Due to the inflexible position of the subject, it was impossible to clear the larynx of the vomitous matter. The cause of death was therefore suffocation by reason of blockage of the respiratory tract."

Silence again.

Silence on both ends of the wire.

Then: "Doc?"

"I'm here."

"That's it, sir. An abstract of the medical examiner's findings."

"Yes. Thank you, Captain McVail."

In Lori's will it was written that she be cremated and her ashes dispersed over the sea. Victor Demarest ordered the cremation of his wife and daughter and on a golden morning the ashes were flown out over the Atlantic Ocean. That afternoon Lori's parents went home to Palm Beach, and Lori's sister returned to her husband in London. Victor asked if Frank could stay for a few extra days, and Frank received that permission from his managing editor. Then Dr. Victor Demarest called Dr. Gary Tennent; they had talked three times on the phone before this day.

"How's Rosenbaum?" Demarest asked. "And Healey?"

"Getting along beautifully."

"You'll stay with them all the way."

"Of course. Now what about you? When you coming back?"

"It'll be some time."

"How long?"

"Six months at the least."

"That's too damn long, Vic. You can't just let yourself drop out like that."

"It could be more. Maybe a year. Maybe, hell, I'll never come back."

Tennent said, "Is Frank still around?"

"Yes. Why?"

"I'd like him to give me a ring."

"What the hell for?"

"Stop biting my ear off, will you? Here's a chap been living in Moscow. Moscow, you know? Russia. The USSR. Heck, right now he's the horse's mouth, and as long as he's still here in the States, I'm dying to hear. Hell, wouldn't you?"

"Yes. Sorry. Forgive. I'm jumpy. I'll see to it that he calls you."

* * *

Dr. Gary Tennent and Mr. Franklin Demarest had lunch in the Four Seasons. "Six months," Gary said. "Six months is a lot, but he also said a year. Then he said it's possible he wouldn't come back at all. Look, we know what the guy's been through. But people bounce back. Vic is the type. Vic would bounce back. He hasn't. In fact it seems to me he's gone all the way the other way. I say he needs help."

"Who in hell can help a Victor Demarest?"

"I mean professionally. A shrink. To kind of carry him through. Me, I wouldn't even *begin* to try to talk to him about it. But you. Don't you think, Frank?"

"Yes, I goddamn do think. But you tell me how. You tell me how in the world I'm going to get Victor to a shrink."

"You suggest."

"I did that. I sort of mentioned it."

"How did he react?"

"Told me *I* was crazy."

"How's he look?"

"Terrible."

"Do you think—would you say—he's suffering from some kind of nervous breakdown?"

Frank Demarest tightened his mouth, shook his head. "Who the hell can say? I mean, his head is clear. There isn't a moment that he doesn't make sense. Of course the grief is there, and a kind of numbness, but there's something else. An anger. A rage. I don't know quite how to express it. He's like a bomb. A ticking bomb. An unexploded bomb."

"What do we do about it, Frank?"

"There isn't a damn thing we can do."

"Might he hurt himself? Something like that?"

"Nothing suicidal about him, absolutely not. He's a strong man, Gary. The strongest man I've ever known. Look, his wife, his kid, his family— wiped out. He doesn't want to go back to work—do you blame him?"

"I think—I mean for his emotional stability—it would be best."

"Do you? The guy's not a shoemaker. You're a surgeon, my friend. Would you like Vic Demarest operating on *you* at this time in his life? He said six months, a year—perhaps he knows better than we do what's best for him. And I can tell you, confidentially, there's no financial pressure. If he never worked another day in his life, there's more than sufficient to keep him living high on the hog until his very last day."

Victor Demarest retired from his medical practice because he was otherwise totally engaged. He was fighting an enemy. He was in the throes of an implacable vendetta, except that his enemy was a phantom. He was alone, he had to be alone, but he did require, at least initially, a modicum of assistance. Which was why he had requested that Frank remain for a while in the States and this morning over their breakfast his reasons became clear.

"Frank, I want to know all about this Nassau Slasher. I want you to find out for me, please."

Frank looked across the table at his brother, at the

face grown gaunt, the sunken eyes. "Why?" Frank asked.

"Look, this son of a bitch killed Lori, killed my Kathy. I want to know all there is to know about him. Don't you think I have that right?"

Frank said nothing.

Victor said, "Are you deaf suddenly? I repeat— don't you think I have that right?"

"Yes," Frank said.

"You're the one guy who can do it for me. You're a distinguished political reporter and you have many cronies who are police reporters. I know there's a lot of stuff that reporters voluntarily withhold, that never gets into the papers, as a means of aiding the authorities. I want it all, and I know you can get it. Just like there's a camaraderie, a mutual confidentiality among doctors—there's the same among your people. *Esprit de corps* and all that crap. Please. I'm not one to beg. Please, will you do this for me?"

"Yes."

No sweat. Frank Demarest knew the top people in his profession and over the years they had exchanged favors, but there were always residual favors, oddments owing one to the other, like outstanding debts waiting to be collected. Frank made his quiet inquiries, the last a long drinking lunch with Hugh Ramsey, and when he came home to his brother in Old Westbury he was loaded with information. They sat in Victor's study. They drank Pinch and Frank talked.

He said that the police privately called the Slasher "Leather Boy." The reason: all his victims were always bound, wrists and ankles, but the bonds were *always* leather thongs. There has never been an actual vaginal rape. Always sodomy: in the mouth or on the body of the bleeding victim. Always the throat is cut and the breasts are slashed. But in this last case—Demarest—there had been a shift in modus operandi. In the instance of Kathy, it was the first time a child had been a victim and the first time the body had not been cut.

"How many victims?"

"Over a period of four years, and all in Nassau County, and including the Demarests—15." Frank took a folded sheet from a pocket and laid it on the desk. It bore, in chronological order, the dates and names and addresses of the victims. He pointed.

"For whatever it's worth, they seem to fall into two categories—nighttime and daytime. The nighttime murders are all single women, and all live in apartment houses. The daytime murders were each committed in a private house and there was a husband who was away at work. As you can see, including Demarest, there were four such attacks. In three there were multiple murders, a mother and daughter."

Victor studied the sheet. "In all, twelve attacks. Eight of them, the preponderance, at night in the apartments of single women."

"And each such single lived alone in her apartment, and there was *never* an elevator man or a doorman in any of those apartment houses."

"Do the police have any idea what his business is?" Victor folded the sheet and laid it on the desk.

"No."

"Any idea what he looks like? The personality. Any kind of, you know, composite picture?"

"Yes. They believe him to be about six feet tall. Very sexy. Good-looking. A smooth talker. A soft voice. A good dresser, tailor-made clothes. They believe he has used the name Don Corbin, they believe he has stated that he's an airline pilot. But neither one checked out. Both are bullshit. The composite has him as young: about thirty. Dark hair, dark eyes. They believe he met most of his victims in bars, picked them up in a bar."

"He didn't meet Lori in a bar. You and I, we both know that."

"He's clever, he's very cautious. The single-girl victims never have a roommate. He's never left a fingerprint that matches up. The police have a composite, they have ideas, but in fact they have nothing. Four years. They've pushed every clue, worked, investigated, done everything possible. The net result to date: zero."

"What else?"

"Nothing!"

"Who's McVail?"

"Chief of the Sex Crime Squad. A genius type, a police officer highly respected by all his peers all over the country. A bulldog cop, tenacious, tough. Supposed to be a guy with a heart, but when it comes to crime and criminals—a martinet. Known to be a loner. Sometimes takes *nobody* into his confidence. His work patterns are unorthodox and he's old and he's an acknowledged eccentric—but his lifetime record is way up in the stratosphere and he's rated an absolutely top cop." Frank paused. "So why don't you leave it alone? Why don't you butt out? Would you approve of an amateur playing doctor and attempting a major operation? Why don't you back off and leave it where it belongs? McVail is a superb pro. Why don't you—"

"Why don't you stop presuming?"

"Me?" A chuckle, innocent. "You think I'm presuming—?"

"That I'm not leaving it where it belongs."

"Are you?"

Victor shrugged. Frank looked at him, straight at him, then he poured more Pinch in both their glasses. "Thank you," Victor said and changed the subject. They talked politics and the Soviet Union and the Middle East and evangelical Christianity and sex and crime and abortion and capital punishment and they went to bed fairly early and fairly drunk. Two days later Franklin Demarest was recalled to Moscow and Dr. Victor Demarest was alone in his house in Old Westbury.

FOURTEEN

The desire for retribution is a disease. It becomes a raging illness when it is complicated by utter impuissance. There was nothing Dr. Victor Demarest could do. He wanted to lay hands on the killer of his wife and child. A personal matter. Between Dr. Victor Demarest and a phantom who for four long years had eluded the police. There was nothing he could do. There was nothing he knew to do. But he knew what he wanted to do, what he must do. But how? It tortured him. *How?* Where do you start? How do you start? He pondered his problem. He brooded. He saw nobody. He remained alone with his passion, aware that a consuming passion is a form of madness. The days passed. Weeks. He knew he must think differently from the police. As Frank had said, McVail was a top cop, a superb professional, a tenacious loner. McVail was the best, but he had produced nothing in four years. Therefore Dr. Victor Demarest must turn it around. Therefore in his vendetta with this phantom, he must think as an amateur, as an *un*professional; he must try to discover a different viewpoint; he must try to ferret for an angle so wildly aberrant that it simply had not occurred to the police. How? Dear Christ, *how?*

Once a week he drove up to Brookville, to the

Weinstein estate in a beautiful area in northern Long Island, sparsely populated. There were rolling hills and tall trees and now in May the woods were thick and green and the wild flowers bloomed riotously. In Brookville the houses were built far apart, with many acres between them. The Weinstein house, set high on a ridge, was surrounded by lovely grounds, and beyond the house and the immediate grounds there were bridle paths and lanes and byways and rustic acres of woodlands. The barn was a distance away, down in a valley, and during these visits Demarest had no occasion to enter it. It was a solid edifice thickly surrounded by tall trees; its windows were boarded up, but of course he had seen the inside. He knew the Weinsteins had established a system of ventilation within the barn that kept the air fresh despite the boarded-up windows. He knew it was excellently illuminated, when necessary, by interior electrical appliances. It had a large single door and a wide gravel road led to it. The key to that door (reposing in the antique desk in the Weinsteins' downstairs drawing room) was a huge, smooth, flat, ancient, iron key. And in a groove on top of the molding of the barn door, as in a groove on top of the molding of the house door, there was the switch that regulated the silent alarm system. Move the lever of the switch to the left and the system was dead: move it back to the right and the system was reactivated. These weekly trips for inspection in Brookville were Dr. Victor Demarest's single recreation; for all else he remained at home in Old Westbury.

On pleasant days he would sit in the sun in the garden at the rear of his house. He was sunburned, he had a healthy tan, but when he looked in the mirror he did not like what he saw. His face was drawn, his expression was grim, there was a glaze of madness in his eyes. He could not forget what he had found in his house that Tuesday in April; he could not rip the pictures out of his mind; but what kept recurring again and again and *again* was the recollection of Kathy, seven years old, tied by thongs, spread-eagled in bed, a child choked to death by her own puke after that bastard had forced his penis into her mouth.

Oh, I want him! Dear God, I want him!
How?

He kept working on it, however helplessly. He studied the sheet Frank had given him, the list of victims, the dates, names, addresses, seeking desperately for some kind of pattern. A single thing emerged, which made no sense and certainly could not help him: there was a period of at least two months, sometimes many more, between the Slasher's murders. So what? So nothing. But he did bestir himself. He drove in the Mercedes at various times to the various addresses. He would park the car a good distance away and walk, inspecting closely. All the single-women victims had lived in apartment houses and all the apartment houses had automatic elevators and no doormen. That was it, and the police certainly knew all of that. The private houses, the scenes of the daytime murders, produced no consistency; they were in different types of neighborhoods, some middle class, some upper middle class, period. The one overall consistency was nothing new: all the Slasher murders were done in Nassau County.

There was nothing out there for Dr. Victor Demarest. The experts had been out there, they had covered that ground, the McVails, the sleuths, the technicians, the professionals. It had to be *here* for him. Here in his house he knew more than the outsiders. He must concentrate here. He must concentrate on the dreadful murders done here in his home. Think! Goddamnit, think!

Dr. Victor Demarest was a veteran of a war, a guerrilla war, and he forced his mind to think along those lines. That Slasher bastard had to have done a full reconnoiter job. He had known where to clip that outside telephone wire, and when he had gone in he must have known that the females were alone in the house. So he must have watched from a vantage point to learn their habits. He must have watched to know what time the doctor left the house. He must have watched in order to know when the kid slept late and where their bedrooms were. But how did it *start?* It was not Kathy. From Frank's list and his own talks with Captain McVail, the guy was not a child molester. So it had to be Lori. It had to have started with Lori. How? How in hell had that bastard ever gotten a line on Lori? According to Frank, the police were quite certain that the guy worked the bars in order to find his victims. Forget it. Out. Impossible with Lori. What else? What else did the police have? What did they have that was incontrovertible, that ran all the way through? Yes. Modus operandi. Thongs. Always leather thongs. They must have worked like hell on that. Thongs. But how in hell can you run down thongs? Anybody, anywhere, in any department store, can purchase thongs, and they don't leave their name and address, and especially if they contemplate using the thongs in murder they will *not* leave a name and address. *Suddenly a thought, all these weeks later, pierced his mind.* He remembered. He remembered that Tuesday when he had found them, both bound in leather thongs, that he had run up to the master bedroom, to one of the deep closets in which they kept their outdoor paraphernalia. He had not known then about modus operandi. He had not known then that this murderer always tied his victims in leather thongs. So he had looked into that closet. He had looked, thinking that bastard had got those thongs out of that closet. But no thong was missing. All those leather strips were there in all the high-topped hiking boots. So he had slammed that closet door shut and had not opened it since. *But now, suddenly, vaguely, a recollection.* What his eyes had glimpsed then had left a picture—and that picture had suddenly registered now. What? Boots. Yes, boots. So? What? Yes. There were a couple of pairs of boots up there that, before that Tuesday, he had not seen up there. So what? Was he going crazy? So what about a couple of pairs of boots up there? What was this blinding flash? What was this great discovery that had suddenly pierced his brain like a dagger? Maybe Frank was right. Maybe all the hints about a shrink made sense. Grief was all right. Rage was all right. A vendetta was all right. A deep psychic need for personal retribution was damn all right. But *really* going crazy was not all right.

He dragged himself up the stairs. In the master bedroom, he opened that closet door. Yes, sir. There they are. Two brand-new pairs of hiking boots, thongs in eyelets. So what? His nerves were tense. A small tight pain quivered down the back of his neck to his spine. So what? For chrissake, so what? He reached in, took out the boots. He set them up, side by side on the floor, and he sat on the bed and looked at them. One pair was beige, the other pair was a deep dark brown. So? What were they trying to tell him? What was he trying to tell himself about Lori's two new pairs of hiking boots? Something was shaking inside of him. Something was lurking inside his brain. Something *was* making sense? What? Was he kidding himself? Was he satisfying some weird psychiatric need? Was he really going crazy? Vendetta. Had the obsessive drive for vengeance finally unbalanced him?

No. No, sir.

Point of contact!

Perhaps the police wouldn't buy it, but Victor Demarest was not interested in the police. Perhaps it was absolutely without significance, but it was certainly worth looking into. Thongs! Whatever the police (and McVail) secretly believed, Victor Demarest *knew* that the murderous bastard had not met Lori in a bar. But here we have something different.

Here we have a *possible* point of contact between Lori Demarest and a killer who always uses thongs in the performance of his murders. Victor Demarest was certain that the police had attempted to run down any clues about persons somewhere somehow purchasing thongs, but he was equally certain that any such channel of investigation had to terminate in a cul-de-sac. It was too wide, too vast. It was simply impossible to accomplish. But we are here in another sphere entirely. We are not contemplating an individual acquiring thongs by anonymous purchase or any other stealthy means. We are contemplating an individual who works in a shop where he is virtually surrounded by thongs. Point of contact. Thongs. Two pairs of brand-new hiking shoes. Contact. Wherever she bought them, even in a department store, there had to be a contact with a salesperson. Thongs. Suppose the salesperson was a woman. In that case, this idea was over. But suppose that salesperson is a man. Thongs. Lori. Thongs. A murderer who invariably uses thongs to bind his victims. Thongs thongs THONGS. He sprang from the bed. He thanked God that Lori had always been a squirrel lady. He pulled open the drawer of her dresser where she stuffed her bills. He searched fiercely, frantically, and found the bill he was seeking. Delanco's Sporting Goods Store in Garden City. Two pairs of boots, one beige, one mahogany, at $55 per pair. Her name was on the bill and her address and the date fit: March three. If that's when he had spotted her and was taken with her, then he knew where to go to watch and reconnoiter and it gave him enough time to set up his plan of campaign to strike during the Easter vacation in April. *If!* I may be out of my head, but I'd be *crazy* not to give it a whirl. We're going to look you over, Mr. Delanco. A new vigor courses through Dr. Victor Demarest. For the first time since the destruction of his family he feels himself to be alive.

He rented a car to use while in surveillance of Delanco's Sporting Goods Store. Although he would not park near, it was senseless to run *any* risk of discovery. If by chance that guy was his man, then he had been out there watching, studying the house in Old Westbury, and he would have seen the Mercedes with the MD license plates. He would also have seen the other cars: Lori's Cadillac, and the Volvo station wagon. *If* the guy was his man. But that's what we're here for—to find out. That's our work now, our only work, and it receives our full concentration. Now it was Victor Demarest who reconnoitered; now he was the watcher, the waiter, the careful, cautious observer. At first there had been that quick shock of disappointment: the salesman in Delanco's was an elderly man. But then had come the reverse: a great high pang of hope! At two o'clock the old man was relieved by a young man: tall and dark and damn good-looking.

Dr. Victor Demarest made his moves slowly and carefully. Time was *not* of the essence; he had all the time in the world; he had his entire lifetime to devote to this cause. He asked a casual question here, a question there. Sometimes he followed quite close to his quarry, at other times he was near a little white house in West Hempstead, but gently, easily, warily, he learned all about Donald Cranford, the dark young man who owned Delanco's Sporting Goods Store. He learned that Cranford was married and resided with his wife and two children, twin boys, in the white house in West Hempstead. He learned that Cranford's mornings were free. The old man, Cranford's assistant, worked from nine until two. Often Cranford came to the store earlier than two o'clock, but his actual work hours were from two to seven; and Mr. Donald Wharton Cranford wore beautiful clothes, obviously custom tailored. Cranford drove a Mercury and also a shiny olive-green van with no markings on it; Cranford's wife drove a Ford. Demarest noted with a strange satisfaction that the license plates of the woman's Ford were scrupulously clean, but the plates of the Mercury and the van (also a Ford) were dirty to the point where the numbers were obscured. Interesting—since all else about the van and the Mercury was shiny-polished and sparkling. And even more interesting, Cranford went out of an evening now and then, and always alone, to the watering holes, stylish pubs and high-type bars. Delanco's Sporting Goods Store closed promptly at seven o'clock. The store had a back exit which opened to an alley and there Cranford parked his car. Usually, after closing up shop, he drove directly home, but not on his pub-crawling nights. On those nights he shaved and re-dressed in his place of business and then out to the car and off to the taverns.

* * *

For almost a month he had been quiet, the family man; but then the blood lust was upon him again and he was moving. And whenever he thought about Paul Mercer, he was proud; that had been a perfect job, clean, a hundred percent. A commonplace mugging murder of an old man, it did not even make the papers. He laughed aloud, driving his car in the night. You are a goddamn important guy, Donald. Because of you they fired the goddamn Police Commissioner, right? So you got to watch yourself, man. They must have plenty plainclothes cops out, men and women, looking to make a score by nabbing the old Slasher. But they can't have them cops out forever, right? There's other fish to fry, right? But fish fries or no, when you are in them bars you play it cool like ice, man. You pick your spots, you wait your turn, you absolutely take no chance at all. Hell, you can always go back to the house and Diana. There's always another night.

A glad madness now for Dr. Victor Demarest. His life was devoted to the hunt and he was pleased with his proficiency. As a successful bird watcher and a successful photographer of wild animals (and a veteran of a guerrilla war) he was an experienced and skillful stalker. He was not certain that Cranford was his man, but he doggedly stayed along with it: the hunter hunting a hunter.

He sold the Mercedes and bought a second-hand Buick. He sold the Volvo and bought a used Dodge.

He sold Lori's Cadillac and bought a used Pontiac. None of the cars had an MD license plate. If Cranford was his man, then during *his* reconnoitering he had seen the Mercedes, the Volvo, the Caddy. But had never seen the Buick, the Dodge and the Pontiac, each of which Demarest utilized on successive days when trailing Cranford, who in fact was an easy mark since he had no idea whatever that anyone was close on top of him, tracking his spoor. A good hunter, Demarest put himself into the mind of his prey. If the police had any idea in the world as to who was the Nassau Slasher, the Police Commissioner would not have been summarily fired because of the failure to apprehend the Slasher. If the police suspected Cranford to be the Slasher, they wouldn't have to be tailing him. After four years and fifteen murders, the Slasher would be wide open, once apprehended, to quick confession under expert interrogation. So if Cranford *was* the Slasher, his psyche delivered him to himself footloose and free. If the police had any suspicion, they would not be wasting their time by stupidly tailing him. They would pounce, arrest, take him in and squeeze him till he talked. Once they suspected him, they would grab. They wouldn't delay the victory, because that kind of victory would catapult the County Executive right up to Albany and into the governor's mansion.

In time, Demarest evolved a system for his surveillance. He would arrive in the vicinity of Delanco's Sporting Goods Store at about seven o'clock. If Cranford closed the store and went out at once to that desolate alley in the rear, then Demarest knew that Cranford would get into his car and drive home to his wife and children. If, however, Cranford closed the shop and did not promptly leave, that meant he was taking off this night for adventure in the taverns; it meant he was in there shaving, cleaning up and changing clothes. In that event the doctor was on the alert in his car and ready to roll.

Aside from his new ownership of three second-hand cars, the doctor had taken other steps, somewhat ebullient, in pursuit of his objective. One day in Greenwich Village in New York City, he had purchased a wig and a matching mustache. Wearing that wig and mustache, he had visited other shops in New York City and had purchased a variety of wigs (he learned that they were now called hairpieces) of different types and colors, as well as a variety of mustaches, sideburns and beards. On occasion, in order to watch his man in action, he had donned a beard, wig and mustache and followed Cranford into a lively bar. He had kept his distance and observed his man in quiet flirtations with handsome women. Cranford's predilection appeared to be mature women. He chose pretty women, but complexion did not matter. They could be dark, fair, blonde, brunette; the one constant was full, upstanding, outstanding breasts. In time Demarest gave up the risk and melodramatics of watching his man in action. The surveillance devolved to a simple system. When Cranford parked and entered a pub, then Demarest, without wig, mustache or beard, parked his car near, and when Cranford emerged and took off to another pub, Demarest would not be far behind. Until this night in June, Cranford had never come out in the company of a woman.

This night in June—it was late, Cranford's fourth bar—he emerged arm in arm with a woman and led her to the parking lot. Demarest, slumped in the seat of the Pontiac and appearing to be drunk or fast asleep, watched. Jauntily, Cranford steered the woman to his Mercury, which meant the woman must live nearby. This late, she would not leave her own car in the lot and go off with the man in his car. Must be a neighborhood woman, Demarest conjectured, who had walked to the pub. Gallantly, Cranford held the passenger door open. The woman entered, Cranford went in the other side, the motor of the Mercury roared, and the car took off. The Pontiac, at first without lights, followed at a prudent distance. Sure enough, Cranford parked at an apartment house quite nearby, but out there, large as life, was a doorman in full braid. The Pontiac rolled past as Cranford and the woman left the Mercury. Demarest drove around the block and parked a distance behind. He put out the lights, turned off the motor, and sat there. It was his feeling that Cranford would be out in short order. It was also his feeling that Cranford, with the woman in the bar, had been unable to establish whether there was a doorman at her apartment house. According to the police, Leather Boy would never subject himself to any hazards. Should the Slasher ever be apprehended, a doorman could pick him out of a lineup: positive identification.

In 15 minutes Cranford came back out into the

night and into the Mercury. The Pontiac remained immobile, without lights, until the Mercury had long disappeared. By now Demarest was thoroughly acquainted with his man's habits. Too late now for another bar. At this hour, Cranford would drive directly to the little white house in West Hempstead.

In time the doctor roused himself. He switched on the motor and turned on the lights and rode home to Old Westbury. He had several drinks of Scotch, ate a sandwich, showered and went to bed—and his dreams were nightmares involving a child bound in thongs, spread-eagled and dead of suffocation.

FIFTEEN

On a hot night in July in a happy crowded bar in Valley Stream, Donald Wharton Cranford finally came up a winner. Her name was Stella Margate. She was a schoolteacher and she was here alone and she was goddamn pretty and she had a pair of bazooms on her like a pair of outsize cantaloupes. She was a talker; wow, an earbender. Told him she had a Porsche parked outside; told him she lived by herself in a big apartment house across town on Grove Street, off Rockaway Parkway; complained that with the high rent and all, there was no doorman, nothing, not even an elevator man; real lousy security. They got along okay, the schoolteacher and the airline pilot, only every once in a while, like for spite, she corrected his English, but before he could get mad, she would tell him how handsome he was, and how he was knocking her out of the box. She was drinking Tanqueray gin, and she sure was drinking a hell of a lot of it.

"Friday night, you know. No work tomorrow." She grinned at him. "You're real cute, Don, but I want to tell you, don't get ideas about a romance. You look just great to me for a *schtup* in the hay, but you're not quite my intellectual cup of tea. No offense. You happen to be a real beautiful *macho* fella and that ought to be enough for anybody. I bet

219

you got a wife and sixteen kids. Wanna know something? I don't *give* a fuck. And something else. If it's any strain for you to pay the bill, just talk up. I admit I'm looking to make out with you—you appeal to my particular type of libido—but I'm not looking to take you for a joyride. I can very well afford to pay my own way. Okay, okay, don't get offended, Mr. Macho. I won't take your balls away. In my time I've been accused of that. Stella the castrator. Don't you believe it. I'm a real pussy cat. And I think you're a real doll, sweetie. Hey, look what time it is. Half past two, by all that's holy. Pay the bill, *macho,* and then I'm taking you home and we'll really give it a run, like the whole weekend. How're you fixed for stamina, baby?''

In the driver's seat of the Dodge, Victor Demarest sat slumped as though he were asleep. He was wearing ordinary summer clothes—slacks, sport shirt, jacket—and of course there was no longer any of the nonsense of wigs, beards or mustaches. He was perspiring. It was a hot night. He wanted to get out and stretch his legs—

He saw them come into the dimness of the parking area. He saw them stop and turn to one another and cling and kiss; then the girl, swaying slightly, went to a red Porsche. Cranford climbed into his Mercury. The Porsche took off and the Mercury took off after the Porsche, and the beat-up Dodge, at first without lights, took off after the Mercury, and soon, with the Dodge some distance behind, the three cars merged into the night traffic on Rockaway Parkway. Demarest's hands were tense, his knees were stiff. In all the months, this was only the second time that Cranford had strolled out of a tavern in the company of a woman.

The Porsche and the Merc turned off the Parkway, and then another turn: Grove Street. The Porsche veered to park near a tall apartment house. The Dodge passed the Porsche and the Mercury and rolled to the end of the street and made a right turn and disappeared.

No doorman. That apartment house had no doorman.

He drove slowly around the block and when he was back on Grove Street the Porsche was parked and the Merc was parked and the girl and Cranford were gone. The number on the license plate of the Porsche was 222-SM. The number on the apartment house was 7412. The Dodge kept going, around the block again, and then back on Grove Street. He looked into the lobby and saw the panel of three automatic elevators. Oh my God, this is it! An apartment house, no doorman, no elevator man. He moved; he kept the Dodge moving; and then once more around the block he parked a distance back, across the street from the Porsche and the Mercury. He cut the motor and snapped off the lights, and at that moment the madness tunneled through to a flicker of sensibility. Why in hell was he parked here? What in hell was he waiting for? Go home and go to sleep. If there is news tomorrow of a Slasher murder at 7412 Grove Street, then your phantom is no longer a phantom: he is Donald

Wharton Cranford and he is the man you want.

He sat there in the hot night in the old Dodge. He had not made an overt move against Donald Wharton Cranford because, despite all the burgeoning suspicions, he did not have a single scintilla of positive evidence that Cranford was indeed Leather Boy. Evidence! He burrowed down in the seat behind the driving wheel. The evidence he required was modus operandi. The evidence he required was a Nassau Slasher killing perpetrated by Cranford. He burrowed deeper. *Dear Jesus, I want him. I do not want him for the police. I want him for me! I have plans for the bloody son of a bitch.* But he needed evidence, and the evidence he needed was *murder*. Until now the madness had obscured it; until now he had not permitted himself clearly to think along that line. But now the man was up there with that girl. What to do? Does the proper vengeance here command a human sacrifice—like an ancient maceration, a ritual slaughter, a burnt offering on an altar? And it was not vengeance for himself alone. What he planned was also proper vengeance on behalf of all the helpless grieving next of kin of all this monster's many victims.

What to do? Dear God, what do I do?

He tried to rationalize. Suppose he called the police. Would they even listen? Look at the insane story he would have to tell them: who he was and why for all these months he had been tailing Cranford. They would probably write him off as a nut. He would have to insist on McVail; and then McVail's people would have to get here in time (and they would have to learn who was the owner of the red Porsche 222-SM). Lord, she would be long dead by then, wouldn't she?

Perhaps there still is time, he thought. Perhaps he's playing sexual games up there with her, before he hits. If she still has a chance for her life, I cannot keep it from her. He switched on the ignition. He had to find a phone! He drove, in the middle of the night, along Rockaway Parkway and he knew in his heart it was a fool's errand, that the girl was dead. That bastard did not play his sexual games while they were still alive. His joy was in the killing, the slashing, the massacre of blood—*then* he played his sexual games. He hoped he was wrong. He hoped—

He saw the sign: VALLEY EXXON SERVICE STATION. The place was closed, but that tiny glimmering light was in the roof of a glass-enclosed public phone booth. He drove up the concrete ramp, passed a dark parked car and braked near the booth. He got out of the Dodge, leaving the door open, and from a corner of his eye he saw the two burly men emerge from the dark parked car. They came toward him swiftly, silently, and he knew immediately that he didn't stand a chance.

"Look," he said. "Please listen."

They separated. One was behind him, one in front.

"Look," he said. "Phone call. Important. Let me make my call and then you can have whatever you want."

"A wise guy," said the man in front.

The man behind grabbed him around the neck in the traditional armhold. The man in front pummeled fists into his face. The man behind released him and he fell. They kicked him in the head, each in turn, gleefully. Then one of them bent to him and yanked out his wallet and pulled off his wristwatch. There was nothing else; he wore no rings, no jewelry. Numbly he felt a final kick and then in the fading blur before he lost consciousness he saw them running like swift transluscent specters toward the dark parked car.

The ambulance called by the Parkway policeman who found the unconscious Demarest drove him to the Franklin General Hospital, 900 Franklin Avenue, Valley Stream. The emergency resident was a five-foot Filipino whose English was lousy but who happened to be as good a doctor as any six-footer who practiced his medicine in English. Dr. Marcos Quezon was assisted by another resident who *was* six feet tall but also did not speak the King's English, Brooklyn-born Dr. Leonard Morse. Between them they got Demarest back to consciousness. He mumbled, but who listens? He kept on mumbling, so they gave him a shot to shut him up.

"Concussion," Quezon said.

"Fracture?" Morse asked.

"Which is what we take to see next step."

"You betcha, Doc. We take to see."

The X-rays showed no fracture of the skull.

"We keep him overnight and then out he goes," Morse advised.

"You betcha, Doc," Quezon said.

They laid him on a cot in a ward with 42 other patients.

Then the cop who discovered the battered Demarest brought the new patient's car to the Franklin General. Up to that point the patient, robbed of all identification, had been John Doe to Dr. Quezon and Dr. Morse. Now the cop came in with the owner's license from the glove compartment of John Doe's car. "Our muggee is a doctor, Lenny," the cop said to Dr. Morse and Morse looked at the license and immediately invoked a new process of treatment. Dr. Victor Demarest was removed from the ward where he was one of 43 and ensconced in a private room. A blonde nurse was assigned to the room. Dr. Quezon and Dr. Morse took turns checking in on their patient.

When Victor Demarest awoke it was Saturday afternoon, and Dr. Morse was in attendance. Demarest had a headache and his doctor told him why. "Concussion," Morse said. "X rays negative for fracture. Contusions and abrasions. The headache figures, but you're A-okay. I'd stick around for a couple of days if I were you, Dr. Demarest." Morse pointed to the automobile ownership license on the bed table. "From the glove compartment of your car."

"I—don't understand."

The young doctor inclined his head. "You have but to ask. I can give you your whole *megilla*. Every test we took. You want to see the X rays?"

"No, I don't mean medically."

"Oh. Well, ask anyway."

"My car. I know they took my wallet and wristwatch. The ownership's from my car, which means, I assume, my car's here. How come they didn't take the car?"

"Because they're shits. I don't know about *your* day, Doctor, but today a resident is part doctor, part cop. These shits that got you are the same tough-guy shits who are out on the streets. The same stupid, violent, petty little thieves who snatch purses, gang up to grab a wallet, and beat up on old men. Out here in suburbia they've figured out a new angle for the late-late show. They've become muggers on wheels. They take you for what you've got and beat up on you for the pleasure of it, but they don't monkey with the car because they wouldn't know how to dispose of a hot car without getting the law down on their asses. What would you like for breakfast, Doc?"

Strangely, he was hungry. "Sausages and scrambled eggs. Fried potatoes, if possible. Buttered whole-wheat toast. Coffee and two aspirins."

"Do you happen to like hash browns?"

"Love them."

"You got 'em." Morse grinned, opened his arms and bowed low.

Demarest fixed the pillows. He lay there thinking of nothing, consciously keeping his mind blank. He dozed.

He awakened when the door opened. A smiling

orderly rolled in a cart with a battery-heated top on which reposed the doctor's breakfast and a folded newspaper. The orderly did not have to serve. The doctor swung his legs off the bed. He pulled the cart close and attacked his breakfast with zeal and fervor and the smiling orderly smiled wider, nodded and backed out of the room. The doctor ate with the gusto of a growing boy, and when he finished nothing remained except the dregs of his coffee and the two aspirin tablets. He no longer had a headache. He took up the newspaper, pushed at the cart so that it rolled crazily away, swiveled on his buttocks so that his legs were back in bed, plumped the pillows, lay back, and opened the newspaper. The Slasher murder was the headline news.

Stella Margate, apartment 14-G, 7412 Grove Street, Valley Stream. Her mother called her at nine o'clock as she always did on Saturday morning. There was no answer. The mother called again. No answer. If Stella did not sleep at home then the procedure was reversed: she would call her mother on Saturday morning. After a third call the mother, Mrs. Helen Margate of Woodsburgh, became apprehensive. She drove to Valley Stream. She had a key to her daughter's apartment. There was no answer when she rang at 14-G. She opened the door and found Stella on the living-room floor. The young woman was nude, her hands and feet were tied, her throat was cut, her breasts were horribly mutilated . . .

* * *

On Saturday at three o'clock a detective named Jeffrey Feinberg appeared in Dr. Demarest's room and politely questioned him about Friday night's mugging. The doctor was of small assistance to the detective. In trying to describe his attackers to Detective Feinberg the best he could do was to state that there were two, they were large and they were Caucasian. No, he had no idea as to the make or model of their car. His wallet had contained approximately two hundred dollars in cash, several items of identification, his driver's license and three credit cards. No, he had not reported the loss to the credit card companies. Feinberg advised him to do that immediately, and Demarest thanked him, and Feinberg closed his notebook and went away.

A tall blonde nurse looked in on him frequently, as did Dr. Marcos Quezon, but Morse took all his breaks in Dr. Demarest's room and they traded stories, and then on Sunday the pleasant detective, Jeffrey Feinberg, appeared again and returned Dr. Demarest's wallet. "A lady going to church found it on the street and turned it in to the precinct," Feinberg explained. The money was gone and the credit cards were gone, but all the rest was there, including Dr. Demarest's driving license.

On Monday Dr. Victor Demarest was discharged from Franklin General. He could have left sooner, but actually he needed the rest, physically and mentally; he needed the feeling, however temporary, of people near him, of people caring for him; he had not yet fully adjusted to being a man alone with no family. On Monday he thanked Dr. Leonard Morse (who lent him twenty bucks) and thanked Dr. Marcos Quezon and thanked the tall blonde nurse whose name was Nancy McGregor. He dressed and studied himself in a mirror: the bruises on his face were already beginning to disappear. He went out to his car and drove to Old Westbury; his first stop was the bank. He drew out three thousand dollars in cash: it was possible he would need cash money quickly available. He mailed a check for twenty dollars to Leonard Morse. Then he went to his jeweler, where he purchased a new (and expensive) wristwatch, highly recommended by the jeweler, to replace the watch that had been stolen from him. Then he ordered the same watch to be sent as a gift to Doctors Morse and Quezon at Franklin General, and a lady's model to be sent to Ms. Nancy McGregor. He signed the gift cards, thanked the jeweler, and drove home. The moment he entered the empty house the madness came back, oppressive, pressing in on him without physical weight, like the still, intense heat of summer—ominous, heavy—just before the torrents and the thunders and the whipping winds of an electrical storm. He took Scotch to the study and sat at his desk and pondered what he knew he had to do and began to know how he was going to do it.

SIXTEEN

On Tuesday Victor Demarest drove to the Weinstein house in Brookville. He reached up to the groove and switched off the silent alarm system. He wore his leather gloves when he entered the house. In the downstairs drawing room he pulled the middle drawer of the antique desk and extracted the huge, smooth, worn, iron key. He drove down to the valley, to the barn shrouded among the many trees. He reached up to the groove in the molding over that doorway and turned off the alarm system. He inserted the big flat old key, turned the lock, opened the door, clicked on the lights. He left the key outside in the keyhole, but locked himself in by sliding the iron bolt inside the door. With purpose he moved about the barn, inspecting carefully. One of the stalls was exactly right. There was an overhead beam of proper height that ran from one wall of the stall to the other, but it was a free beam, not annexed to the ceiling. He continued his intensive inspection, cool in the barn, silently complimenting Leon Weinstein on the excellence of the ventilation apparatus. He walked about, touching gloved hands to objects; he peered, he looked, he smiled, satisfied. There were boxes, stools, chairs: everything necessary was here in this barn. In the rear, a locker room. It had a sink with running water. It had showers in faultless working condition. Couldn't be better, he thought. Ideal. It was the perfect place.

He slid back the bolt, opened the door, clicked off the electric lights. Outside, he slammed the door shut, locked it, withdrew the key, reached up to the lever and switched on the silent alarm system. He drove along the pebbled roadway and then up the ridge to the house. He returned the barn key to the desk, locked the door with Weinstein's keys, raised his hand to the groove and reinstated the silent alarm system.

On Wednesday in the garden in Old Westbury he sat in the sun, deep in thought, and then abruptly he sprang to his feet. He trotted up to the master bedroom. He opened the closet that contained their outdoor paraphernalia. A pain shot through his chest like angina. He had postponed this action for a full day. Too rough, too goddamn dreadful. Kathy's things; Lori's things. God, it was like entering a mausoleum and disturbing the objects, the memorabilia, of the dead. He reached in and took out the two new pairs of boots that Lori had bought at Delanco's, and he swung shut the closet door. On his knees he pulled the thongs, eyelet by eyelet, from the high-top boots. He was perspiring, his armpits sticky. It was difficult, enervating, somehow a despicable operation, like grave robbing, but for Victor Demarest it was exigent, it was work necessary to be done, because for him it would provide in its own special way a form of poetic justice. He required only three of those sturdy leather thongs, but he pulled all four. It gave balance. For him, at this moment in his life, it would be improper to dispose of Lori's four boots, three without thongs in the eyelets, but one with. For him, at this moment in his life, that would be indecent, an injustice, a displacement, an imbalance. He retained the four thongs and threw into the garbage bin the four thongless boots. Then he ran back upstairs and into the bathroom for a cleansing shower.

On Thursday, it was not poetic justice. On Thursday, it was cream of the jest. He had disposed of the silly wigs, the sideburns and beards and mustaches—except for one dark long-haired wig and one dark matching Zapata mustache. He wore those in the morning when he drove the Dodge to Garden City. He parked the car far away and he walked. In Delanco's Sporting Goods Store he purchased a hunting knife of ordinary quality from the polite old man who attended the customers in the morning. On the way back to Old Westbury, Demarest got rid of the dark wig and the dark Zapata mustache. In the house he burned Lori's sales slip for the two pairs of boots she had purchased at Delanco's Sporting Goods Store.

On Friday, in the Pontiac, he was suddenly struck with a new thought. He tried to shake it off but he could not. One must make sure. One must be dead certain. He smiled grimly at that last phraseology. He was driving to New York but he detoured. He stopped in Hempstead at the Motor Vehicle

Bureau and checked license plate 222-SM. It was
registered to Stella Margate, 7412 Grove Street,
Valley Stream. He returned to the car. He had
sealed off any margin for error.

In New York City he visited his offices on Park
Avenue. The receptionist and the nurses were sur-
prised to see him. He had not called, he had not
given any advance notice. Their greetings were
tremulous; pleasant but not hearty. He understood
their ambivalence. They were glad to see him, but
how in hell can you be cheerful with a man whose
wife and child have been horribly murdered?
Lyons, the internist, was busy with a patient, and
Tennent was at the hospital, so, thank God, he was
able to duck both of them. His visit was brief. In his
own office he picked up a pair of surgical gloves, a
roll of surgical tape, a vial of sodium thiopental and
a hypodermic syringe. He said good-bye to the
ladies of the office, went out to the car, drove to the
Stage Deli, double parked, went in and came out
with a brown bag that contained two thick pastrami
sandwiches and a can of beer. He ate, hungrily,
while driving, and at home his dessert was two
Alka-Seltzers in a tall glass of water.

He climbed up to the attic and searched and
found the old portable typewriter. He had bought it
as a gift to Lori 14 years ago. It had not been used in
recent years. It had been supplanted by an electric
typewriter; but of course Lori had saved the old use-
less relic. Up there in the attic, while looking for the
portable, he had been pleased to discover a battered, dusty, ancient, anonymous attaché case. He

came down with his trophies. He dusted off the attaché case; he opened and closed it. The case was okay; its locks snapped smartly, like a flag in a breeze. He tried the portable, but he could not test it because the desiccated ribbon immediately fell apart. So it was out to the Pontiac again. And he drove all the way to Garden City, to one of those immense self-service stationery stores, where no one could ever remember another customer who bought another lousy little typewriter ribbon. At home he fixed it into the portable, rolled in a sheet of paper and tested. The type came through black and blurry, but the old machine was in excellent working order.

Saturday. Sunny and hot. Into the battered attaché case he packed the hunting knife, the surgical gloves, a pair of scissors, the roll of surgical tape, the leather thongs, a plastic cup and two Turkish towels. He drove the Buick, the biggest of the cars, to Brookville. At the Weinstein house he switched off the lever in the groove over the door, entered the drawing room, and took the huge flat key from the desk. When he left the house he switched the alarm system back on. In the car he pulled on his leather gloves and drove down to the valley and along the long, wide, pebbled pathway to the barn. Once again he reached up to a lever in the groove in the molding over the door. And now it was all rapid movement, quick action. He inserted the key, he opened the door, he clicked on the lights. He set away the attaché case in a secure place. Then he opened the door, turned off the lights, locked the door, switched on the alarm system and returned to the car, tossing the barn key into the glove compartment of the sturdy second-hand Buick. On the way home he stopped at a stationery store in a strange town and purchased some cheap, standard 8½- x 11-inch paper and some cheap, standard 4½ x 9½-inch envelopes.

On Sunday, the day of rest, Dr. Victor Demarest was exceedingly restive. His naps were interrupted by nightmares of a child suffocating on semen and vomit. Monday was dank, dim; there was rain, thunderstorms. He wandered about the house in T-shirt and boxer shorts. He ate bread and cheese and turned on the radio. The weather report stated that the rain would end by early evening. At five o'clock, when he began his preparations, it was still pouring rain outside.

He dressed in dark slacks, black loafers, russet sport shirt, charcoal-gray jacket. He folded his brother's list of the Slasher's killings and folded several sheets of the cheap stationery. He placed them into an envelope and slid the envelope into the inside breast pocket of the gray jacket. He hooked in a ball-point pen. Then he loaded the hypodermic with the sodium thiopental and went into the garage. He carefully placed the hypodermic into the glove compartment of the Buick. He slipped on his leather gloves and started the car. On his way to Garden City he stopped at a service station to fill the tank with gas.

At six-thirty he drove into the alley behind Delanco's Sporting Goods Store. Cranford's Mercury was at the far end, near the exit of the alley. There was no other car. There was nothing but rain. A desolate alley. Dr. Demarest parked his Buick directly in front of the rear door of Delanco's Sporting Goods Store. Should the man come out to complain, it would be to Demarest's advantage. It would mean Cranford had had the time to notice; that there was no last lingering customer. Should he come out, it would help; ancillary to the plan, it would improve it. But the man did not come out. As Demarest knew from long observation, he was now beginning to close up shop. On this rainy Monday, business had to be poor.

At a quarter to seven he left the Buick and stationed himself under the eaves by the rear door. At five minutes to seven, Cranford emerged. As he turned to lock the door of the store, he received a blow to the nape of the neck and fell unconscious. Dr. Victor Demarest had been a trained field medic in a guerrilla war. He was a decorated veteran of action and a lieutenant-colonel in the Army Reserve. He knew exactly where and how to strike with a karate chop in order to render a man senseless.

He dragged Cranford through the doorway and left him prone on the floor. He went out to the Buick and came back with the hypodermic. He yanked up a trouser leg of Cranford's pants, injected intravenously. He was a surgeon; he was certain of the dosage. His man would be comatose for at least an hour.

Rapid action now. The door to the trunk of the Buick was flung open. The unconscious man was carried out and dumped in. The trunk was slammed shut. The door to the store was quietly closed. The hypodermic was thrust into the glove compartment, and the Buick purred out of the alley. The driver was smiling, a fixed smile, a rictus of madness. His gloved hands were easy on the wheel.

On the way to Brookville he unscrewed the needle of the hypo and threw it away; several miles farther along the way he tossed the syringe into a clump of shrubbery. He removed the leather gloves and laid them away. He shut off the windshield wipers. The rain had ceased, the sky was beginning to clear. He turned on the radio, listened to the news and got the weather. Fair and warm and clear. And that was also the five-day forecast: fair and warm and clear.

Pebbles crunched under the wheels as the Buick drew up and stopped near the door of the tree-shaded, boarded-up barn. They were in far country. No glimmer of light would show. The smile diminished, but his head bobbed. He nodded approvingly. They would be unmolested. They would be alone: the sole remnant of a family and the monster who had slashed and violated and murdered the other members of that family.

He reached up and turned off the alarm system. He used the flat smooth key and unlocked the door. He removed the man from the trunk compartment, shut the trunk and pulled him into the barn. He lay limp as Demarest switched on the lights and kicked the door shut; with his elbow he pushed the bolt and the door was locked from the inside. He strode to his attaché case and snapped it open. He slipped on the tight, strong surgical gloves.

He grasped Cranford's ankles and dragged him to the selected stall. He tied a thong securely to each wrist, but left loose a sufficient length of the leather. The man was beginning to moan, to blubber. Soon the bastard would be coming around. Standing on a low box, Demarest pulled him up, spread the arms wide and tied each wrist to the overhead beam. Now Cranford was hanging, but all of his weight was pulling down against the bound wrists, cutting off the circulation. No good. Demarest kicked away the low box and pushed higher boxes under the dangling feet and rejected them until he had one of the right height. He removed the man's shoes and socks and tested. Good. He was hanging from his wide-spread wrists, but he was in fact standing, the soles of his feet supported, although barely, by the wooden box.

Demarest returned to the battered attaché case and came back with the hunting knife. He cut away the dark man's clothes and pulled them off and let them fall. Now Donald Wharton Cranford was naked and hanging by the wrists; the thongs did not cut into the flesh because the weight of the body was supported by the feet. Demarest tightly bound the ankles with a thong; but now there was still that extra thong from Lori's fourth boot. He used that thong to tie together Cranford's knees, and at that moment the eyes fluttered open. A frown mottled the handsome face. A squint narrowed the dark eyes.

"What the hell is going on?"

"Soon," Demarest said.

"What the fuck is going on?"

"We shall get to that, Mr. Cranford. Soon you'll be more awake. And more aware."

"I'm thirsty."

"Yes. Rightfully."

Demarest brought out the plastic cup from the attaché case. In the locker room he filled it with water and then in the stall he held it to Cranford's lips. The man drank.

"All right?" Demarest asked.

"What the fuck is going on?"

Demarest set the cup away. He undressed. He folded his clothes carefully and placed them on a box a good distance away from Cranford's stall. "Don't want to get them soiled," he explained. "I suspect you know about that sort of thing."

Naked. Two naked men facing one another: the savage animal whose record was spread over four long years and the constrained, evangelical, obsessed avenger. One man, naked, bound by leather thongs, and the other man, naked, strangely frightful to the hanging man because his sole attire was a pair of surgical gloves. "What the fuck is going on?" said the hanging man and he kept repeating: "What the fuck is going on?"

The naked man in the surgical gloves drew up a chair near the stall. A box in front of the chair would serve as his desk. He sat in the chair and looked up. "Don't you recognize me, Mr. Cranford?"

"What the fuck is going on?" said the hanging man and Dr. Victor Demarest finally recognized it for what it was. Unconsciously, a litany. A dying man, not yet knowing, but impelled by something mysterious, had begun to chant his own elegy.

"Look at me. Don't you recognize me?"

"What the fuck is going on?"

"Demarest."

"What the fuck is going on?"

"Dr. Victor Demarest."

"What the fuck is going on?"

"Old Westbury."

The squinting eyes suddenly opened round. A clear expression of comprehension gleamed in the dark eyes.

"Hey, Doc. *You're* the doc."

"Well, we've come around, Mr. Cranford."

Now the man knew. The eyes were intelligent. But no fear showed in the face. "Holy fucking Jesus. How'd you get me, Doc?"

"Tracked you down."

"So why didn't you give me to the cops?"

"I'm the husband of a woman and a seven-year-old whom you sodomized, you cut and killed." Emotion thickened his voice.

"I'm the husband and the father and I want you for myself, Mr. Cranford. No cops. Me."

Now the hanging man knew it all, and stated it. "You're gonna kill me, Doc. Right?" No fear.

Somehow a release, a relief. And an arrogance.
"Right, Doc?"

"No cops, no lawyers, no plea bargaining.
Maybe inside you, you were banking on that. A
nice little prison sentence. They feed you and give
you exercise. And fresh air and baseball in the yard.
Hell, after a while, maybe even the right to conjugal
relations. Not for you, Mr. Cranford. For once, one
of you bastards is going to get back exactly what he
handed out."

He stood up from the chair, went to his jacket,
and came back with the envelope and the ball-point
pen. He opened the envelope and extracted Frank's
list. He sat and flattened the blank sheets on the
box. They were the extras, the spares, in the event
there was more to write. He took up Frank's list.
"Now listen—"

"I gotta go to the john. I—gotta take a leak."

"No john. Whatever you have to do, do."

The man in the stall urinated. Demarest, a hospital veteran, was not unaccustomed to the acrid odor.
He waited, looking at the paper he was holding in
his hand. When the splashing sounds ceased, he
said: "I'm going to read. I want you to listen very
carefully." He read the names, the dates, the addresses. The last names he read were Lori Demarest
and Kathy Demarest. Then with the pen he wrote
another name on one of the sheets and read it:
"Stella Margate. Now that's your bill of indictment, Mr. Cranford. Fifteen women and one child.
You cut their throats, you ripped their breasts, you
violated, you mutilated. How do you wish to plead,

Mr. Cranford? You've heard the indictment. How do you plead?''

The man laughed. Demarest couldn't believe his ears. The guy up there was laughing. Then after the laughter the man said, ''Total recall. I got total recall. I got a mind like a fucking hair-trigger pistol, mister.''

''Recall?''

''I'm gonna croak anyway, right? So what's the difference? I'm gonna give you more, Doc.'' Braggadoccio. The voice grew full, round with pride. ''You got some of them, Doc.'' The chuckle was a boast. ''I'm gonna give you more. Total recall. Write. Write them down. Write them for your fucking indictment.'' Another laugh. Brief. Raucous. ''I plead guilty. Write. This is six-seven years ago. Chicago, Illinois.''

Demarest's body was wet. Perspiration trickled in rivulets, accumulating in pools at the hollows: navel, crotch, armpits, the cleavage of the buttocks, the sockets of the eyes. He stank. They both stank of sweat: the laughing, hanging defendant, and the sitting, scowling prosecutor. ''Write,'' the man in the stall commanded. The man talked and the doctor wrote. Six names. The man stated six names. The dates were approximate, but the addresses were precise. ''And I got one more for you, Doc. A man. Recent. Paul—''

''Enough!'' Demarest thundered. He was up off the chair. He was on his feet. ''Enough!'' he screamed. He grabbed the hunting knife and ran to the hanging man. ''No more! Enough!''

The eyes were arrogant. A lip lifted in a smile of upper teeth. The voice mimicked a Southern black. "You the boss, man."

"If you want to pray, Mr. Cranford, this is your time."

"Not me. I don't pray. I don't give a shit for God. Okay. Stick that thing into me and let's get it over with."

"That's not the way it's going to be, Mr. Cranford."

He went to the attaché case. He used the scissors to cut a long strip of the surgical tape. He attached the tip of the tape to his left shoulder and came back with the knife to the man in the stall. The hanging madman looked intently at the madman in the surgical gloves. Madness recognizes madness. Finally there was fear up there. The voice broke. It quavered. "No, please no, Jesus, no."

"Yes."

"You can't do it like that, Doc."

"Oh, yes I can. So, do you want to pray?"

"I'm praying to you. Don't do it like that."

"Would you like to know why the hunting knife? Why not a scalpel?"

"Why?" A rationale shivered through the madness of the naked man in the surgical gloves. We're a strange breed, the homo sapiens. Here is a man at the point of death, the arrogance finally out of his eyes because he has become aware of the penalty: the trading of horror for horror. But in these last moments, finally in terror, a dry tongue lolling out of the mouth and saliva drooling: the imperative of human curiosity, like a stiletto, pierces through. "Why?" Cranford asked.

"A hunting knife hacks. A scalpel is a delicate operative instrument. I'm a surgeon. A proper surgical procedure would be a giveaway, don't you think, Mr. Cranford?"

"Look, man, stick it into me. Cut my throat. You caught up with me; you're entitled. But, Jesus, do it right. Show some mercy, for chrissake."

"Mercy! What the hell mercy did you show to the twenty-two people you killed?" Demarest swallowed, seeking breath. His voice came out guttural, a croak. "What mercy did you show to a child?" He reached up and, backhand, slammed his knuckles against Cranford's mouth. "Pray, you bastard. I tell you, pray. Because whatever you think is going to happen to you, it's even going to be worse than that, I promise you."

"I don't pray to God. I fuck God."

"No more. Shut up. Don't talk anymore. I advise you to close your eyes."

He did not look up to see if the eyes were closed. He attended to what he had to do. Hacking with the hunting knife, he amputated the man's penis and his testicles. The hanging man was howling, but the howling ceased when the penis and testicles were shoved into his mouth and were locked in with the surgical tape. It was over. Demarest fell back into the chair. The retribution was fulfilled. In symbol he had avenged his child, the innocent little Kathy. This man's genitals had caused her to choke to death. Now the same genitals will cause him to choke to death. Victor Demarest was a physician; he knew the man would choke to death before he bled to death. So. It was done. It was ended. It was over. He closed his eyes; limply, he lay back in the chair, and suddenly he recalled a quote from the Bible study days of his youth: "The revenger of blood himself shall slay the murderer." He sat up and breathed deeply, a long sigh. Then he rose to his feet and stood upright, his shoulders braced, and faced the dying hanging man and another quote welled up from the distant depths of memory: "The righteous shall rejoice when he seeth the vengeance."

He did not rejoice, but he could not reject the encompassing aura of justification. He had avenged his Kathy and Lori but also all the others who had been ripped and slashed and violated and mutilated, and he had served as surrogate in vengeance for all their suffering next of kin.

It was done.

SEVENTEEN

Swiftly now. The towels from the attaché case. Then in the locker room he removed the surgical gloves. He washed the blood from them. He washed the blood from the knife. He turned on the shower and washed the blood from his body. He stood there under the shower, breathing deeply, letting the water run hard. The amputation certainly would not disclose professional skill. The autopsy would show traces of the barbiturate but insufficient to reveal professional injection. The man had urinated. And by the time they discovered him the other factor would come into play: an enormous amount of blood would have drained out of the body. He had done what he had to do.

Out of the shower, he wiped thoroughly with a Turkish towel. In the other room, he dressed. He folded the sheets into the envelope; placed the envelope in his jacket pocket. Now everything was returned to the attaché case: the hunting knife, the surgical gloves, the tape, the scissors, the plastic cup, the Turkish towels. He shut the attaché case. He pocketed the ball-point pen. He left the lights burning; to hell with the lights. He pushed the bolt with his elbow, stepped out into the warm night. He slammed the door and turned the lock. He did not put on the alarm system. He climbed into the Buick and placed the attaché case on the seat beside him. He started the car, switched on the lights and took off slowly along the pebbled road. It was late at night, but he still had a long circuitous journey before him. Out of the area, he picked up speed but he broke no law. He slipped on his leather gloves and opened the attaché case. He drove many miles in many directions as in the waning light he disposed of the contents of the attaché case. The hunting knife was thrown out in Jericho. One surgical glove was flung out on a tree-lined road in Greenvale. The other surgical glove miles away in Sea Cliff. The roll of tape in Flower Hill. The scissors in Munsey Park. One Turkish towel in Port Washington. The other Turkish towel in Great Neck. The plastic cup in Manhasset. And the empty attaché case in Strathmore. It would be absolutely impossible, ever, to link any one of these objects to the other.

When he came home to Old Westbury the sun was brightly shining. It was twenty after seven, Tuesday morning. He drank a Scotch. He was fatigued. His muscles ached. He buttered a slice of bread and ate it with a piece of cheese. He showered again. There was still so much to do, but he was exhausted. He fell into bed at eight-thirty, but roused himself to set the alarm for twelve-thirty.

At a quarter to eight on Monday evening Diana had had that first flash of prescience. Until then, in truth, she had not really looked at the clock. She was cooking. It was a dark rainy day. She had promised Don a pork roast; he *loved* roast loin of pork. They had talked on the phone in the afternoon; he had said he'd be home about seven-thirty. So she had figured the pork roast for eight o'clock. With it they would have string beans, applesauce, candied sweet potatoes and a bottle of Chianti. Now she looked up at the wall clock: a quarter to eight. She frowned. She felt a pang. Had something happened to him? She shook it off. Crazy. Would it be the first time he had come home late? When a customer lingers, when the customer keeps you, you can't just throw them out, can you? At eight o'clock she called the store. No answer. Good. He was finally on his way home. But at nine o'clock, the pork roast out of the stove, she was frankly worried. She had called the store again: no answer. And again: no answer. What to do? What do you do?

First she had called Don's assistant, Natie Silver, the sweet old man who had replaced Paul Mercer, the poor man who had been murdered by those loony muggers who are everywhere, all over the place these days. There had been no answer at Natie's, and that had frightened her further. No answer at the store, no answer at Natie's—had something happened? No. Why should it be that something happened? Natie could be at a bingo game, or a movie, or something, and Don could have stopped off somewhere necessary. Necessary for the business. But he would have called. The pork. They had talked in the afternoon. He knew about the roast pork. He would have called. Why didn't he call? By nine-thirty she knew something was terribly wrong.

She knew she would have to call the police, but she hesitated. She postponed. In all her life she had never called the police, she had never had anything to do with the police: they scared her to death. But at ten o'clock she made the call. The man at the other end sounded very nice, very sweet, sympathetic. She told him the whole story. He took her name, her address and her phone number. She told him she was alone in the house with two little children who were asleep. Then he took down Donald's name, and the address of Delanco's Sporting Goods Store, and that phone number and Natie's name and address and phone number. He said for her to sit tight, not to worry, she would hear from them.

At twenty-five after ten the phone rang. It was the same voice, the nice man again. He said not to worry, there had been no stickup in the store, nothing like that. He knew she could not come to the station house because she was alone with two small children. So a policeman would come to her. His name would be Jonathan Clark.

At eleven o'clock Jonathan Clark rang the bell at the white house in West Hempstead. He was a bald man with a polite smile and a quiet voice. He told her first not to worry. They all kept telling her not to worry, but where was Donald? Clark told her he was a detective from Missing Persons.

"Why Missing Persons?" she asked.

Detective Clark explained. After her call, a policeman from a patrol car had checked out the store. Nothing wrong there. No evidence of violence. No robbery. Nothing at all like that. The front door was locked, but the rear door, although closed, was not locked. There was a Mercury parked in the alley in back. It checked out to be owned by Donald Wharton Cranford. All was in order. The Mercury was in perfect shape. They had found Natie Silver at the apartment of his girl friend, a lady 68 years of age named Carrie Avalon. Mr. Silver had supplied a key to close the rear door. Mr. Silver had said that Mrs. Cranford had duplicate keys to the store in her home.

"Yes," Diana said.

Mr. Silver had said that Mr. Cranford had been in good humor and fine fettle when Mr. Silver had gone home for the day. Mr. Silver had said that Mr. Cranford was a tall young man, dark and handsome.

"Yes, very handsome," Diana said.

That's why it was Missing Persons, Detective Clark explained. There was no evidence of robbery or violence or anything like that. However, it was not yet formally a Missing Persons case. A period of 24 hours must elapse before a missing person is officially a Missing Person. At that time, if Mr. Cranford didn't show up—which most probably he would—then all the data would be collected and put into the computers and put out on the wires. But Mrs. Cranford must not worry. The store was in excellent order. There was absolutely no evidence of violence. Men are men—you know how it is, Mrs. Cranford. A friend of his may have dropped in and taken him to a party or something, or maybe a charity affair, or maybe a political gathering or something, and he had a few drinks and he just forgot to call home. Detective Clark wrote down a phone number for her. If Mr. Cranford didn't show up by tomorrow twelve o'clock noon, then would she please call that number, and Detective Clark himself would again be in touch with her.

He said good night politely and went out to his car and drove away from the little white house. He lit a cigarette and shook his head dolorously. The graph was going up. More and more missing persons became Missing Persons, male and female. He felt sorry for that ordinary-looking chick in the little white house. His vibes twanged out a dirge for the little lady, a sad story repeated day after day every day these days. The spouses kept lighting out, they kept disappearing, the graph going up and up. The little lady was a fair-to-ugly little chick. The husband was described as tall and very handsome. Detective Clark flipped his cigarette out the window and looked at his watch. He had time. On a house call like this, he could write up his report for as long a period as he liked. Detective Clark had a good solid wife named Phoebe in a good solid house in Massapequa. He also had a long-legged blonde waitress who lived in an apartment in Farmingdale for which he paid most of the rent (and food and clothes and so forth and so on) who went by the name of Phyllis although her real name, honest to God, was Philomena. He looked at his watch again and chortled. He decided to drive out at this weird hour and drop in on Phyllis in Farmingdale.

* * *

At twelve-thirty the alarm wrenched Victor Demarest from sleep. The alarm kept ringing because he was incapable of turning it off. In his own home, in his own bed, he did not know where he was. He was floating in a void, chimerical, a limbo, his brain reluctant, his body heavy with exhaustion. Then suddenly, as though in spasm, he sat bolt upright. He shut off the alarm. His mind meshed, the gears turned. There was much to do.

He staggered out of bed and into the shower. He toweled briskly. He swallowed a Dexie spansule, and that spawned a memory. There was this old professor in med school who was adamant against any stimulant, even caffeine. *"You can flog a dead horse, gentlemen, but you cannot make him run."* That was *your* hangup, Professor. Dr. Victor Demarest remembered in 'Nam on emergency nights when the Dexies went down like jelly beans at a kiddy party. And they were medicine; dear Lord, they did a job.

He pulled on a T-shirt and a pair of Jockey shorts and then he stood rigid, frowning, his mind once again disoriented. What was today? What day was it? Wednesday? No. It was Tuesday. He had gone to bed Tuesday morning. Four hours. Now it was Tuesday afternoon. Yes. Right. Much to do. Work to do. He pattered barefoot down to the kitchen and made a pot of coffee. The very first cup brightened him. He grinned. The coffee had a helper. The Dexedrine was popping off and beginning to flow through the bloodstream. He placed the pot of coffee and a cup on a tray and took it to the study. He took the old portable. He took a pair of gloves. He took the envelope from the inside pocket of the charcoal-gray jacket. He took the cheap stationery and the envelopes he had purchased in the strange town. He sat down at the desk and did the first draft of the letter in longhand. He did it again and again, draft after draft; and he was suddenly admiring his brother Frank. Writing, getting it down the way you want it; that's one hell of a tough job. It took a long time, picking out sentences, taking out words, until finally he had it the way he wanted it, terse and compact.

He put on the gloves. He took the portable out of its case and set it on the desk. He rolled in a sheet of the cheap paper. The gloves made it awkward, but the gloves would prevent fingerprints. He typed slowly, with the index finger of each hand. He addressed the letter to Captain Jackson Brendan McVail, Police Headquarters, 1490 Franklin Avenue, Mineola, New York. He referred to the anonymous writer by the editorial *We*. He informed McVail that we had captured the Nassau Slasher, that the said Slasher was dead, and that the cadaver reposed in the barn of an estate owned by one Leon Weinstein in Brookville. We are enclosing, on a separate sheet, a list of the persons the Slasher had admitted killing. We are requesting—since we have succeeded where you have failed—that you fully inform the public of *exactly* what you find in the aforementioned barn. We believe that thus the next of kin of the many murdered victims will receive what they have prayed for and what they justly deserve: the compensation of retribution, the quid pro quo, the measure for measure. We have come the full circle. It is time to avenge the victim, rather than pamper the perpetrator . . .

On another sheet he typed the dates, names and addresses of the persons murdered and ravished by the Slasher in Nassau County, and the approximate dates and the names and addresses of the persons the Slasher murdered and mutilated in Chicago. He rolled in an envelope, addressed it, marked it PERSONAL. He folded the sheets, inserted them and sealed and stamped the envelope. Finished. It had been a tedious, devious, fatiguing, damn long job. It was four o'clock.

He was perspiring. His T-shirt was wet through, his shorts were wet. Much more to do. He replaced the portable in its case. Still wearing the damn gloves, he carried the sealed letter through the house to the garage and laid it in the glove compartment of the Pontiac. Certainly that letter could not bear a postmark that was anywhere in the vicinity of Old Westbury. He came back and now it was all physical labor and he worked swiftly. He disposed of what was left of the cheap stationery and envelopes purchased in the strange town. He disposed of Frank's list. He disposed of the list that had been Cranford's addenda. He disposed of the vial that had contained the sodium thiopental. He was clean. The house was clear. He removed the gloves and went up for a shower again, a long, warm, soapy shower; then gradually cool; then icy cold.

He dressed carefully: a conservative suit, black shoes, a white shirt, a quiet tie. He put on the gloves again and drove all the way to Brooklyn Heights, where he posted the letter.

Suddenly he was starved. Dexedrine will inhibit the appetite, but it cannot destroy appetite, and he had eaten nothing—not a bite since awakening—and it was verging on evening. He knew where to go, Gage & Tollner, a landmark in old Brooklyn, a fine restaurant. He ate. Lord, did he eat—but slowly, leisurely. And then he found a movie and sat there and digested food and watched, without erotic reaction, an erotic film, and then out to the car and home to Old Westbury and he parked the Pontiac in the garage and it was eleven o'clock, but there was still more to do. Survival is man's paramount instinct. Again the gloves. He wiped the portable typewriter and carried it out to the car. This last trip, and then his journey was over. He backed the car out of the garage and he drove a long way from Old Westbury to the bridge that spanned Reynolds Channel and there in the night he dropped the typewriter into that deep water, and it was done. When he drove away he was not wearing the gloves.

He drove slowly because his vision was beginning to blur. Of course. He was dead tired. He kept shaking his head, to shake off the wisps of fatigue that whirled around him like fog. The Dexedrine had long exhausted itself. He drove doggedly, squinting through the windshield, his hands perspiring on the steering wheel, and at long last—it seemed hours—he was home. It was one o'clock in the morning. His feet dragged as though they were locked in fetters. He drank down a couple of Scotches. He realized he had slept only four hours in the last thirty-six. He undressed. He had one more Scotch, and then he took *two* Nembutals. He knew all about the synergism of alcohol and barbiturates. It was a heavy dose in combination, but not lethal, and it would damn well keep him sleeping for a hell of a long time and that was what he wanted. A quick thin pain, like the stab of a needle, cut through his head. He fought away from it. He fell asleep.

He awoke at two-thirty, blinking against the sun on the blinds. He had slept for thirteen hours. He stretched, shuddered, got out of the bed and into the shower. He slipped into T-shirt and jeans and moccasins. He brushed his teeth, shaved, combed his hair. He went down to the kitchen and made coffee and bacon and eggs and he was relishing his midday breakfast, his mind still placidly somnolent, when of a sudden his jaws shut and the food in his mouth was occluded.

He had never removed the key from the door of the barn in Brookville.

He sat there at the kitchen table. The immediate problem was whether to spit out the food or swallow it. He swallowed. He sipped coffee. He squinted, smiling crookedly. Was there indeed a basic truth in the tired old bromide that every criminal unconsciously wants to be caught?

He had turned the lock in the door of the barn,

but he had not removed the key. The plan had been *not* to reinstate the alarm system at the barn. He would lock up, withdraw the key, take it back to the house, wipe it clean of prints, replace it in the desk, quit the house, switch on *that* alarm system, and drive away. But in his hurry to get moving, to get away from that grisly business in the barn, he had failed; he had bungled the few final simple steps. Now the big flat key was there in the door, and it was quite possible that his fingerprints could be lifted from it. What to do? Nothing. There was nothing to do. The plan had been perfect and the execution perfect, except for that one last slip; and he had prepared and rehearsed the appropriate answers to any questions. He speared a piece of bacon; let it fall back to the plate. Think! We must assume new stances and contrive additional answers because it was now far too late to go back and try to retrieve that key. In surgeon's language: too late to rectify. He poured more coffee. How strange. But how, in symbol, correct. A circle. The eternal circle. The schema of life goes on without end. Or beginning. It goes around and around: always the circle. This adventure had shifted in axis. It had turned itself all the way around. Cranford the hunter had become Cranford the hunted when Victor Demarest had learned beyond doubt who Cranford truly was. Now Victor Demarest the hunter will himself become the hunted, and the new hunter will be the wise, penitent, implacable Captain Jackson Brendan McVail. But! Always the but. The surgeon in despair gives up on a patient; then God moves things about, and the patient outlives the surgeon. Yes, we must begin to plan again, to rehearse the additional answers, to prepare for the new exigencies, but we must also consider the possibility and pray that there is no decipherable fingerprint on the huge flat key extruding from the barn door in Leon Weinstein's tree-shaded valley.

EIGHTEEN

On this Wednesday morning McVail was even more grumpy than usual. A bursitis in his left shoulder had exploded into excruciating pain; his internist, Gelfand, a good guy and a great doctor, had stabbed in a long *long* needle that had killed the pain. "Why?" McVail had demanded. It was not a new bursitis. For almost a month now the doc had been treating it, and it had cooled off—until this morning. "Why, for chrissake?" McVail demanded. And he received a reply that had become the standard when a doctor had no answer; an empirical reply, it was impervious to dispute.

"Stress," Gelfand said.

"Yeah, here we go with the bull again."

"Believe me, Jake, stress can do it."

"Okay. I'll see you. When it starts hurting, I'll be back."

He went out to the car and started for the office. The doc had used the right word for the right guy, although stress was of course in some form or another universal to everybody (which was why the learned physicians had picked up on the word). Gelfand, however, was a bright guy and he was not wasting his words: he knew that anybody in McVail's business had to be under *heavy* stress. But the doc could not conceive of the bull's-eye he had

261

achieved. Stress! Since 12 days ago, since the Margate killing, he had been under more stress than he ever experienced before.

When a succession of similar crimes is widely spaced, they are insulated within the focal site: they remain local news. An ax murderer in Bridgeport is not news in Miami. A child molester in Peoria is not news in San Francisco. A mugger-killer in Fairbanks, Alaska, is not hot news in Atlanta, Georgia. Unless the space narrows down. The frequency makes for sensationalism and that is what sells newspapers.

The Nassau Slasher was hot news with the wire services. Since the Haskell murder in late December (and the subsequent suicide of the husband), and the Demarest murders in April and the Margate murder soon after the Fourth of July—four horrible same-type modus operandi sex murders (and a related suicide) within two hundred days—the Slasher had contracted his space and expanded his despicable prima-donna status. He was a nationwide item, and the editorials, locally and nationally, excoriated the authorities who had been unable to apprehend this nefarious criminal. (Within the Department it was known that these authorities did in fact funnel down to a single authority: Captain Jackson Brendan McVail.) And the new Commissioner, ex-FBI and formerly police commissioner in Pittsburgh, and withal a very young guy (39), was insisting to the County Executive that in the interests of both efficiency and economy the Sex Crime Squad be disbanded. At their last conference in the County Executive's office, the Commissioner had repeated this demand and McVail, hot and harassed, had threatened to resign.

"It's an interesting thought," Commissioner Quincy Parrish said. "In fact, it jibes with my theories as to promotion in police departments. I believe that certain police superiors, grown old before their time and rather poor physical specimens, *should* retire, although not yet technically at the retirement age. It makes for room at the top. It provides the opportunity for younger and more vital men to move up and fill those ranks."

But at that moment S. Lloyd Jutland proved his mettle. He stuck a finger in the face of his sprightly new Commissioner. "Lay off those tactics, Mr. Parrish. Jake McVail, by total unanimity, is the finest superior officer we have produced in the Nassau County Police Department. There are certain boundaries we should not cross, certain easy ploys we simply should not utilize. Not me, seeking the Governor's chair, nor you, trying to make a name for yourself in Nassau County. I sought you out. I appointed you. But if I'm compelled, I can admit my mistake and discharge you. I should like to advise you, Mr. Commissioner, of a fact you possibly know and probably don't like. A new Commissioner likes to sweep clean; he especially likes to sweep out the hot-dog heroes who can, by whatever mystical process, undermine the new man's authority. Now this is my fact, Mr. Commissioner. Captain McVail *is* one of our hot-dog heroes. But he is an absolutely brilliant police officer who over the decades has had many great successes and he has acquired, and rightfully so, an enormous reputation. You simply cannot blow a man like that away like a loose hair on the back of your hand.''

It was vindication but it did not mitigate the stress. Sexual assaults had not ceased in Nassau County, but Sergeant Caldwell and Sergeant Emerson (with aides) ran them down and reported to McVail. McVail himself stayed in the kitchen where the heat was: the Nassau Slasher. Since the Margate homicide, nine different crazies had confessed to being the Slasher, and it was McVail, in person, who conducted the intense interrogations. And McVail, in person, who followed through on every clue, no matter how preposterous. And McVail, in person, who ran down the crank letters wherever possible, and since Margate there had been one hell of a spate of crank letters.

He arrived at the office at ten-thirty. He answered several phone messages, then he separated the mail, the regular mail from the crank letters—a simple procedure because the crank letters usually came in cheap envelopes, were almost always handwritten and never bore a return address. He set aside the crank letters—there were 14—and opened his mail. He called in his secretary and dictated replies. Then he closed the door and settled back alone with the missives from the crazies. Thirteen of the envelopes were handwritten, some in almost illegible scrawls.

The 14th was typewritten, blurry but neat, and he saved that one for last. The 13 went quickly. They were really from crazies and they simply made no sense. Now he slit open the 14th envelope. It contained two typewritten sheets; one appeared to be some sort of list, the other a letter. He laid aside the list, began to read the letter, and immediately experienced an acceleration of the heartbeat. The impulse for his excitement was simple: the letter was unusual because it was phrased in excellent English. But as he continued to read, his pulse rate continued to quicken—with damn good reasonable cause.

Where you have failed, we have succeeded. We have captured the Nassau Slasher. He is dead. His cadaver reposes in the barn of an estate owned by one Leon Weinstein in Brookville. On a separate sheet we are enclosing a list of the persons the Slasher has admitted killing. We are requesting, since we have succeeded where you have failed, that you fully inform the general public of EXACTLY what you find in the aforementioned barn. We believe that thus the next of kin of the many murdered victims will receive what they have prayed for and what they justly deserve: the compensation of retribution, the quid pro quo, the measure for measure. Our society has finally come the full circle. We demand that the victim be avenged and we demand the extreme penalty for the vile perpetrator.

*He that strikes with the sword shall be beaten
with the scabbard.*

He put down the letter, took up the list. His muscles tensed, his jowls shook, he felt himself quiver.
The dates, names and addresses of the Nassau victims could easily be acquired—but on this list were
the names and addresses of six murdered women in
Chicago, Illinois. *How could any crazy know anything about any of that?* He lurched out of the
swivel chair, took his keys, went to the steel-walled
file room and used the two keys necessary to open
one of the TOP CONFIDENTIAL files. He compared
dates, names and addresses. The dates were close,
but the names and addresses were absolutely precise. He returned the data, locked the file. He went
back to the office, let the typewritten list flutter to
the desk, and slouched into his swivel chair. He sat
there. He closed his eyes and sat there.

He had been through all the mills. He was an old
cop; a policeman for almost 38 years. He knew not
to jump like a kitten when the catnip is dangled.

What's up, kid? What's going on here? Was
somebody trying to pull a rib on good old Jake
McVail, or was someone in the Department pulling
a wingding? There are crazies in police departments
like there are crazies everywhere else. It has to be
the Department. Because nobody else knows about
the Chicago six who were cut and assaulted and
mutilated and killed in Leather Boy's irrefutable
mode of procedure. None of the news boys was
ever made party to any of that information. So,

Christ, *who* in the Department? Now hold it. Just hold it. He opened his eyes and leaned forward.

It does not have to be the Department *per se*. There is always the possibility of a slow leak. Okay, slow down. Who knows about the Chicago Six? Sex Crime Squad: Pam Medford, Mary Caldwell, Bill Emerson. Then Marge Wyckoff. And the former Police Commissioner, Arthur Dumont. And of course the County Executive, S. Lloyd Jutland. And Jake McVail, who can positively speak for Jake McVail: he did not leak. But any one of the others could have talked to a dear one, a confidant, and so it could go, leak by leak, from a dear one to another dear one, from a confidant to another confidant and so on to a crazy.

Hold it.

Once more, hold it.

More ominous. A ruse to trip you up. Make you stumble. Flaunt you as a fat old codger whose shutters are starting to flap in the wind. You have an enemy, Jake, upstairs in the executive suite. Quincy Parrish, the young and dynamic new Commissioner. You are a fishbone in his craw. You are a roadblock on his march to unimpeded authority. You are an immovable object resisting the sweep of his broom. Without meaning to, you showed him up in front of the County Executive. He had to back down. He had to take water. He is the new Commissioner. He is entitled to all the information in all the files. So, without your knowing, he plucked the Chicago information and planted it in a crank letter and like that he sets you up to take a pratfall. So easy to do. Watch your step, protect your flanks. This thing can be a trap that can snap and bite your ass off.

Or, is it legit?

Crazy deals do happen.

In any event, go easy. No hurry. If the thing is legit, then the guy is dead and he won't go roaming out of a barn up in Brookville. He looked at the envelope. It was postmarked Brooklyn. Lightly he restored the sheets to the envelope and went over to the lab and let Jack Skinner, the best in the business, scan the stuff for fingerprints. Nothing. As expected, nothing on the sheets; and on the envelope, just a bunch of smudges. McVail took the envelope to Casey Lane, who knew more about type and typewriters than anyone at Smith-Corona. Casey slipped it under a microscope and came up with a judgment.

"I'd say an Underwood portable, maybe fifteen-twenty years old. I won't say, on this quick reading, that I'll take an oath on Underwood. But I will take an oath on a manual portable vintage fifteen-twenty years."

"Thanks."

He returned to his office. He checked with Information. He called Leon Weinstein in Brookville. He was informed by a telephone operator that the phone was disconnected. He hung up, lit a cigar. Brookville. He was not going to call in the village cops. Not yet. Not while it could still be a rib, or a ruse for a pratfall. He rocked in his swivel chair.

Thirty-seven years with the Nassau P.D. Brookville. He knew Nassau County like he knew his own face in the mirror. Now, who in Brookville? He snapped his fingers, stopped rocking. Ezio Elberon. Owns Ezio's General Store on Chicken Valley Road in Brookville. He blew smoke, grinned. That's a real name, folks. Chicken Valley Road. And Ezio's been there for 40 years, and he has the nosiest nose in Brookville.

McVail made the call. He kidded with old Ezio and they made idle conversation and then he slipped his question in roundabout and of course he got his answer. Leon and Elaine Weinstein, an old couple alone, very rich. Went off on a cruise in March; around the world for like a year. Swedish-American Line. Luxury liner, the S.S. *Kungsholm*.

McVail made some confidential telephone calls to friends in the realty business. He learned about the Weinsteins, the Weinstein estate, the address of the house, the position of the barn. He hung up, sat there, squinted, shrugged. He went out to his car. He drove north in the glaring sun to Brookville. He looked at the Weinstein house and then he swung the car down to the valley and up the pebbled road to the barn. He clambered out of the car and saw the large flat key in the huge keyhole of the barn door and that stopped him short. For moments he stood there in the heat of the summer sun, cogitating a fourth hypothesis. There had been no rib, no ruse. Legit—why in hell would they leave the key in the door? And the kind of old flat key that, like glass, figured for a print? Was this deal even more convoluted than he had thought? Legit—was somebody trying to set somebody *else* up?

He pushed fingertips against the door. It did not yield. He used his handkerchief and turned the key, pressing only on its outer edges. He wrapped the key carefully, loosely, and laid it into the glove compartment of the car. He returned to the barn, pushed the door, opened, entered, and stood transfixed. He saw the hanging man. But he could not see clearly. He had come from blazing sunshine to the flicker of electricity. The barn door was open, and the lighting, the mix of lights, did tricks. What he saw appeared abstract, unreal, an apparition, a vision supernatural.

A crucifixion.

As his eyes grew accustomed, his gorge rose. He clenched his hands and held his breath and swallowed hard in order not to vomit. Not a crucifixion. No cross. No nails. The man was nude. Arms outstretched he was hanging from an overhead beam, his wrists secured to the beam by leather thongs. His ankles were bound together by leather thongs. The soles of his feet rested on a wooden box. His mouth was covered by a wide strip of surgical tape. He had no genitalia. Where there had been genitalia, there was a dark-clotted ragged hole. His inner thighs and legs were covered with blood. The top of the wooden box was full of blood. The eyes were closed. The head was bent forward, the chin resting on the chest. McVail knew—he knew!—what was inside the mouth that was locked behind the wide strip of adhesive tape.

He was a cop. There was work to do. He worked.

He tore his eyes away from the hanging man, who, no matter, because of the outstretched arms and the way the rest of him was bound, was hanging as though upon a cross.

McVail shook his head. He remembered a prayer, but did not say it. He stooped and examined the clothes on the floor. The man's name was Donald Wharton Cranford. His address was on his driver's license. In his wallet there was further identification. His wife's name was Diana (to be notified in case of accident). He was the owner of Delanco's Sporting Goods Store in Garden City.

McVail went out into the sunshine. He opened his mouth and filled his lungs with air. He kept breathing like that, deeply, momentarily enjoying the good clean smells out there: the smell of loam, the smell of the green trees, the fragrance of flowers. Then he crunched on pebbles to the car and leaned in.

First he called Homicide in Mineola, and then he talked to the local police in Brookville.

The barn was crowded with the village officials, who were superseded by the county officials, but the highest official, the man in charge, was Captain Jackson Brendan McVail. It was the medical examiner who stripped away the tape from the man's mouth and what the medical examiner found in there was what McVail had expected he would find. The medical examiner's verdict was death by suffocation, and it was the medical examiner's opinion that the amputation of the man's pudendum had been a crude, hack-type action, probably with a hunting knife. McVail delivered all of his information to the reporters, to the village officials, and to the county officials, except the matter of the key. Jake McVail here. McVail, the loner. McVail, the unorthodox. It was his case. The Nassau Slasher, now deceased, had been his case, and now the *murder* of the Slasher was his case, and he refused to let it get screwed in the grinding mill of police establishment. There was something goddamn weird about this business of the key. No murderer leaves evidence *that* obvious. Who is trying to set who up? Is somebody presenting a fall guy for the cops to pick up a quick credit and close out the case and lay a sure-thing conviction on the D.A.'s platter? Is somebody trying to work a con? Is somebody playing for the twist? Is somebody trying to outsmart a smart old cop? Maybe yes, maybe no, but it's worth a whirl, and that has to be all-alone inside, once again a loner job, a very private whirl.

NINETEEN

The front pages of most of the newspapers all
along the Eastern Seaboard (and the front pages of
the Chicago papers) headlined the sensational de-
nouement of the Nassau Slasher case and the stories
contained all the gruesome details of his demise.
The murderer's letter, word for word, appeared in
the newspapers, as did the list of victims to which
the Slasher had confessed, and the police stated definitely that the dead man was indeed the Nassau
Slasher. The public's opinion was unanimous:
*"Couldn't have happened to a nicer fella! It's
about time one of these sonsabitches got what was
coming to him!"*

Diana Cranford, of course, refused to believe,
but a photo of Donald Wharton Cranford, displayed
by cops in restaurants and pubs, was recognized by
numerous bartenders all over Nassau County. "Always came in alone. Always made a quiet pitch for
a good-looking dame. Seemed to be a real nice guy,
soft-spoken, well-dressed, never a disturbance."
McVail noted (and it appeared in his report) that
Cranford's olive-green van, a Ford, and his Mercury were kept spick-and-span-shiny, except for the
license plates, which were covered with sufficient
grime to make them indistinct and unreadable. A
check on his background revealed that in his

younger days he had worked as a repairman for the telephone company in Nassau County. The van contained two pairs of telephone-company coveralls and a pair of professional wire cutters. That must have been his means of entrance to some of the private homes. The olive-green van bore no markings: it could easily be mistaken for a phone company truck. He must have cut the wires, and then pretended (wearing the coveralls) to be from the phone company. The glove compartment of the van contained a pair of gloves, but under the front seat there were many strips of leather thongs and a switchblade knife. The glove compartment of the Mercury contained nothing more incriminating than a pair of gloves, but under *that* front seat: strips of leather thongs and a switchblade knife. Cranford's background disclosed that he was living in Chicago during the period of the six murders with the identical modus operandi of the Slasher murders in Nassau County.

McVail called the Swedish-American Line in New York City. He was informed that the S.S. *Kungsholm* was in the Ligurian Sea, at anchor in Genoa. He put through a call to the *Kungsholm*. He identified himself, but the English-speaking man on the other end was cagy. He said he would call back to Captain Jackson Brendan McVail of the Nassau Police Department in Mineola, New York, USA. In time the return call came through and now the man at the other end was courteous and cooperative. McVail inquired as to whether a Mr. and Mrs. Leon Weinstein were passengers. There was a pause and then a reply in the affirmative. McVail asked to speak to Mr. Weinstein. He was informed that the Weinsteins, among a great many other passengers, were off on their own, sightseeing and living on their own in Genoa, but that they would be back aboard ship by Sunday at four o'clock P.M. Eastern Daylight Time. McVail thanked him and told him he would call again to the *Kungsholm* when it was Sunday and four P.M. Eastern Daylight Time.

On Thursday McVail reviewed all of the sales slips at Delanco's Sporting Goods Store, but there was none with any nexus to any of the Slasher's victims. On Friday, the Slasher storm beginning to abate, McVail brought a flat old iron key to Jack Skinner to learn whether there were any fingerprints on it. Skinner, one year younger than Jake McVail, was light-years more taciturn. Skinner never asked any questions and never vouchsafed a remark unless it was in answer to a question. But Skinner was famous in the Department for a single remark that was said while attending a conference, though his statement was in fact an answer to a question. It was at the time that Arthur Dumont was appointed the new Police Commissioner and, like all the new ones, he was wielding the broom. When it got down to Jack Skinner, it was a whisk broom. Skinner, even back then, was the best fingerprint man in the Department, and he was earning a sergeant's pay, and during this crowded conference of the little-shots, the new Commissioner wanted to know why. Was Skinner a college graduate? No. Had Skinner gone to college for special courses in fingerprinting? No. Had Skinner taken special courses in high school? No. Then why in hell was Skinner earning a sergeant's pay and what in hell made Skinner such a big deal in the fingerprint department? Skinner's answer was short and sweet. "Mr. Commissioner," he said, "you don't have to lay an egg to know how the hen does it." Skinner remained on sergeant's pay and grew old and lost his hair and never learned to talk a lot, but he was still the best damn fingerprint man in Nassau County, and now on this Friday he dusted and squinted and came back to McVail and said, "There's only one, but it's a beaut. A thumbprint." McVail asked for a small photograph of the print, and Skinner obliged.

On Saturday, McVail slept.

On Sunday he was in his office in Mineola and at four o'clock he put through the call to the S.S. *Kungsholm* and he talked to Mr. Leon Weinstein. He said there had been an accident in Mr. Weinstein's barn, but nothing important enough to disturb the Weinstein's around-the-world cruise, and he asked mild questions and Mr. Weinstein proffered mild replies and that was how Jake McVail learned the name of the good friend to whom the Weinsteins had entrusted the care of their home while they were away on their long vacation. Captain McVail thanked Mr. Weinstein. He hung up. He sat there in his swivel chair. He did not once get up. He sat for a long time. The street noises faded away. The windows grew dark. In the black silence he sat there in his swivel chair.

TWENTY

In Old Westbury, day after day, Victor Demarest was cleaning house, washing dishes, cooking meals, mowing lawns, tending the garden, keeping busy—but where in hell was McVail? Why was he stalling? Was this some type of police torture with intention to soften him up? It was Monday; five days since that body in the barn had been discovered. But no McVail. Nobody at all. Nobody had been in touch with Victor Demarest. They must know, from the Weinsteins somewhere, that Demarest had the keys to the house in Brookville and was serving as limited custodian, the selfsame Demarest whose wife and child had been killed by the Nassau Slasher. So? Where was McVail?

Originally the prepared story had been simple: total negation. Yes, he was in charge of the Weinstein home and he had the keys. Yes, he knew of the alarm system in house and barn. Yes, he knew where the key to the barn was kept. Yes, periodically he had checked the house, but there had been no occasion to go to the barn. (Which was the reason he had been so careful not to leave fingerprints within the barn.) That had been the original story and it followed, therefore, that whoever had committed this crime had known all that Demarest had known: how to get into the house, how to operate

277

the silent alarms, and where the key to the barn was kept. He would stick to his story, and that would be it. No matter what their suspicions, they would simply have no proof.

On purpose he had not switched on the alarm of the barn. He did not want the local police to pour in on McVail when he came to investigate in response to the anonymous letter. But he had *not* purposely left that damn key in the door—and that certainly stank up the original story. He had taken no special care about prints on the key, because after he locked up he was *then* going to wipe the key before returning it to the desk drawer in the drawing room. So, perforce, a new story. He would now state that he had checked the barn as well as the house and, unwittingly, he had left the key in the barn door. He must have been preoccupied with his own troubles that day because, as it would turn out, he had also forgotten to switch on the barn alarm system. But now, of course, his initial precautions would work in reverse—against him. If he had checked the barn, how come there were prints on the key—how come on the key and not inside? Was he in fact the murderer? Had he taken care on the inside to protect himself and then in haste, in error, in panic, on the outside he had left the key there in the barn door. That, ladies and gentlemen, is the contention of the prosecution. So? What says defense counsel . . .?

What *about* the key? The newspapers had been astonishingly thorough on every aspect of the story, but there had not been a single word in any of the newspapers about that key to the barn door.

And not a single word from McVail. Demarest had been home every day, 24 hours a day, but no word from McVail. Frank had called from Moscow. Hugh Ramsey of *Newsday* had cabled the Slasher murder story to him. Victor thanked Frank for the call, but he had little to say to him except to acknowledge the fact that the Nassau Slasher no longer existed.

He rehearsed his new story, imperfect in comparison to the original story. It is possible, in a cursory look-see into the barn, not to leave fingerprints, and still leave prints on the key forgotten in the barn door. What about the doctor's three new cars? Answer: because the old cars reminded him too sharply of his family. Why were they used cars? Answer: because he simply could not think in terms of bright new cars. Why *three* cars? The answer to that was—I don't know. Some kind of inertia. Three for three. After his tragedy he was not thinking too clearly. He was on sabbatical. Preoccupied. Like leaving that key in the barn door.

He wondered if McVail had learned about the mugging and the hospitalization of Dr. Victor Demarest (during the very night that Stella Margate had been killed). Probably not. Minor crimes do not filter through to the county police and certainly not to Captain Jackson Brendan McVail at Headquarters. But if McVail knew and questioned him, he had the answers. Funny, no cop back there at Franklin General had asked him any personal questions. He was a doctor, and they gave him respect. The fact that his name was Dr. Victor Demarest had no point in this ubiquitous-type mugging. The murders of Lori and Kathy were then already long-ago and obscure. They had been killed in the cool springtime of April, and this mugging had happened in the heat of July. But he had been ready for the questions never asked when his wits returned at Franklin General. That evening, restless, he had been cruising about in his car; without patently admitting it even to himself, he was seeking sex. Somewhere he picked up a girl. She directed him to a quiet place, they had sex in the car, and he paid her. She had then politely requested that he drive her to a phone booth; she wished to make a call. It was not too far away, a service station on Rockaway Parkway. No question she was the decoy, setting him up for the two men waiting in the dark car. They had mugged him and left him unconscious. He had spent three days at Franklin General and upon his return he had remained at home and had not once ventured out.

The phone rang. He looked at his watch: four o'clock.

He picked up the receiver. "Hello?"

"Doc?"

"Demarest."

"Jake McVail here."

"How are you, Captain?"

"May I come see you, Doctor?"

"Certainly. When would you like?"

"Today. This evening. What time would be convenient for you?"

"Anytime at all, sir. You name it."

"Eight?"

"Fine. See you then."

TWENTY-ONE

At last the confrontation. The hunter and the prey.

The huge man sat in the huge chair, the red morocco-leather thick-cushioned wing chair. On a tray on the end table beside him was a bottle of Jack Daniel's, a shot glass and a can of beer. The slim blond man sat in his swivel chair behind the desk and on the desk was a tray with a bottle of Pinch, a tall glass, a small keg of ice cubes, and a pitcher of water. The slender man was attired in casual summer clothes: white slacks, white shoes and a white sport shirt open at the neck. The fat man was attired in casual summer clothes: brown rumpled slacks, a brown rumpled jacket, brown shoes and a tan shirt open at the neck, which revealed the thick wattles that wobbled when he spoke. "I'm sure you've been expecting me, Dr. Demarest."

"You're long overdue, Captain McVail."

The old man smiled. The fat face was a network of wrinkles.

"When *did* you expect me, Doc?"

"As soon as that guy was found. I would imagine that all the survivors—the family, the next of kin—of that bastard's victims would quickly be interviewed. I would imagine they would be the prime suspects. I mean, motivation. The intense

283

motivation. And then the very manner of his execution—''

"Execution." McVail drank a Jack Daniel's. "That's an interesting word you're using. Unusual in these circumstances. Execution. I mean it implies, in a sense, a formal penalty."

"As the sole survivor of two of the bastard's victims, I kind of expected you sooner than five days. What held you up, Captain McVail?"

"Actually, no hurry. No hurry with any of the suspects. They don't—they won't—run away. The first part of the job, Doc, is collecting the hard evidence, if you know what I mean. It's like with you guys. You have to first do the X rays before you operate. Right?"

"Yes."

The old man grinned. He knocked back another Jack Daniel's and drank beer from the can. The gravel voice said, "In point of fact, Doc, you've turned out to be a rather special person in the line of suspects."

"Me?" Demarest said innocently.

"But not until I spoke with Leon Weinstein. Took me a heck of a time to get through. S.S. *Kungsholm*. The Weinsteins were in Genoa for days, doing kind of a free-floating sightseeing. *Kungsholm*. Anchored in the Ligurian Sea in the harbor of Genoa. Wanna know something? I never in my life ever heard of the Ligurian Sea. I looked it up. Italy. The boot. Well, on one side of the boot there's the Adriatic Sea, and we all know about the Adriatic Sea, right? But on the other side of the boot there's *two* seas. There's the Ligurian Sea, and there's the Tyrrhenian Sea. I never heard of either one of them.''

For some reason, a lecture in geography. Demarest drank his Pinch and water.

''Did you, Doc?''

''Pardon?''

''Ever hear of them?''

''Weinstein?''

''Those seas.''

''Vaguely, I think . . .''

''I talked with Leon Weinstein. Yesterday. He told me you and he were old friends. Told me you have the keys to his place up there in Brookville. Told me kind of as a favor you were kind of taking care of the place while they were away on the cruise. Told me you knew all about the switches for the silent alarm systems and you also knew where they kept the key to the horse barn. True?''

''Yes, all true.'' The thin sharp pain stabbed through his head.

''Which is what I mean that you turned out to be rather special in the line of suspects.''

Demarest drank Pinch. McVail drank beer from the can.

''Dr. Demarest, somebody who was hell-bent after a murderous assailant has himself become a murderous assailant. You know how the Slasher died?''

''I've read.''

''Genitals hacked off. Stuffed into his mouth. He choked to death.''

"Yes. Couldn't have done it better myself."

"Did you, Doc?"

"What do you think, Captain?"

"I think you did." McVail settled down in the red leather chair. His stomach lumped up like a huge tumor. "Hacked. The genitals hacked off."

"Yes. I read. Wouldn't quite say it was the work of a surgeon with a scalpel."

"Damn right. Wasn't meant to be. Do you own a hunting knife, Doc?"

"Never in my life."

"Own a portable typewriter?"

"No, sir."

"Do you have a typewriter here in the house?"

"Yessir. IBM electric. Standard."

"How about the office? Any portables? We can check on that. I mean, if any disappeared lately."

"No portables. All standard electric typewriters."

McVail drank. He clasped his hands on his stomach. "Lemme ask you something, Doc. Philosophically. What's your stand on vigilantism? Taking the law into your own hands?"

"That's a tough question to ask me, Captain McVail. I'm a man who lost a wife and child to a murderous animal."

"Perhaps that's why I'm asking it."

"Before this—this damned thing happened, I suppose I would have said I'm against vigilantism. The very word has an evil ring. I'd have been pure in heart."

"That was before."

"Since . . ." Demarest sipped his highball. "I've done a lot of thinking on the subject."

"That's why I'm asking, Doc."

"I don't believe there can be a general answer. No question, the courts seem more concerned with the perpetrator than the victim. But there exists in all of us, instinctively, a desire to balance the scale—and that desire is the meaning of vengeance. In our times, the law has turned it the other way. It rejects instinct, it tampers with balance, it pampers the criminal, it skims over the awful sufferings of the victim and the victim's survivors. That makes for a climate of what you call vigilantism, don't you think?"

"Yes."

"The murderer of Senator Robert Kennedy eats, drinks, reads, watches television, exercises, takes the sun and in time will be eligible for freedom under parole. The same applies to the murderer of Dr. Martin Luther King. The same for that Charlie Manson guru and his 'family' of murderers. They were convicted of shooting, stabbing, slicing and bludgeoning seven persons to death, including a woman, Sharon Tate, who was eight months pregnant. Yet, by law, that Manson is eligible for release on parole in seven years from his sentence."

"He won't get it."

"Well, the women who were convicted as the actual murderers in this mass slaughter—the District Attorney who obtained their conviction has predicted that all of these murderous animals will be free within fifteen years. So, Captain? Where is the balance? What has happened to justice in these United States?''

McVail produced one of his thin, gnarled, black cigars and lit it. He drank Jack Daniel's. He chased it down with beer from the can. ''Hypothetically, Doc. Between you and me. Would you have killed this Slasher bastard if you were able to lay your hands on him?''

''Hypothetically—yes!''

The whiskey rasp grated against his vocal cords. ''If we live long enough, we must all do something, sooner or later, which we know in our hearts is wrong.''

''Are you talking about me, Captain? Or, perhaps, you.''

The jowls quivered. ''Each of us. Both of us. Hypothetically.''

They were silent, looking across at one another, the craggy wrinkled man and the slim blond man in the swivel chair. Demarest poured more Pinch into his glass. The man opposite him was fat, flabby, probably not as old as he looked, but of all of him, the eyes were the most interesting. Because they were the youngest part of him, and yet the oldest. They were strong; the clear bright eyes of a bird, an eagle. And then suddenly Demarest understood. It was the expression. The eyes were old because their expression was the oldest: compassion. Strangely, a tenderness. A sadness. The cynical mouth, the bushy eyebrows, the furrows, the hanging flesh on the jowly face, none of it could obscure that expression of sadness in the deep-set eyes.

"Tell you something, Doc." McVail drank, smoked his cigar. "This assailant sure made a monkey out of me. Succeeded where I failed. He, not me, caught up with the Slasher. The only way I can reestablish myself, at least with the people in the Department, is for me to catch up with this one. Right?"

"Whatever you say."

"I'd like to take you into my confidence. Impart some confidential facts."

"Whatever you say, Captain."

McVail sighed. The wattles fluttered. "Our assailant, he sent me this mail in an envelope postmarked Brooklyn. There was the anonymous letter that you read in the papers, and the list of the Slasher's murders which you read in the papers. On that list were the six murders in Chicago. Nobody knew about those Chicago murders except the Slasher himself and a small number of persons right inside the Department. I receive this anonymous letter, but I'm too old to jump right at it, to hit the gong, to set all the bells ringing. I look at it, I read it, I sit there and consider. There are three possibilities. It could be, number one, a fun game, a hoax, a rib by a crazy in the Department who knew about the Chicago six or a crazy to whom that information had been leaked. Then, number two, I have enemies—don't we all?—in the Nassau Police Department. So number two can be an enemy who sticks that confidential information onto that list and I go bonkers and start ringing bells and call in the reporters and call in the Brookville cops and we open up that barn, and there's nothing in it. Which sets me up as a senescent old geezer who's beginning to go soft in the head." McVail grinned. "Which some pretty high-up people in the Department *are* beginning to think. Then we come to number three—that the whole deal is straight and legit. N , therefore." The grin again. "What you must understand, Doc, that this is one time— there've been other times—that Jake McVail must tread light and easy." He lifted the can of beer to his mouth. There was no more beer in the can. "Doc, if I may trouble you. Can I have some more beer, please?"

"No trouble at all."

He was glad to get up. His pants were stuck to his underpants and his underpants were stuck to his buttocks. He went past the kitchen, to the bathroom. He urinated, washed, combed his hair. He took two cans of beer from the refrigerator, laid them on McVail's end table and seated himself in the swivel chair behind the desk.

McVail pulled the tab of a can and drank thirstily. "Where were we?" he asked.

"You were treading lightly and easily."

"Yeah, I'm just built for that, huh?" He laughed. He tapped out the cigar in an ashtray. "Okay. So I go up there by myself. And I get to the barn and there's this key sticking out the barn door. Now there's a whole new *shtick* going. Now suddenly we got number four. If it *is* legit, then somebody could be setting somebody else up to take the fall. Not with me. I'm an old hand, you should pardon the expression, at my game. Nobody pulls *shtick* on Jake McVail. So once again we got to keep it covered up; once again we've got to tread light and easy. Am I boring you, Doc?''

''No.''

''I didn't think so.'' He knocked back a Jack and drank beer. ''Now let's go back to hypothetical, Doc. A killer with any brains at all doesn't leave a hunk of evidence sticking out like that. So now on this new one we have to break it up to a new number one and a new number two. Number one. An assailant smart enough to track down the Slasher doesn't figure to be dumb enough to leave the evidence sticking out the barn door—unless he panicked, which is always possible. Number two. The smart assailant left this hunk of evidence in order to set up somebody else for *his* crime. So even before I call in the Brookville cops, I take the key and say nothing about it. To nobody. Are you with me, Doc?''

''I'm right alongside you, Captain.''

''Without saying nothing to nobody, I have it tested for prints. Let's say, hypothetically, the last overprint is a clear thumbprint and it's the thumbprint of Dr. Victor Demarest, and I have a picture made, and that's it: a single picture of the thumbprint, and the key to the barn door from which the print was dusted and photographed. How'm I doing, Doc?''

''It's your story, Captain.'' The thin pain again through his head.

''Okay. Then we learn that Demarest had access

to the premises because the Weinsteins had given him the keys and left him in charge. We know our doctor had more motive for killing that killer than anyone else. Let's say, hypothetically, the doc had hunted down the Slasher and hung him up and got the confession, which included the six Chicago murders and then the doc killed him. Are you with me, Doctor?''

No answer. Demarest drained his glass of Scotch and water.

"The method," McVail rasped. "Let us consider the method of the killing. It is a precise action of symbolic retribution. The doctor did a hack amputation, but arranged it that the child's murderer died, symbolically, as he had made the child die. The son-of-a-bitch of a Slasher choked to death on his own genitalia. What say, Doc?''

"It's still your story, Captain.''

"Okay. Suppose in these circumstances I put the collar on the doc. I would say, hypothetically, that Jake McVail would be reestablished among his own. He brought in the killer of the killer. And I can tell you definitely, Doc, on the stuff we'd have to give to the grand jury, they would have to bring in an indictment. After that, not my concern. The cop makes the arrest and delivers the evidence. What happens at the trial is up to the District Attorney and the judge and the jury and defense counsel.'' McVail looked at his wristwatch. He knocked back a last Jack Daniel's, chased it with a last suck of beer from the can, slapped his knees and stood up from the wing chair. "Time to go now.''

"Yessir." Demarest rose from the swivel chair.

"I'd like you to think about all of this, Doc. I'd like you to try to remember everything we said here tonight."

"I'll try. I certainly promise to try."

"Yes, you do that, Doc."

The huge man did not stagger. He walked steadily to the door, Demarest beside him. He had knocked back an enormous amount of Jack Daniel's, but there was no sway in his gait and no slur in his speech. Demarest opened the door and they shook hands and the policeman trundled down the long pathway toward his car.

Closing the door, Demarest nodded, to nobody. *Noblesse oblige.* Captain McVail, the martinet of the sad eyes, had given him time. To get a lawyer. To prepare a defense. I thank you, sir. You are wise and good, a gallant old man.

He moved quickly toward the study. He would call Frank now, immediately, whatever time it may be in Moscow. Frank must come home and together they would select a lawyer and the three would work out a defense. Obsession. Justifiable homicide. Who in heck knows; that's the lawyer's business. I will be indicted and we will have the trial and quite possibly I'll be sent to prison. I don't care. It was worth it. I did what I had to do and whatever happens with the rest of my life really doesn't mean a damn thing to me anymore.

In the study he was almost at the phone when a side of his eye glimpsed white where there should only be red. He grimaced, his head veered, his eyes

sought. There was a corner of white in the red of the
morocco-leather wing chair. What the devil! Had
the old man lost something; had he left something
behind? Squinting, Demarest turned from the desk
and strode to the chair. The corner of white pro-
truded from between the thick leather-cushion seat
and the back of the chair, and he took hold of that
corner of white and pulled. It was an envelope. It
was a slit-open envelope. It was the envelope, now
postmarked Brooklyn, that he had addressed in the
blurry type of the portable to Captain Jackson Brendan McVail, Personal. He held it away from him, in
his left hand, as though not to be contaminated, as
though it were some evil portent. It was bulky. It
was heavy. He kept looking at it from arm's length,
and then he drew it to him, and the fingers of his
right hand entered into the slit-open envelope and
extracted two objects. The first was a snapshot-size
photo of a blowup of a thumbprint and the second
was the old iron key to Weinstein's boarded-up barn
in the tree-shaded valley, and right then as he
realized the significance of his find he forever lost
all meaning of significance and he stumbled toward
the desk, his mouth opening wide and the laughter
erupting.

The laughter.

Laughter!

McVail in the car, about to turn the key in the ignition, heard the howling, piercing, insane laughter:
peal merging to peal until it was one long sustained
shriek; and he ran out of the car and up the path and
all the while the frightful keening screaming

continued, until quite suddenly—silence.

He rang the bell. He rang again, and again, and then he went around to the side and kicked in a screen and squirmed through and ran to the study and when he saw him he knew immediately, in his long lifetime as a police officer he had seen them before—in Creedmoor, in Nassau Medical, in Central Islip—the irreversible catatonics.

Demarest was slumped in his swivel chair at the desk. His mouth was open, his lips were stiff, his tongue hung out. His eyes were vacant; his body was rigid. And there on the desk lay the white envelope and the iron key and the photograph. Perspiring heavily, McVail stood there. For moments he just stood there, like a mourner at a bier. There was no need for motion, no need for action. This was no emergency; there was time, a long, *long* time.

The poor bastard, twisted by tragedy, certainly at the edge of madness to have wrought that fearful vengeance, had nonetheless clung to his sanity right up until the end of the line, and perhaps it was the act of kindness that had pushed him over, or perhaps it was his comprehension of that act of kindness. He himself was already a criminal; perhaps unconsciously he had wished to turn off the act of compassion that on his account would also make a criminal of Captain Jackson Brendan McVail and therefore the wild laughter, the uncontrollable howling had been his call, an outcry for McVail's return—before he had snapped off into the final release of catatonia.

Who in hell knows how the human mind works?

McVail yanked out a handkerchief. He wiped the perspiration from his face. He folded the handkerchief and brushed it at his eyes. He sighed, shuddered, put away the handkerchief. He bent to the desk and collected the key and the photograph and placed them into the envelope and slid the envelope into a pocket of his jacket. He touched the doctor's head, patted it lightly, gently, as he would pat the head of a suffering child, and then he reached to the telephone and called for an ambulance from the psychiatric ward of the Nassau County Medical Center.

OTHER SELECTIONS
FROM
PLAYBOY PRESS

THE MINOTAUR FACTOR $1.95
STUART STERN
A mysterious killer disease is striking teenagers all over the world, turning them into raving maniacs and bringing sure death in a matter of days. The only way to stop it is a hideous experiment using human guinea pigs. Only one person knows the cause of the disease and he is on his deathbed.

NIGHT CROSSING $1.50
KEN KOLB
A Vietnam vet is hired to fly $50,000 worth of marijuana across the Mexican border. Wild, hair-raising and sexy.

TIME OF RECKONING $1.95
WALTER WAGER
A young American Jew becomes the avenging executioner of convicted Nazi murderers, until a CIA agent in Berlin—a specialist in violence—crosses his path.

CITY OF MASQUES $1.75
ALAN BRENNERT
A bone-chiller about a Hollywood studio that could make anyone a star—simply replace thought patterns electronically with those of the person you want to become. The results: overnight fame—and overnight terror.